MILLINERY ACADEMY

Ghost in the H.A.T.B.O.X.

Ghost in the H.A.T.B.O.X.

BOOK 1

Frank Beddor

with Adrienne Kress

PUBLISHING

9200 Sunset Blvd, PH 22, Los Angeles, CA 90069
automaticpublishing@gmail.com
automaticpublishing.com

Cover Logo and Type by Cale Burr
Cover Art by Maciej Kuciara
Millinery Academy and H.A.T.B.O.X. art by Tae Young Choi
Design by Debbie Berne

Distributed by Publishers Group West

Manufactured in the United States of America.

Summary: An exciting new adventure for Middle Grade, featuring a teenage Hatter Madigan, the most popular character from the *New York Times* best-selling *Looking Glass Wars* trilogy by Frank Beddor.

First edition 2016
9 8 7 6 5 4 3 2 1

ISBN 978-0-9912729-2-1

To my Queen
Long Live Marilyn!

WONDERLAND MILLINERY ACADEMY

CADET HONOR ROLL

In Recognition of Superior Imagination

Cadet Rune Barredbelch

Cadet Bud Hullporter

Cadet John Ambersnit

Cadet Sonnet Hashnu

Cadet Cravat Teedwheedled

Cadet Van Exitodds

Cadet Talavas Druid

Cadet Tales Crier

Cadet Cabova Ioni

Cadet Curiae Aimjack

Cadet Dire Beenebb

Cadet Scar Rucklit

Cadet Hazel Calibre-Vitae

Cadet Janus Lacunas

Cadet Cur Blare

Cadet Bantam Shoon

Cadet Ice Young-Oath

H.A.T.B.O.X.

They came at him from all directions—razor-cards, glinting in the dusky light of what appeared to be the Volcanic Plains, two decks' worth at least, dicing the air. He fell as flat as he could onto his back, activating both sets of wrist-blades, positioning them parallel to his body to shield himself with the centrifugal force of coptering Wonderland steel, just as—

Razor-cards smashed into one another and fell, hailing down on him, ricocheting off the blades.

The enemy was converging: a Four of Clubs from the east, a Five of Spades from the south, an Eight of Diamonds from the west, and a Ten of Hearts from the north.

Thirteen-year-old Hatter Madigan leaped to his feet and charged the Four of Clubs, his left forearm horizontal in front of him, wrist-blades spinning to provide cover. He snapped shut his right wrist-blades and reached for the weapons jutting from his Millinery backpack: spikes, rapiers, daggers, double-edged corkscrews. He sent a spike tumbling end over end at the Four Card.

Thwack!

The spike pierced the card soldier's armor and lodged in its wiry guts. The soldier folded, dematerialized.

No longer surrounded, Hatter ran. If he could just reach the pile of black rocks up ahead, he'd be able to get above them and maybe—

Something came whistling at him from behind. He ducked: wrong move. His feet tangled in a double-weighted tripchain and he fell hard to the knobbly, crusty ground, the ill-fitting top hat tumbling off his head.

The card soldiers were less than a few spirit-dane lengths away. No chance he'd be able to free his feet from the bruising, heavy tripchain. He lunged for the top hat, flicked it flat, and winged it at the Ten of Hearts. It wobbled briefly in the air—the blades curving out from its edges weren't rotating as fast as they should've been—and hit the ground. The Ten Card stomped on it, and now they were on him, all of them—the Five of Spades, the Eight of Diamonds, the Ten of Hearts—with swords drawn, and Hatter could only twist and writhe, contort his body to avoid the weapons stabbing at him, unable to find time or space to manage an offensive maneuver. He couldn't even get his wrist-blades to work.

As one, the card soldiers raised their weapons, about to skewer him, when—

Fwip! Fwip! Fwip!

Attacked from behind, they folded, faded into nonexistence.

"You didn't have to do that," Hatter said after he found his breath. "I was about to take them out."

Dalton Madigan, saber in one hand, stood looking down at his

2

little brother. He lifted his free hand to catch the disc of blades he'd picked off the ground and just used with great efficiency, and which now boomeranged back to him. "And you didn't have to help yourself to my gear. Give me the rest of it."

Hatter surrendered the backpack and two sets of wrist-blades. "You might want to lock them somewhere safe next time you shower," he said.

"Do you think this is funny? You could've easily been killed. How did you turn on the machine?"

"I didn't know you had to turn it on. It was working when I got here."

Dalton's mouth twisted with doubt. He looked around but saw no one. "Shimmer?" he called.

No answer.

"Get up," he said to Hatter, "before—"

Dalton spun, his long coat flaring out as he sent his disc of blades at a black knight who'd appeared from nowhere.

The knight fell, headless, and vanished.

Dalton's signature weapon circled back to him; he caught it, and with a quick shake of the hand, returned it to its innocent incarnation as a top hat, which he put on his head. He reached toward a burned-out tree, flung open a door in its trunk, and pulled Hatter into a gray outer hall.

"Listen. I'll admit it's impressive," he said. "Your stealth. To get into my room and 'borrow' my gear as you did. But just because you can do something, it doesn't mean you should. You have to be more disciplined."

It wasn't the first time Hatter had been told this, but now that he was about to officially begin his Millinery training, it seemed more important than ever.

THE FIRST DAY OF THE REST OF YOUR LIFE.

Dalton offered the hat with both hands, formally presenting it to Hatter as the younger Madigan sat on his small cot in his small room. The hat was, for want of a better word, *unimpressive*. Blue. A stovepipe. The edges of its brim ragged and frayed. There wasn't even a ribbon. And it was thick with dust.

"Uh, thanks?" Hatter said.

"Don't be too proud, little brother."

How long would Dalton stand there, his arms extended, waiting for Hatter to take the thing? Those strong arms wouldn't give out anytime soon. Hatter often hoped that one day—when he wasn't so skinny, when he wasn't shorter than most Wonderlanders his own age—he might have his brother's strength. It was that strength, both of muscle and character, that had enabled twenty-year-old Dalton Madigan to graduate at the top of his class and be awarded the post of Queen

Theodora's personal bodyguard, the highest possible honor a Milliner could receive in all of Wonderland.

"I just . . . it's pretty old, isn't it?" Hatter took the hat and studied it more closely. The brim's left side, where it met the stovepipe, was patched with some sort of faded brown cardboard. He wiped a palm's width of dust from the crown, but it did nothing to brighten the dull satin.

"It was Father's," Dalton said. "He'd want you to have it, to inspire you to great things."

"Father's?"

Had Dalton secretly been keeping its existence from him, in expectation of this day? Hatter should have felt honored—to have his father's gear! It was, after all, one of very few of their parents' belongings to be left behind after Belmore and Lydia Madigan had gone missing and been presumed dead eight years earlier. But honored? Hatter felt sad more than anything—the worn-out hat a stinging reminder of his parents' glaring absence.

"You'll make your own in class, of course," Dalton said, nodding at the headgear. "Assuming you get that far in the curriculum."

Hat-making was midterm stuff, and this was Dalton's way of reminding him that becoming a professional Milliner wasn't guaranteed, despite his bloodline. Sure, only children of Milliners could attend the academy, but that didn't mean they would graduate. Becoming a member of that elite group of Wonderland protectors, whether as a guardsman, warrior, or—Hatter's dream—a spy, was no easy task. Even if you passed your

classes and excelled physically, you could still be kicked out of the academy if the eeries thought you were somehow lacking. Hatter had witnessed it many times: young Wonderlanders with their cases and bags packed, tears streaming down their faces as their humiliated parents arrived to take them home.

But if he didn't make it through training, where would he go? He and Dalton had lived at the Millinery Academy ever since their parents' disappearance. If Hatter failed to become a Milliner, not only would he disappoint his brother and tarnish his parents' memory, but he'd be forced to spend the years until he came of age in a place that no longer wanted him.

"And now he's gone into silent mode. Honestly, Hatter. Stop thinking so much!" Dalton sat down on a stool and looked at him with concern. "I wish I could be around for you."

"You don't think I can make it on my own?"

"I worry about you, that's all."

Hatter felt a burning sensation in his gut—a raw, red thing. He hated that his brother thought he was too soft and couldn't take care of himself. But part of him was scared that Dalton might be right. His mind journeyed back to his very first day at the academy. It was a hazy memory, vague and insubstantial. Just flashes of scenes.

"Oh my, he's so little!" Cook commented when they'd first brought the brothers down to her. Two hungry boys with wide eyes and empty stomachs.

Dalton, twelve years old, had placed a protective hand on Hatter's shoulder. "He's the son of two of the greatest Milliners who ever lived."

"Of course," Cook had said, and handed them each a plate piled high with food.

That night. Lying alone. On a cot. So much fear. So much sadness. Sneaking into Dalton's room. "No, little brother, no. We have to be strong."

"I don't feel strong."

"It doesn't matter. Don't show weakness."

"I miss them."

"Don't. Show. Your. Weakness."

Returning to his bed. Curling up tight. Tears on his cheeks.

From that point on, Hatter had done his best to hide his fears, but he hadn't always succeeded. And though he'd frequently been told off by his older brother, Dalton had still always been there to take care of him. When Hatter got in trouble for trespassing into the Wonderground, Dalton had defended him to Tutor Wren. When he injured himself playing with a stray wrist-blade he'd discovered in the Banquet Plaza, Dalton had tended his wounds.

"I have to go and get changed," Dalton said, rising to his feet. "I'll see you out there." The brothers shook hands, staring at each other a moment. "This is the first day of the rest of your life," Dalton said. "Work hard. For Mother and Father. And for me."

Hatter nodded. Of course he was going to work hard. He'd been waiting for this day for as long as he could remember.

Alone in his room—a cramped basement room in the tenders' wing—Hatter jumped onto the stool to peer out his one window. Shadows had been passing it all morning, and various tenders were scrubbing the courtyard's alternating black and white marble tiles to an impressive gleam in anticipation of the cadets' arrival.

Soon. So soon.

Hatter jumped off the stool and studied his reflection in the mirror above his cot. He was dressed in Cadet Blue, the Millinary Academy's traditional undergrad uniform. A short, form-fitting jacket with horizontal rows of silver braid lining the chest. The fabric was an amalgam of caterpillar silk and jabberwock hide, allowing for ease of movement while being tough enough to withstand the cadet's intense martial training. His trousers were triple-reinforced at the knees with patches of pure jabberwock hide and tucked into the regulation academy stompers, triple-buckled, black, calf-high boots famous for their traction and force. But the element which most excited Hatter was the Millinery Academy insignia which had been woven in faint colors of caterpillar silk on the back of his jacket. The insignia was barely visible, because he was a Cap, but the insignia would become increasingly vivid as he progressed to graduation. He had worried at one point that he might have to wear an old hand-me-down uniform from a Cap who'd been sent packing, and the potential humiliation had burned in his cheeks. But Cook and the former Grand Milliner's chauffeur had surprised him on his birthday with this brand-new one. His face in the mirror might have looked a little too thin—Cook often praised his "high cheekbones," which made it sound like they were up somewhere in his forehead—but like Dalton, he had his father's floppy brown hair and brown eyes. His reflection in the mirror gave him confidence. He was a true Milliner. He would prove his worth to everybody.

He tried on his father's hat; too large, it slipped down over his brow. Caps didn't wear headgear anyway. Maybe his skull would grow by the time he became a Brim. He tossed the hat onto his duffel, which was packed with his few personal possessions and sat by the door, ready to be carried by a tender to the South Needle dormitories.

Hatter took a last look at what had been his room for eight years. In a way, he'd been lucky—getting to live at the Millinery after being orphaned, a place so special that few Wonderlanders ever even got to visit. But he felt no love for this room. It reminded him of the timid child he had once been.

Υ

The low-ceilinged hallway led to a large vaulted kitchen where tenders were running this way and that, undercooks and assistants stirring pots and cutting vegetables. Steam and smoke mingled and created all kinds of appetizing aromas. Cook stood in the midst of it all, hands on hips, shaking her head. "How do you manage to burn water? How do you manage to burn water three times in a row?"

"Hi, Cook," Hatter said.

Cook's exasperated expression turned happy at the sight of him. "My goodness, Hatter, look at you! You're the spitting image of your brother. Such dashing young men you are," she said, handing him a tarty tart with a wink.

Hatter's cheeks grew pink, and he wished he could hide his emotions better; an academy cadet was meant to be stoic at all times. Hatter knew that he felt too deeply—worse, too uncontrollably. It was something Dalton had never quite succeeded in helping him overcome. "Have you seen Weaver?" he asked.

"She said she'd meet you 'you know where.' And while I don't condone this sneaking about the academy, seeing that it's your last day as one of us, I suppose I can pretend ignorance this time."

"Can I take a tart for Weaver?"

"Of course!" Cook handed him another tissue-wrapped treat and kissed his forehead. "Now off with you. I've got several hundred hungry mouths to prep for."

Hatter ran down hallway after hallway, turning left and right and left again until he reached a narrow wooden staircase. Taking the steps two at a time, he flew up out of the tenders' door and then was in the grand foyer—a large curved room with buttresses that rose to a skylighted ceiling framed and filigreed with orange caterpillar thread. Hatter never tired of the academy's beauty and was as awed by it now as he'd been the day he and Dalton first toured it with Tutor Wren, when he had reached out to feel the walls and found them surprisingly soft to the touch.

Tutor Wren had smiled. "Ah yes, you thought rock, maybe? Brick? No, the Millinery Academy has been woven together, made of silk from the caterpillar oracles, each color of which has its own unique property that protects the academy and its residents. Only the academy's outer wall is stone, but even there the mortar has been mixed with orange thread—the thread of strength."

Young Hatter hadn't believed it possible that a whole building could be made in such a way. But having lived at the Millinery awhile, he now knew: much of what he once believed untrue or impossible was the opposite.

How many times had he snuck into this very foyer late at night, the room dark save for the glass bowls of light that hung from a girder far above? How many times had he stood here in meditative silence after all the cadets were back in the Needles, and wished to be the best Milliner ever?

He closed his eyes and made the same wish, and then darted down a passage that led to the administrative offices. He stopped at a tapestry woven into the main fabric of a wall. It was of Grand Milliner Tortoise, one of the Millinery's founders. The artwork was, to Hatter's eye, kind of ugly. Or maybe it was just that Grand Milliner Tortoise had been ugly. Hard to say. Hatter cast a quick look around to make sure he was alone, then faced Tortoise and gestured as if he were doffing an imaginary hat. With the slippery sound of thousands of threads unraveling, an opening materialized in the tapestry. Hatter stepped through it and sped along a maze of connected passageways, deftly avoiding the gnarled webs that clogged the shadows and the occasional gaps in the floor's fabric. He had gotten to know these passageways so well he could probably find his way in complete darkness. He had heard a tutor once refer to them as "seams," and that was exactly what they were: seams that held together the academy, that a Wonderlander could travel quickly along from one end to the other. Hatter raced way upward in the seams until he reached a beam made of threads so tightly compressed that it might have been mistaken for Wonderland steel. The beam led him out under the arched roof of the northeast wing, high above the Textillery. Down below: the oversize table around which cadets would work; cabinets full of materials, tools, and everything needed to fashion headgear; vests and suits, even armor.

The Textillery roof was outfitted with fifty-two alcove windows. One of these afforded the best view of Wondertropolis, and it was here that Hatter and Weaver met in the evenings, Weaver being pretty much the only Wonderlander who listened to Hatter and didn't criticize his obvious shows of feeling.

Hurrying to this "you know where," Hatter noticed movement out of the corner of his eye. Across the wide empty space under the roof, on the other side of the Textillery, a boy was standing in a window. Hatter stopped, unbelieving. No one ever came up here except him and Weaver—it was their secret spot. The boy seemed to be about thirteen, like Hatter, and was completely bald. Instead of hair he sported a complex tattoo of curling lines that swept over his head and down the right side of his face and neck. He was staring openly at Hatter with almost perfectly round eyes. Who could he be? Cadets hadn't yet arrived for the term, and besides, he wasn't dressed in any Millinery uniform Hatter had ever seen. His garment was loose and draped over his body, a robe of green and blue. Was he a new tender?

"Hey there!" Hatter called, but the boy didn't say anything, just continued to stare. "Are you stuck? Wait, I'm coming over!"

Hatter ran nimbly back along his beam to another, which led to the boy—who watched him approach, expressionless. At various points in the cross section of beams, trusses rose up to help support the roof, and Hatter occasionally had to maneuver behind them to reach the boy. But when he finally did . . .

The boy was gone, the alcove empty.

Fearing the worst, Hatter glanced down. There was no sign of the boy anywhere. Hatter looked out the window at the courtyard below—empty save for the tenders finishing their preparations for the opening ceremony, at which the Grand Milliner would stand and welcome the cadets.

Strange.

Hatter shook his head as if to erase the boy's image from his mind. He didn't have time for this.

"Took you long enough," Weaver teased when he met her in their favorite alcove.

"Yeah, sorry. Dalton gave me a little speech—you know, about working hard and all that. Like I don't already know. Here." He passed her the tarty tart.

"Thanks." She took a big bite and, with a mouth full of flugelberry, said, "He only does it because he loves you."

Backlit by the window, Weaver's strawberry-blond hair created a kind of halo effect. It was normally a mess of curls and tangles, but today it was done up in a braid that crowned her head.

"What's with the hair?"

Weaver gave him one of her classic eye rolls. "What's with the suit?"

"It's the academy uniform—you know that."

Weaver popped the final bite of tart into her mouth and brushed crumbs from her hands. "And this is the hairstyle worn by apprentice alchemists."

"*What?*"

"I wanted to tell you last night, but I couldn't find you anywhere. They're sending me away. I thought I'd be apprenticing with Cook if I were lucky, or more likely I'd become a tender. But they have other plans, I guess. It's really flattering. Don't you think?"

Hatter felt his insides run cold. "I don't get it."

Weaver faced him, crossing her legs. "It was Tutor Wren's suggestion. He saw my abilities—my love of creating things that are useful to others. So instead of a life in service, I'm being sent away to train at the Alchemist Tower. I'm very fortunate."

"But you can't leave."

"I have to. I *want* to."

A lump formed in Hatter's throat.

"I am going to miss you," Weaver went on. "I'm going to miss you like crazy, even though I'm also excited you're going to finally learn what it's like to be down there." She pointed at the empty Textillery. "But for a street urchin Cook took pity on, getting to do more with my life than being a tender, to do more than serving cadets and sweeping floors, is amazing. It's all happening so quickly, I know. I wish we had more time together."

Hatter tried to accept what he was hearing; couldn't quite. "I . . . I don't know what to say."

"Say you're happy for me."

The lump in Hatter's throat got smaller. "I'm happy for you."

"Say you'll miss me."

The lump got bigger. "I'll miss you."

"Great. Now let's sit here and pretend like you're not about to become a cadet and I'm not leaving to become an apprentice. Tell me more about Dalton's speech."

Hatter nodded, and with a great deal of effort said, "It started with him giving me Father's hat . . ."

SOME OF YOU QUITE SIMPLY WILL NOT BE GOOD ENOUGH.

On the courtyard dais, Hatter stood with Wren among the tutors, the old fellow's hand on his shoulder. Dalton, wearing a new hat and uniform, was on the other side of the dais with the Master Milliners. His chin held high, he looked very much like a master, not at all like a recent graduate, and Hatter couldn't have been more proud.

From beyond the gates came the rhythmic beat of marching feet. It was an impressive, thrilling sound: parents were escorting their children in a regimented fashion up the steep mountain road that led to the Millinery. They marched— Diamonds, Clubs, Hearts, and Spades mixed together—in a silent parade. This was the only time all seven levels would be together in a formal ceremony until the end of term: Caps, Brims, Cobblers, Bonds, Crowns, Tapers, and Peaks—all one formidable-looking unit.

It's happening.

Hatter kept his eye on the courtyard gates. They had been forged from molten silver and ingrained with yellow thread, the thread of energy, to electrify them so they would fry anyone who attempted to scale their daunting height. Rising up on either side were two guardhouses that pierced the sky with lancet roofs covered in reflective silver shingles. To unknowing eyes, the academy might have appeared a prison. But to the Milliner race, these gates and towers were the bright beacons of an exciting future.

The marching stopped. The courtyard gates began to open, the smooth quartz wheels on either side of them turning slowly. The incoming cadets waited on the other side, a mass of blue save for the rainbow of different-colored caterpillar-silk hatbands and the white shirtsleeves of the Caps. The march began again, parents splintering off to stand on the fringes of the courtyard while cadets formed eight platoons in the center.

Tutor Wren gently squeezed Hatter's shoulder. "Go," he said.

Hatter didn't need to be told twice. He rushed to find a place among the Caps and stood facing the dais, firm and straight, head held high, hands clasped behind him. All was silent and still. Almost. A Cap with turquoise hair one row back and three across from Hatter scratched her nose. He felt embarrassed for her.

The large glass doors of the academy opened. Out stepped Grand Milliner Victus, tall and broad. He wore an enormous tricorn hat sprouting multicolored jubjub bird feathers. An iridescent veil flowed from its sides, parting dramatically in the

18

middle to reveal the Grand Milliner's deep scowl that matched the deep furrows at the corners of his mouth and across his brow. It was Reginald Victus's first year in the post, and the little Hatter knew about him was that he'd been the queen's personal bodyguard up until Dalton had been requested as his replacement.

Accompanying Victus was a Wonderlander in a long red brocade coat decorated with golden hearts. His gwormmy-thin mustache was carefully waxed and turned up at the edges, his shoulder-length blond hair carefully coiffed, curling upward in solidarity with his mustache. On the dais, this Wonderlander was first to speak. He removed a white handkerchief from his coat pocket and sniffed, and then:

"Welcome, cadets. I am the Knave of Hearts, a member of the royal family, and the royal liaison for the Millinery Academy." He paused as if expecting a reaction, which was silly of him, considering his audience. "Yes, anyway. How glorious, another term! Yet more opportunity for you all to hone your skills, to become the elite of the elite. The true guardians of Wonderland and her people. It is an honor indeed, and we— the royal ruling family, of which I am a member—thank you." He paused again to sniff once more into his handkerchief. "And now, it is my privilege to introduce your new Grand Milliner, Reginald Victus!"

Victus stepped forward, glaring at the cadets. "Speeches are for politicians. We are Milliners, Wonderlanders of action. So all I will say is that it is my job to train you to be the best. Some of you quite simply will not be good enough. If you fear you should not be here, you will not be here long. Be the best. There is no second place." The silence seemed to become even more silent, if that were possible. "No time to waste. Let us begin the new term."

There was a handkerchief-muffled cough from behind him, and Victus pressed his lips tightly together. Then he said, "But first, it is time to pass the honor of being the queen's official bodyguard to . . . Dalton Madigan."

In any other crowd, during any other ceremony, applause might have followed that statement. And indeed, as his brother stepped onto the dais, Hatter had to hold himself back from cheering until his throat went raw. But Milliners didn't cheer. They stood in respectful silence. Sometimes they stood in determined silence. At other times they stood in frustrated silence. As long as it was silence, they were doing it right.

The Knave of Hearts approached Dalton. He removed a crimson rose from a small box he carried. "Dalton Madigan, on behalf of Queen Theodora of Wonderland and the entire royal family, I present you with the rose of the Hearts. May it protect you as you protect them." The knave pinned the flower to Dalton's lapel. Thin green vines immediately grew out of the stem, twisting up around Dalton's arm and creating a band of thorns around his right biceps. Its petals blossomed, hardened to indestructibility.

Dalton and the Knave of Hearts turned, and they stood side by side on the dais.

"And now," Victus announced, "we recite the Millinery Code of Honor."

In one swift movement, all cadets who had hats took them off and placed them over their hearts. The Caps, who had no hats yet, placed their right hands instead. Hatter had murmured the Millinery Code to himself countless times, but it was for real this time, official, and the words shivered with adrenaline as they left his mouth.

One hat, one hatter.
Absolute allegiance to White Imagination and its ruling queen.
To serve and sustain White Imagination,
To master the forging of immaculate blades,
To excel in personal combat,
To contain and control all emotion.
If you promise, you must fulfill.

To contain and control all emotion. Hatter was finding that rather difficult to do right at this moment. He was so happy, he wanted to cry. Finally, finally his dream—the day he'd been longing for, when he'd become one of them and live in the South Needle with other male cadets—was becoming a reality. No longer was he primarily an orphan, some youngster who got underfoot. No longer was he just Dalton Madigan's younger brother. He was Hatter Madigan, Cap cadet, soon to be the greatest Milliner of them all.

"And now," Victus said, "the HATBOX."

DOES ANYONE ELSE HEAR THAT?

The HATBOX?

Every cadet was confused. Every cadet except Hatter, since he knew what the HATBOX was. Sort of. All during the hiatus, he'd seen workers traipsing around the academy and down the side of the mountain, and he'd heard talk of something that relied on both thread tech and imagination. *Science* was the word he'd heard mentioned. And at the end of the last lunar cycle, after construction had ceased and everything had returned to an almost too-quiet calm, he and Weaver had walked down the steep mountain path and stared at the new building in awe.

Inside, they had seen Dalton talking quietly with MM Haymaker before pushing open a door and stepping into . . . what exactly, they had no idea. But before the door closed, half a deck of card soldiers had materialized to advance on Dalton and the Master Milliner, both of whom flicked their top hats flat in preparation for a fight. Hatter then guessed that the HATBOX was some kind of combat-training arena and decided to sneak into it the first chance he got.

Just wait, he thought now, marching with the other cadets past the North Needle. *You're going to be amazed.*

The cadets entered a tunnel that led through the academy's thick outer wall, to a path carved into the mountain itself—a kind of gully of a path, with stone banks rising high enough on either side to camouflage its existence from all but the sky. After a steep, twisting descent, the path leveled out. Again, even though he'd seen it before, Hatter was filled with awe; he couldn't help himself. The mountain melted away on either side, opening up to a jagged, rocky vista. Protruding from the middle, tall and imposing, was the HATBOX—like the academy, designed in the shape of a massive top hat. A white mist swirled around it.

The cadets filed through the entrance, across the concourse, and into the HATBOX proper. Hatter had never seen the room in its inert state. It was as long as two Wondertropolis blocks and at least one block wide. The floor and walls were covered with chessboard tiles of white and blue, as was the ceiling four stories above their heads. The massive room was empty except for a grandstand, on which the cadets were instructed to take their seats.

Before them, standing in a shaft of light in the center of the room, were MM Haymaker and a man Hatter didn't recognize. Haymaker was the Master Milliner in charge of hand-to-hand combat, and her exploits as a Club on the field of battle were legendary. It was said that she had taken out a jabberwock with one punch to the jaw. She was broad across the shoulders, with a shaved head hidden under her deep-orange hat, which her frock coat matched in color. The man next to her was of unremarkable height and build. His wavy blond hair fell to the lobes of his ears. The most curious thing about him was his outfit—what looked like slippered pajamas. MM Haymaker did not introduce him.

"Welcome to the HATBOX," she said, greeting the cadets, "your new combat-training facility."

She and her colleague joined the cadets on the grandstand. Dalton Madigan entered and stood in the center of the room. Hatter leaned forward, excited. Whatever was about to happen, he knew it'd be awesome. Dalton was wearing his Millinery backpack.

But nothing happened.

Nothing at all.

"Does anyone else hear that?" asked a voice behind Hatter. It belonged to the turquoise-haired girl he'd seen fidgeting during the opening ceremony.

The tread of boots, the clank of armor—they were faint at first but getting steadily louder. Dalton remained still and didn't even flinch when fourteen card soldiers from the Spades deck materialized before him.

Cadets gasped, held their breath. Hatter grinned.

The card soldiers stalked forward, the pointed ends of their shields as deadly as any of the weapons in Dalton's backpack, which he had shrugged open, blades at the ready. No one was as gifted in combat as Dalton, Hatter thought, watching his brother cut and thrust and parry with such speed that his weapons were blurs of silver. Card soldiers collapsed all over the place. Only a couple were left. Dalton speared one as he somersaulted over it. Landing on his feet, he thrust a J-blade into the last of them.

The tiles on which the folded soldiers lay flipped to reveal a complete set of white chessmen at arms.

Dalton immediately removed his hat, and with a flick of the wrist its four brim-blades appeared. He sent his hat flying at the nearest pawn, striking it in the head, and the hat continued on, taking out two more pawns and slicing through four crenellations of an attacking castle before boomeranging back to him.

A cannonball landed in front of Dalton, sending him flying toward the stands. From within a smoking crater, sharp points began to protrude from the ball as it doubled, tripled in size. The points grew too, turning into long, spindly legs. The whole thing grew at such an alarming rate that Dalton barely had time to get to his feet before the arachnid ran at him. Another cannonball spider landed to his left. Dalton fought the first one with his double-blades as it backed him toward a wall, its pincers snapping at him. He finally thrust a blade down the spider's gullet, but instead of dying, it swallowed the weapon whole. Meanwhile, more and more cannonballs were falling from the sky, and more and more spiders were growing at a sickening pace. Not to mention the remaining chessmen who were advancing quickly. In short order, Dalton was surrounded by

black spiders and white chessmen, all intent on his complete and utter annihilation.

Dalton looked at the ceiling, and just as the spiders and chessmen came at him, he leaped upward. The blades from his backpack extended and acted as a propeller to get him to the very top of the room. And then Dalton dove—a corkscrew dive into the scrum of spiders and chessmen, both his pack and wrist-blades cutting into ribbons whatever they came in contact with.

Black-and-white goo sprayed everywhere, even onto the front row of cadets in the stands. Hatter was happy to be a mere Cap, forced to sit in the back, not a higher-level cadet whose seniority would mean he sat closer to the action.

For a moment the spiders and chessmen lay dead on the floor. Then they vanished, leaving a clean room. And, Hatter noticed, the front row was no longer gooey either.

It wasn't over yet. There was a massive roar, and a bandersnatch materialized. It was huge, much larger than any Hatter had seen in pictures. The beast stood on four thick legs, its sagging belly scraping against the floor and its hide patchy with scales and fur. Its head was small, which no doubt explained why the bandersnatch was notorious for being incredibly stupid. What brain could fit in such a tiny space? But stupid didn't mean *not* deadly, and Hatter stared as its jaw, which unhinged like a snake's; in its mouth were dagger-sharp teeth.

Dalton whipped off his hat again and threw it at the bandersnatch. The beast slashed at it with its tail, covered along its length with poisonous spikes, and sent the hat flying to the other side of the room. Dalton threw two short C-blades at the beast and charged forward. One blade hit the bandersnatch in the side of its face; the other, the tough hide on its back. It reared up with a roar of pain and launched itself toward Dalton, but just when the two were about to collide, Dalton leaped and caught his hat as it came sailing to him from the other end of the room, brim-blades spinning, and with a powerful swing embedded it in the back of the bandersnatch's skull. The beast fell. Dalton yanked the weapon free, flapped it so that it was once more a hat, and put it on his head. The dead bandersnatch was gone.

Surely that had been the climactic fight. Surely there could be no more. But then a heavy *thud* could be heard. And then another. There was a loud roar, so loud Hatter couldn't help but cover his ears.

He knew what was coming next. Knew what beast could top the bandersnatch.

A jabberwock.

There was another loud roar, but still the beast didn't appear. There was also the sound of a footfall. And another. What was happening? Was it invisible? That didn't seem fair, especially since jabberwocky weren't capable of invisibility in real life.

Hatter glanced at MM Haymaker, who was looking at the man she hadn't introduced. The man, however, had eyes only for the ceiling, where the faint strobe of what might have been light crystals played along its nubbled surface like quartz fragments strafed by sunlight. Dalton meanwhile stood waiting, his face betraying no emotion whatsoever.

Finally, MM Haymaker rose and walked to the man. They had a quiet, apparently heated conversation. The man left the HATBOX and, shortly thereafter, the sounds of the approaching jabberwock ceased.

"That's enough of a demonstration for today," MM Haymaker announced to the cadets. "Upper levels, head to the Needles to unpack and prepare your rooms for inspection. Caps, make your way to the academy foyer."

Dalton remained a moment in the middle of the room, and then stepped over to join MM Haymaker. Hatter, exiting with the rest of the cadets, felt as if he should be congratulated for having such an exceptional Milliner as a brother.

YOU ARE NOT AS SMART AS YOU THINK YOU ARE, AS TALENTED AS YOUR PARENTS HAVE LED YOU TO BELIEVE, OR AS BRAVE AS YOU WILL NEED TO BECOME.

The Caps stood at attention in the academy's foyer, Hatter determinedly staring forward, trying to ignore the turquoise-haired girl at his side who kept turning to look at him. Which wasn't proper, not proper at all. Especially with Head Tutor Orlage pacing in front of them.

Orlage was small, only a few gwormmy-lengths taller than Hatter, but still a formidable presence. She wore a white tunic and loose-fitting white pants that almost blended in with her pale skin. She stood in stark contrast to the sea of blue cadet uniforms.

"Your education here will be as straightforward as any in Wonderland," she was saying, her voice somehow both soft and severe. "In fact, it is arguably the simplest of educations. You learn new skills; you move on to new levels. You don't, and you don't. So do."

"I will," whispered the turquoise-haired girl.

Hatter focused his gaze even harder on Tutor Orlage—the blue-green veins pulsing visibly beneath albino skin, the ice-white eyes, and the large, pointy ears common to all tutors. With those ears, Orlage could hear faraway sounds, the faintest of sounds. Certainly, she could hear a whispering turquoise-haired Wonderlander who should have been standing mutely at attention.

"You will learn all of the academy's glorious history in time. It was founded by the four royal suits. It is in their honor that the four disciplines you may find yourselves streamed into—should you survive the cut—have been named. Spades."

"Spies," the turquoise-haired girl whispered.

"Diamonds."

"Strategists," came the whisper.

"Clubs."

"Military."

"Hearts."

"Royal bodyguards."

Hatter's face burned. He couldn't be the only one bothered by the girl speaking out like this.

"You cannot pick and choose," Orlage continued, "although through experience I know that you all likely already have your preference. The decision will be made by the eeries. Remember, cadets at every level fail and leave the institution, but none more than Caps. You are not as smart as you think you are, as talented as your parents have led you to believe, or as brave as you will need to become if you are to graduate. If you get homesick, I don't want to hear about it. I am not your mother."

Head Tutor Orlage stopped, standing in an impressive silence. She stood a little while longer. And yet a while longer still. Until rushing footsteps and panting were heard approaching from a hallway to the right, and into the foyer came another tutor. Though taller than Head Tutor Orlage, he hunched over so much he seemed shorter. He was extremely skinny except for a round potbelly, and the only hair on his head was a small tuft of white sticking straight up from the middle. His ears flapped about as he ran, and he wore an old graying shirt underneath a vest made of patchwork, and a purple jacket. His trousers were a dark tweed, and Hatter noticed a hole in the knee.

"Tutor Mars, you're late."

The tutor looked at her for a moment and then pulled a pocket watch from within his vest and looked at it. His ears drooped considerably. "Apologies, Head Tutor Orlage—I was reading and lost track of the time. Are we ready?"

"Past ready."

"Right, okay, good. Cap boys, follow me then."

"And Cap girls, with me," Head Tutor Orlage said.

For the first time there was disorder as the boys and girls separated and lined up single file behind their tutors. Hatter fell in quickly behind a tall boy with a light-blue cane that almost seemed to be glowing. The fact that he had a cane was unusual, as it wasn't a tool in a Milliner's arsenal.

The boys followed Tutor Mars back along the wide hallway, past the administration offices, and then outside through the large diamond-shaped doors into the south courtyard. There looming before them was the South Needle, a wide corkscrew of a tower, the dormitory for all male cadets. Unlike the main academy building with its pristine lines, angles, and curves, the Needles were more naturally shaped, almost as if they were sagging rock foundations that had grown out of the formidable exterior walls of the academy. Windows were arched but soft at the edges, and no two were exactly the same shape and size. In general, the tower looked like a melting candle.

Hatter had of course snuck into the South Needle before, though the throb in his veins now was wholly different from what he'd felt previously, when his heart had been pumping fast in fear of getting caught somewhere he didn't belong. Now his every fast-thumping heartbeat seemed to say *I belong*.

Entering, cadets all around him gasped at what they saw. The inside of the Needle in no way resembled the outside. It was the work of an architect with powerful access to White Imagination. The room before them was vast and tall. It speared the sky, and light spilled down into its depths from a skylight above. Looking up, you could see doors to rooms on level after level, and cadets walking along balconies that did not have any railings. The cadets didn't seem to care, though—some stood with the toes of their shoes over the edge so that they could better call out to another across on the other side. A dozen swifties, starting from the ground floor and rising up to the very top, broke up the pattern of doors. Several were in motion now, cadets balancing themselves carefully on their glass platforms and being whisked up or down to the appropriate balcony.

Though the walls and foundation of the Needle were made of thread just as the academy was, the inside had been decorated

34

with quartz and granite, and when the light touched the surfaces at certain angles, they gave off an exquisite iridescence.
Swirling around the structure far above them were threads so
fine and light, they were almost invisible. These ethereal wisps
powered all the mechanisms of the Needle.

The common area stretched out before them. Tables of
bleached pine, their legs carved with decorations representing
the four suits, filled the middle of the room where homework
could be done. At the far end was a large area with plush chairs
and couches where cadets could relax. But there were also a
dozen chessboards set up to help them practice strategy.

"Now then," Tutor Mars said, "who here has ridden a swifty
before?"

Only a few hands went up, including Hatter's; swifties fea-
tured in very few Wonderland buildings.

"Caps live in the dormitory on the main floor until they've
been successfully streamed. However, I suggest you practice
using the swifties, because the streaming ceremony will be on
us before you know it, and you may then be officially assigned
your room and roommate for the duration of your time at t'
academy. And believe me, depending on how high up yo'
you won't want to take the stairs."

His audience nodded earnestly.

"Not because there are so many steps, mind yo'
there are so few."

In confusion, his audience stopped nodd'

"All right! This way."

They walked the perimeter of the ⌐

double doors that opened at their approach. A long room with bunks lining each side was revealed. This room had no decoration. Just floating globes for light and gray plastered walls. The beds were equally gray, each outfitted with a single thin coverlet and a flat pillow. Hatter didn't mind—this was pretty much the exact same kind of bunk he'd slept in the whole time he'd lived in the academy.

"You are ordered alphabetically. Inspection will take place in"—Tutor Mars pulled an oversize pocket watch from within his purple jacket—"forty-three minutes. Get unpacking, everyone!"

The cadets watched as the tutor turned and exited through the set of double doors into the common area. He turned and stared at them. They stared back.

"Go on, go on, go on!" he ordered, waving his hands at them almost as if to shoo them away.

The doors swung shut, and they were on their own.

SO I GUESS I HAVE TO HATE YOU.

All chaos broke loose as cadets scrambled about the room, trying to find their bunks. They talked loud and fast with one another, creating a wall of sound that reminded Hatter of the tenders in the kitchens.

He walked down the rows of bunks, trying to ascertain which kind of alphabetical order he was supposed to use. Was it A to Z? Was it Z to A? Was it H to T, U to G? Was it maybe the version of the alphabet where the letters rearranged themselves in order to play pranks on one another?

"M is down at the far end," said an assured voice.

Hatter turned to see a Wonderlander with dark hair parted so precisely down one side it looked almost threatening. "Thanks."

"Rhodes Victus," the boy said, sticking out a hand.

"Victus? Like Grand Milliner Victus?"

"Got it in one. And you're Hatter Madigan. Like Dalton Madigan. Like Belmore and Lydia Madigan."

Hatter's stomach clenched at the mention of his parents' names. "Uh-huh."

"So I guess I have to hate you."

"You do?"

"Your brother stole my father's job."

"I'm not sure that's how it works, really."

Rhodes laughed and put his arm across Hatter's shoulders. "I'm just messing with you. No, my father is honored to serve as Grand Milliner, and hey, it doesn't hurt to have him in charge just as I'm starting at the academy, now, does it?"

Rhodes had been subtly escorting Hatter to his bunk; *Madigan* was stenciled at the foot of it. But a small pale-blond boy was unpacking.

"Uh, I think you have the wrong bunk," Hatter said.

The boy glanced worriedly at Rhodes.

"No, this is Twist. He's getting your things ready for inspection."

"But . . . why?"

"Because he's being helpful. Aren't you, Twist?"

Twist nodded, his eyes growing wider, his expression changing from concern to fear. "What should I do with this?" he asked, holding Hatter's father's hat in his hands.

"Oh, come on, Twist," Rhodes replied. "That old ugly thing? It's clearly not his. Get rid of it."

"No, no, it's mine." Hatter took the hat from Twist and held it awkwardly before him. "It was my father's." It felt more like an apology than an explanation.

"Ah. Okay, well, I mean, I suppose every family has its . . .

heirlooms." Rhodes raised his eyebrows at the hat and shook his head. "Why don't you just put it somewhere out of sight, Twist. Under the bed or something."

Twist reached for the hat, and Hatter took a moment before handing it back to him. He had no love for the hat, but hidden away on the cold dormitory floor seemed disrespectful—if not to the hat itself, to his father's memory at least.

"So," Rhodes said, sitting on Hatter's bed as Twist got back to work. "There must be some pressure with that name. Madigan. Expectations."

"I intend to live up to them." Hatter hoped he sounded sure of himself.

Rhodes laughed. "Me too. So what do you think of everything? The knave and that handkerchief of his? The HATBOX? Head Tutor Orlage? Finally getting to officially train in this place?"

Hatter thought it was all was pretty fantastic, but he didn't want to gush. And anyway, he got the sense that Rhodes was fishing for something else. "Did you see that girl who kept shifting?"

"Yes, I did!" Rhodes said with enthusiasm. "She's from the Vost family, so she'll be gone pretty soon. No Vost has made it past Cap. Her parents are actual milliners. I mean, they make hats. For regular Wonderlanders. No caterpillar thread. No imagination, just pretty party hats for ladies and caps for men to keep their heads warm."

"That explains it. She was so embarrassing." Hatter was starting to relax.

39

"You don't know the Vosts? They're infamous for being total failures."

"Well, I just . . . I haven't spent much time in the rest of Wonderland. I was raised here, in the academy."

"You were?"

"Yeah, me and Dalton. After our parents . . ." He couldn't finish the sentence.

"*That's* why you were standing with Tutor Wren. It makes sense now. I mean, I knew you didn't live in the old neighborhood anymore, but I didn't realize you'd grown up here. So," Rhodes said with a big grin, "when you say you're familiar with everything . . . "

"I know the academy pretty well, yeah."

"Do you know what went wrong with the HATBOX?" The voice came from the bunk beside them, and Hatter turned to see the tall boy with the cane. In an instant, the cane retracted within itself, getting smaller and smaller, and vanished into a small box attached to a blue leather wristband the boy wore. The boy stared in their direction but didn't make eye contact. It was creepy.

"Uh, no, not really. Do you really think something went wrong?"

"Something wasn't quite programmed correctly, possibly," the boy replied.

Rhodes sighed hard. "Ugh," he said. "Science is just so common."

"Well, it's not just science." Hatter was a little taken aback. He hadn't really thought much about science one way or the

40

other. "I know a bit about how it was put together. Workers were installing it during the hiatus. It has something to do with thread tech. It's the future of imagination. Mixing thread, imagination, and science together."

"I don't trust it," Rhodes admitted. "My father says that science and technology are invented by people, and people make mistakes. As I think we all witnessed just now with that jabberwock—or the non-jabberwock, I should say. Imagination exists with or without us and is infallible."

Hatter thought about that. The Grand Milliner made a very good point.

The doors banged open and instantly the cadets were on their feet, beside their bunks. In swept a short, square man wearing what Hatter had always considered to be the tallest stovepipe hat in Wonderland: Master Milliner Clout, who was in charge of Caps.

"Inspection!" he bellowed, and he began the long slow walk, eyeing cadets carefully, grabbing an ear here, a lapel there, slapping the top of a bed to see if the blanket was tight enough. He withdrew a small magnifying glass on a chain from inside his coat pocket and examined the hairline of a cadet. And as he passed each one, he found some fault, something the cadet had done wrong.

"Shoelaces not equal length! Pillow a gwormmy-length too close to the wall! Loose thread in the seam of your collar! Your hair is too wild! Who do you think you are, a member of the royal family?"

Hatter was in a mild panic, realizing he'd been chatting the whole time and so hadn't examined his uniform for creases or put a comb through his hair. He hadn't even checked whether Twist had unpacked his things properly. *Badly done, Hatter*, he chided himself.

MM Clout inspected Rhodes, who stood across the aisle from Hatter. In the shuffle, Rhodes had somehow managed to straighten his vest and tie and brush back any stray dark hairs from his forehead. MM Clout wandered along the side of his bunk, looked underneath, sat down and bounced a couple times on the mattress, and stood.

"Well done, Victus. Your father will be proud."

Rhodes didn't smile in relief or pride, just kept his gaze fixed.

Hatter was next. He felt his body start to shake. He tried to steady himself but couldn't. There was nothing he could do. MM Clout studied his bunk first, and then his cubby where Twist had perfectly folded and placed his clothes. He glanced under the bed. *Father's hat!* Hatter remembered. But MM Clout said nothing and began to inspect his person, looking closely at Hatter's uniform and, using his small magnifying lens, at Hatter's right eyeball. Finally, he stepped back and said, "Not bad, Madigan. But you have a few stray hairs, and your right iris could be a richer shade of brown."

Hatter felt his face flush with pride.

Suddenly MM Clout grabbed his arm and glowered fiercely. "Hadn't noticed these emotions on your sleeve, Madigan. You get a pass this time, but keep your feelings under control. Got it?"

42

Hatter nodded, but the flush in his face only deepened, now from embarrassment. MM Clout saw it and shook his head, and then moved on to the boy with the cane.

The boy's bed was made, but the corners were uneven and a pronounced crease ran down one side of the blanket. The top was tucked under on a sharp angle. His clothing was folded neatly in his cubby, but a stray sock lay in front of it. At least the boy's uniform was neat and his curly light brown hair nicely groomed.

"Cadet Ezer, your bunk is a disgrace!" MM Clout said.

"I'm sorry. I'll improve."

"You'd better. For practice, you'll spend the next week making the beds of all Brims."

No emotion registered on Cadet Ezer's face, though Hatter did observe the boy's hand squeeze the top of his cane tighter.

"In all my time at the academy," MM Clout said at the end of inspections, "this is the most disappointing group of Caps I've ever seen. Aside from one or two of you, you do not exhibit the core values of the Millinery Academy. I expect most of you will be booted out before you even make it to streaming. Your schedules are on your bunks. Let's see if it is possible to teach you anything."

He stormed out of the room. The cadets remained where they were, looking at one another in uncertainty for some time. Slowly they turned, and sure enough, schedules had miraculously appeared on their beds. Hatter eagerly looked at his. *Yes!* he thought, seeing that his first class was a combat workshop.

"I've got combat too," Rhodes said, reading over his shoulder. "And check it out." He pointed to where the schedule listed the workshop's location.

"The HATBOX!" Hatter smiled. Whatever he thought of science, it wouldn't change how he'd perform in a fight.

6

THAT IS A COMPLETELY
UNACCEPTABLE REACTION!

In the HATBOX the next morning, Hatter, Rhodes, Cadet Ezer, and twenty-five other Caps formed a circle around MM Haymaker. The room was bright with light. The fellow in pajamas, whom Hatter had seen earlier, stood off to the side.

"Welcome, cadets," MM Haymaker said. "You have the distinct honor of being the first Caps in Millinery history to use the Holographic and Transmutative Base of Xtremecombat, otherwise known as the HATBOX. The HATBOX represents a huge leap forward for combat training. And we have this man to thank. Cadets, meet Sir Isaac Shimmer."

The man in the pajamas gave them a thumbs-up.

"Sir Isaac, would you like to tell us about your invention?" MM Haymaker asked.

Shimmer shrugged. "I guess. So the way it works is a combination of Maynor's third theorem and the latest innovations in lepidopteral filamental fusion and wave-band molecular dichotomy. I dunno; it's pretty straightforward."

MM Haymaker looked blankly at Shimmer and asked, "Perhaps you could explain exactly what lepidopteral filament fusion means . . . to the cadets, of course."

Shimmer's eyes lit up. "Thread tech!" he whispered as if he were telling a shocking secret. "For ages caterpillar silk with all its remarkable qualities was relegated to use in Milliners' wimples and weapons and whatnots. Not since the days of the Great Weavers, when the Millinery was built, has it been utilized to its true potential. But now, modern science has tapped into the thread at the center of the thread. We call it TNA: Thread Nexus Axis. Thread can be incorporated into any number of objects—yellow thread to conduct vast amounts of energy, blue thread to relay unimaginable data, orange thread to build impregnable structures! The future will be built with thread tech!"

Hatter and his fellow Caps stood in uncomfortable silence.

"Fascinating," MM Haymaker said. "Maybe tell the cadets how the machine will enhance their training?"

"Oh, that. You'll be fighting tangible simulacra of organic and inorganic life forms."

That uncomfortable-silence thing happened again.

"A projection or hologram," Shimmer said. "You'll be fighting what, for lack of better words, you can think of as holograms with temporary bodily substance."

"Yes, exactly. Thank you, Sir Isaac," MM Haymaker said. "Over time, cadets, you will have a chance to work through various levels of difficulty, ultimately facing off at the highest level with a jabberwock—who *will* actually appear, I promise."

MM Haymaker glanced at Shimmer, but he didn't seem to notice. "As Caps, you'll each get a sparring partner with whom you can learn and practice your moves. These partners have been calibrated so as to be slightly above an average Cap's skill level. This is a more efficient means of training compared to pairing you off with each other. But first, let's review what you should already know: basic punches and kicks. The Millinery style is very particular, very precise. Technique is everything. Stand before me in a line."

What followed was a rehash of hand-to-hand combat fundamentals—how to throw a jab, an uppercut, and so forth. The same with kicks: roundhouse, forward, back, side. None of the more complex moves. All stuff that Hatter had learned long ago from Dalton. MM Haymaker spent a while walking up and down, correcting cadets' form and posture, helping perfect their movements. She showed particular interest in Cadet Ezer, which annoyed Hatter because Cadet Ezer didn't seem any better at combat than the rest of them. In fact, he seemed a fair bit worse.

"Right. I think we have the basics covered. For the last ten minutes let's see you spar with your HATBOX partners." MM Haymaker nodded toward Shimmer, who shuffled from the room.

Hatter took a deep breath. What would they be facing? A card soldier? Maybe an imagination vampire? Something terrifyingly fearsome?

Hatter glanced down the row of cadets. Appearing one by one before them in a line that mirrored their own was a group of kids around their age. Oh. That was kind of anticlimactic. The holograms seemed to match their cadet partners in height and weight. It made sense, Hatter supposed, though it wasn't particularly exciting. But when his partner materialized before him, he stepped back in shock.

"Cadet Madigan!" MM Haymaker scolded. "That is a completely unacceptable reaction! Do something like it again and you will have detention for a week!"

Somewhat shakily, Hatter returned to his starting position, trying his best to conceal how he felt, to make his eyes less wide, to lower his heart rate. But it was impossible; standing opposite him as his sparring partner was a boy with tattoos covering his bald head—the boy he'd seen yesterday morning under the Textillery roof.

I SAW SOME OF YOUR MOVES. YOU'RE GOOD.

"**B**egin!" MM Haymaker ordered.

The holograms approached, and the cadets took up defensive postures, Hatter with his fists in front of him though they felt heavy and far away. How could he have seen his HATBOX sparring partner in the Textillery?

The boy darted left and punched him in the kidney.

Hatter staggered, stunned at how much it hurt.

The boy swung at his head; he ducked and countered with an easily avoided uppercut. As he continued to spar, Hatter was able to focus more on the fighting than on the boy himself, and sooner than he expected, the ten minutes were over and the holograms vanished.

Glancing around, Hatter saw that many of the students were definitely the worse for wear, covered in cuts and bruises. But no one had been more badly beaten than Cadet Ezer; blood was pouring out of his nose, and both of his eyes were darkening with bruises.

"Well, that was interesting," Rhodes said after class, in stride with Hatter as they walked to the Banquet Plaza for lunch.

"Changing your mind about science?" Hatter asked.

"I'm withholding judgment," Rhodes replied.

"Yeah, me too. You get hit?"

"Once. Total sucker punch, though. You?"

"Couple times," Hatter admitted.

"Nothing to be ashamed of. I saw some of your moves. You're good. Did you see Cadet Ezer?"

"Who *didn't* see Cadet Ezer?" Hatter guffawed, feeling pretty pleased with Rhodes's compliment. Being the son of the queen's former bodyguard, the kid had to know quality when he saw it.

"I think we need to start a pool for who we think is getting kicked out first," Rhodes said.

The Banquet Plaza was teeming with cadets: some stood in line at the various food stalls whose colorful awnings and banners competed for their attention; some were eating already, seated at the round tables that circled the central hat-shaped fountain in the middle; some were just standing around, staring at it all as if overwhelmed by so much commotion, so many choices.

At an aquamarine booth, tenders piled Hatter's and Rhodes's plates high with pixie whistle pasta and jollyjellies. The two new friends made their way over to a table in an area where Caps had congregated. This area was noisier than the rest. Unlike the older, more disciplined cadets quietly eating their lunches, the Caps were excitedly talking about their first day of training.

Hatter sighed at how noisy his fellow Caps were. Hadn't they been disciplined at home? "Ever feel embarrassed to be a Cap?"

Rhodes nodded. "Since the moment I marched up that hill."

They dug into their food, and just as Hatter was almost done working his way through his pasta, the turquoise-haired girl plunked down into the seat beside him.

"Hi!" she said brightly.

Hatter looked at Rhodes, who raised an eyebrow at him. He reluctantly turned to the girl. "Uh, hi," he said.

"I'm Astra Vost. You're Hatter Madigan," she said with a smile.

"Yes, I know who I am."

"Our parents were friends."

Hatter knew he shouldn't judge, but considering how this girl had behaved during the ceremony as well as everything Rhodes had told him in the dormitory, he found that hard to believe. Belmore and Lydia Madigan had been top-notch Milliners who'd fought in two long wars. They'd never have had time for anyone who hadn't graduated from the academy. And he seriously doubted they'd have been interested in the kind of hats that the Vost family made—frivolous, fashionable things, utterly useless in battle.

"We should be friends too," Astra said.

Rhodes lowered his face into his hands.

"I don't know," Hatter replied, shifting in his seat.

Astra watched him for a moment, then shrugged and bounced back up to standing. With a quick turn, she skipped off toward one of the food stalls.

Embarrassed by her attention and the implication she had made about his parents, and sensing Rhodes looking at him hard, Hatter said, "Add her to the pool list?"

"Oh, she was on the list before the list even existed."

Hatter smiled and was about to scoop up the last of his pasta when suddenly Cadet Ezer was sitting beside him.

"Wow, you're popular," Rhodes said. "Newton, what do you want?"

"I want to eat." He placed his tray on the table and sat down, and once again his cane retracted into the little box on his wristband.

"Saw you trying to fight. Pretty laughable," Rhodes said. "They fixed you up, though."

"Well, they fixed the broken nose. Left the cuts and bruises."

"You can't learn if you don't feel pain."

"Just reporting the facts."

Hatter watched Cadet Ezer—or Newton, as Rhodes had called him—feel around his tray until his fingers closed on a can of winglefruit juice.

"You're blind!" Hatter blurted, suddenly understanding.

Newton paused, holding the can at his mouth. Then: "Yup." And he took a sip.

"That explains a lot. Wow, you must be looking forward to when you can go home." Hatter felt kind of bad for the cadet. There was something unfair about every single Milliner's kid having to attend the academy. Especially ones for whom there was no hope of advancing any further.

"What are you talking about?" Newton asked.

"When you're cut from the program."

"I'm being cut?"

Hatter just stared at Newton. The whole point of becoming a Milliner was to become the ultimate Wonderland warrior. How could you fight someone, how could you protect someone, if you couldn't *see*? He no longer felt bad for Cadet Ezer. This kid was obviously delusional.

"Look, Newton," Rhodes said, "you'll try to make some point about how capable you are but it won't be enough and then you'll be sent home. You know it. I know it. Hatter knows it. Why don't you save the tutors and MMs the trouble and fail now?"

Newton felt around his tray for his sandwich and leaned back in his chair, taking a big bite. "I'm a Milliner," he said with his mouth full, "and I'm going to be one of Wonderland's protectors."

"Blind *and* stupid," Rhodes hissed. "Go away. You're not wanted at this table."

Newton dropped his sandwich onto his plate. "Fine." He stood, his cane telescoping out of the wristband until it locked firm, fully extended. With his free hand, he picked up his tray, then turned and walked right into a Taper girl. Both of their trays flew out of their hands and crashed to the ground, food spilling over the two of them. Newton slipped in the greasy slick of food and fell onto his back. The girl stared at him in horror, though she tried her best to contain her emotion, while every other cadet turned to see what was going on.

Newton pushed himself up to standing and brushed off his uniform. Then he turned and walked with slow, deliberate steps toward the exit. This time all the cadets gave him a wide berth.

"Pathetic," Rhodes said.

Hatter said nothing. It had been pretty awful to watch, but he felt bad for Newton again. He'd have been completely humiliated if that had happened to him.

I JUST THINK EMOTIONS
EXIST FOR A PURPOSE.

After lunch, Rhodes was off in Enemy Recog 101, and Hatter didn't know anyone else in his History class, so he sat by himself at a crystal-topped hovering desk for two. The room was windowless, seemingly airless, with such a low ceiling that some previous cadet had been able to carve *When will it stop?* into it.

Tutor Mars smiled at the students. "History! Isn't it frabjous!?"

The answering silence was not firmly in agreement.

"So much to learn! So much to know! What a delight. What a—"

The door opened and Astra's head appeared. "Oh, good!" she said, entering. "This is the fifth room I've tried. The way they keep moving about, it was difficult to find." She took the only free seat remaining, which unfortunately happened to be next to Hatter.

"Cadet Vost," said Tutor Mars, looking serious for the first time, "a moving room is no excuse for your lateness. No one else had difficulty."

"I'm sorry, sir."

"Good. Be grateful that I'm feeling lenient on this, your first day."

Astra nodded and then looked sidelong at Hatter, who was doing his best to ignore her. "Hi," she whispered.

"As I was saying," Tutor Mars resumed, "the history of our academy is a fascinating one and just as exciting as the history of our great land itself. It tells the tale of how the Milliners came to be. But I thought we'd begin by looking more closely at the principles described in the Millinery Code of Honor, which you all recited at yesterday morning's ceremony. Now, 'Absolute allegiance to White Imagination and its ruling queen.' What does this mean? It means that our queen depends on you. You are going to become the backbone of this world. There are many out there who would love to steal Queen Theodora's rightful place, usurp her crown, and throw Wonderland into chaos and darkness. Without you to protect and serve her, the very core of Wonderland would crumble. You are its foundation. The core. The rock. The . . . you get my meaning. Your allegiance is therefore paramount."

"But isn't that dangerous?" Astra asked.

Hatter wanted to disappear. She hadn't even been called on. She'd just spoken out. What was wrong with her?

"I beg your pardon?" If Tutor Mars's jaw could have unhinged like a bandersnatch's, Hatter was pretty sure it would have been on the floor.

"Absolute allegiance. That's all great if you like what the queen is doing, if she's a great Wonderland queen. But what if she isn't? What if she's doing bad things?"

"A queen only becomes a queen after she's passed through her Looking Glass Maze and White Imagination has chosen her. There is no way for a queen to do 'bad things.' Moving on. 'To serve and sustain White—'"

"Yes, but what about war?" Astra interrupted. "What about someone who would kill the queen and take her place? Then there's no maze for her to pass through. She isn't the chosen one then. Do we still owe absolute allegiance in that case?"

"Enough of this!" Tutor Mars squeaked. The blue-green veins crisscrossing under his translucent skin throbbed with anger. "One more outburst of this kind and you'll regret it, Cadet Vost!"

It didn't sound particularly threatening, but Astra kept silent as Tutor Mars worked his way through each phrase in the Millinery Code. Until he reached, "To contain and control all emotion."

"Emotion is the enemy of reason," he said. "Fear causes panic, and a Milliner cannot panic even in the most fearsome of circumstances. That is why, since you were born, you have been working with your parents to control your emotions and why we here will see that you do so."

"I don't think that makes sense," Astra commented.

Tutor Mars sputtered at that. Sputtered, but could find no words in response.

"I just think emotions exist for a purpose," she continued.

"To ignore them is denying a tool that we could use. I mean, they say that those with a lot of feeling are those best able to imagine. And we as Milliners need to have excellent imaginations. Doesn't our gut tell us when something isn't right? Isn't it wise to listen to it?"

Tutor Mars slammed his fist on his desk—which Hatter had never seen a tutor do before. Tutors were not known to be in any way aggressive.

"Cadet Vost, you will leave this classroom immediately!" Tutor Mars's voice cracked as he spoke. "You will proceed to Head Tutor Orlage's office, and she will come up with an appropriate punishment for your outbursts. Never, ever, ever, ever, have I encountered such a spectacle. Not when your parents were Caps or even when your grandparents were. We all know what we should expect from the Vosts. But this is too much!"

Out of the corner of his eye, Hatter watched Astra stand on shaky legs. She walked with head held high, though, and if he hadn't been feeling quite so embarrassed for her, he might have been impressed by her dignity.

She opened the door to the classroom and turned to Tutor Mars. "You shouldn't have said that about my family. That wasn't nice." Then she left.

Tutor Mars stared after her a moment in disbelief before walking around his desk and collapsing into his chair. There was a charged silence as the students waited. Finally, he leaned forward and opened the book in front of him.

"I shall now read aloud a most respected historian's view on the establishment of the Millinery Academy. You will all listen and then write a paper on what you've learned, due next class. No note-taking. We are here to sharpen your memory as well as impart knowledge to you."

The rest of the day was less eventful. Exercises in the yard: hop arounds, spiral winders, flailing drubles, and so forth. Another history class. Dinner. By the time Hatter fell into his bunk, he was more than ready for sleep. For years he'd helped Cook in the kitchen and assisted various tenders in their duties. He had trained with Dalton in the unkempt yard where deliveries were made. He had kept himself busy and had enjoyed it. But he'd never been quite this busy before.

On top of which, there was his sparring partner from MM Haymaker's combat workshop. The tattooed boy. How had the boy appeared in the Textillery, outside the HATBOX? Maybe he hadn't. Not really. It must have been his mind playing tricks on him. Yes, best to pretend it had never happened, Hatter decided. He had more important things to worry about. Except for a couple of emotional missteps, he'd been doing well. He enjoyed having a new friend in Rhodes, who respected his abilities and was himself clearly talented. No, Hatter wasn't going to let his imagination run away from him. He needed as much of it as possible for his classes.

Keep it contained.

And for the love of everything, stop feeling so much!

ARE YOU TELLING ME YOU CAN'T DO IT, MADIGAN?

Hatter sat bolt upright in his cot. It was still dark. His heart was beating fast. He had no idea what had jarred him awake, or what had caused the panic coursing through his veins.

"You are Hatter Madigan?"

The tattooed boy was sitting at the end of his bunk. Hatter stared at him for what seemed like forever. Then the boy opened his mouth wide. It kept opening, wider than any Wonderlander's mouth could open. A scream, not of fear but of great pain, rose out of the boy's throat, low at first but getting increasingly louder until Hatter covered his ears.

Then boy launched himself forward—flew toward Hatter, *into* him. And Hatter's whole body screamed.

"Madigan!"

Hatter opened his eyes. The dormitory was black as pitch, and the cold of night stung his nose and ears. His body was sore, heavy, recovering after his first day of training.

A nightmare. It had only been a nightmare.

But it had felt so real.

"What? What's going on?" he asked in exhaustion.

"With me. Now," the fierce whisper said, and Hatter recognized the voice as MM Clout's. Was he in trouble for something?

"Don't make me wait, cadet," Clout said.

In a daze, with the rest of the Caps sleeping soundly, Hatter followed the Master Milliner from the dormitory, through the common room, and out into the night.

"Run twice around the academy. Go!" Clout ordered.

The sentence sounded like a fairy-tale task to Hatter; it didn't make any sense. "Sorry, sir, I don't understand."

"Get running, cadet!"

Hatter knew he wasn't supposed to question *why*. He remembered Astra in History class. He definitely didn't want to act like her, so . . .

He ran. The Millinery grounds were long and wide. The institution was meant to be daunting, intimidating. To run around it once would have been torture enough. Hatter inhaled the cold, piercing air. His feet were soon heavy with mud. His lungs burned. The steam of breath seemed to spell out *Help me!* Clearly, he wasn't as fit as he'd supposed, despite all his sneaking about the academy's seams. By the end of his first lap, a deep blue was creeping up over the sides of the high gray outer walls. MM Clout stood waiting for him, frowning, arms crossed. "One more, Madigan, and you'd better make it back to me by dawn."

It didn't seem possible—to go around the academy another time, let alone do so by dawn.

"Sir, I . . . " Hatter bent over, gasping for breath, his sides cramping up hard.

Clout towered over him. "Are you telling me you can't do it, Madigan?"

Hatter hated to admit it, but he didn't know what else to do. His body was giving out on him. "I am," he said, his voice low. "I'm sorry. I can't do it."

He braced for punishment. Would he be given detention for the rest of his days as a Cap? For his entire cadet career? For the rest of his life? *I'm sorry, Your Royal Highness, I would love to go to war this evening, fight for queen and country and all that, but I'm afraid I have detention.*

"You disappoint me, cadet. I'll see you this time tomorrow morning."

And that was it.

When Hatter next looked up, Clout was gone. Relief washed over him. He walked back to the dormitory. Opening the door to the South Needle, he glanced off at the two suns rising above the horizon. A figure was coming toward him from across the academy's grounds. A figure Hatter hadn't noticed before. Was MM Clout returning?

"Keep fighting," it said.

The tattooed boy. Hatter blinked and the boy was gone. *It can't be real*, he told himself. *Just a lingering phantom from my nightmare.*

BUT THERE IS NO GREATER TOOL TO A MILLINER THAN WHITE IMAGINATION.

Dawn came too soon. Hatter ached all over—in his thighs, calves, triceps, even at the front of his shins. He was worried that MM Clout might have thought better of his late-night leniency and would still punish him, but no. He passed inspection, as did Rhodes—the only two Caps to do so. When it came to maintaining pristine living quarters, Newton had improved, but not enough, and he was given another week of making up the Brims' bunks, on top of the one he had only just started.

History of Imagination was the first class of the day, and when Hatter entered the room he was immediately put off by the sight of Cadet Vost sitting in the front row, waving for him to sit next to her. She couldn't take a hint, could she? Rhodes, who had saved Hatter a seat, was at the back of the room.

"This is Drummer," Rhodes said, introducing him to a stocky cadet in a nearby desk. "My second cousin on my mother's side."

"Nice to meet you," Hatter said.

Drummer grunted back at him.

"So how do you think she'll embarrass herself today?" Rhodes asked, eyeing the back of Astra's head, her turquoise hair in a ponytail.

"Just as long as she doesn't embarrass us."

"Hey, Astra!" Rhodes called out.

Astra turned and smiled brightly at him.

"Let's see if you can go a whole class without asking a question."

Astra laughed and shook her head. "Very funny, Rhodes." And she turned happily back toward the front just as Tutor Wren entered the classroom.

Hatter sat up a little straighter in his chair. Tutor Wren had been the one to take it upon himself to teach him and Dalton about Wonderland and their Milliner lineage. He had sought them out at the end of their first week living at the academy, two scared boys who were pretending to be anything but, and promised that he would watch out for them, promised that they would not fall behind in their education and that he would prepare them for that day when they became cadets themselves. Why he'd done this, Hatter had never found out. Though he had asked once. Tutor Wren had just looked down at the large worn book he was reading and turned the page.

He owed a lot to Tutor Wren. He wanted to do him proud.

The tutor's classroom was also his office. The ceiling seemed to be held up by walls of books. His desk supported a single, humongous book: The Complete and Ever-Changing History of Wonderland. Behind it was a tall gemstone writing board, though it was almost completely obscured by yet more books. Tutor Wren never used it. He was known for expecting every word he spoke in class to be remembered by every cadet. Shafts of green light from the board pierced the bent pages and small spaces, almost like sun falling through leaves in a forest, making the room mottled. Dust danced its way toward the students in the bright beams.

Tutor Wren sat behind his desk and interlaced his fingers. He examined his students for a moment. And then began to speak. "From your earliest days you have known about imagination. You have seen your parents, strangers, the royal family, and everyone in Wonderland either use or be touched by White Imagination. Some of you, unfortunately, have seen displays of Black Imagination. There is nothing more powerful or more dangerous. But there is no greater tool to a Milliner than White Imagination. His hat is imbued with it. His fight skills informed by it. His heart full of it. And so you must understand it."

Despite his soft, slow, steady voice, Tutor Wren managed to grab their full attention with his words. He somehow made the air buzz. Tutor Wren might not have been Head Tutor, but he was special, no doubt about it. He didn't just recite facts from memory the way the other tutors did.

"Who can tell me of the origins of imagination?" he asked. It was an unusual technique for a tutor. Hatter knew from his brother Dalton that tutors normally just lectured, expecting cadets to listen and absorb the way they themselves listened and absorbed.

And for this reason no one raised their hand. No one except . . .

"The imaginations have existed for as long as Wonderland itself," Astra said. "But the discovery of their existence was made by the caterpillar oracles. They also gifted Milliners with their silk thread so that we could wield imagination ourselves."

"Well done, Cadet Vost," Tutor Wren said, and Hatter felt mild annoyance at the compliment. "Now then, imagination—"

"What do you think about science, sir?" Astra asked.

And it was happening again. Hatter shrank down in his seat.

"Science, cadet?" Tutor Wren spoke calmly, but Hatter knew the man well and noticed the slight twitching of his ears, indicating he'd been thrown a bit by the question.

"Yes, like the science used for the HATBOX. Does that make imagination unnecessary? Or can they work together? Or maybe science can't be trusted, and so we still need imagination, but that doesn't make sense because then why would the academy allow the HATBOX to be installed. So maybe—"

"Cadet Vost," interrupted Tutor Wren, "questions are questionable at the best of times, but not waiting to hear an answer is certainly disrespectful."

"Oh. Sorry." Astra fell silent.

"Science and technology have always been with us, but

they have always been secondary to imagination. Now that there have been certain technological advancements, many believe that science is dangerous, unpredictable, and subject to human error. But imagination can also be dangerous, and those who have thought they had complete control over it have caused just as much damage as a mathematical miscalculation in a new scientific invention. My thoughts are that science and imagination are compatible. And the existence of one oughtn't erase the existence of the other."

"But do you really think so? I mean, I've heard some of the tutors talking about the HATBOX, and they seem to think it's the beginning of the end of Wonderland culture and history and tradition and—"

"Thank you, Cadet Vost. That will do. There are two sides to imagination, and they are the light and the shadow," Tutor Wren continued. "The white and the black. Imagination is organic. It grows from within all of us, every plant, every beast, every person. It is wisdom itself, and when we do not force our will upon it, it is White Imagination. It is like a rushing river that we guide our boat on, following the current. We can steer, we can change course, but we do not bend the river to our will. When we do that, we face Black Imagination.

"Black Imagination is powerful but unstable. Its strength derives from a presumptuous effort of will. It's tempting to use Black Imagination because we don't have to make any sacrifices. We can choose to have whatever we want, and we can claim it. This is why the use of Black Imagination is outlawed in Wonderland. Not only is it dangerous, but its power is seductive. A person practicing Black Imagination finds it hard to stop, and as they do more and more with it, as they create larger and larger manipulations, eventually Black Imagination consumes the entire person and possesses the body. Perhaps you are familiar with Tutor Vollrath?"

There was a charged silence at the mention of the name.

"He was a brilliant tutor, graduated second only to the famous Bibwit Harte, tutor now to the royal family. However, he devoted his great knowledge and intellect to the service of Black Imagination. He became entangled with an evil and social-climbing smuggler, and it became necessary for him to jump into the Pool of Tears."

Hatter noticed his fellow cadets were looking as uncomfortable as he felt.

"Have no fear," Tutor Wren said kindly. "It is so difficult to control Black Imagination that none of you will have to worry about its temptation so early in your training. But you will have to learn how to recognize it. In Brim level, not only will you continue to be taught how to harness White Imagination, but you will personally learn the effects of the Black."

Hatter had heard stories from Dalton of those lessons. But the most frightening had been just before the hiatus, when Dalton was testing for the position of queen's bodyguard. He'd been given a rogue hat to wear. A hat imbued not with White Imagination, as was normal, but one tainted with Black. He had returned from the test pale and shaken. And Hatter had had a rare glimpse of what was beyond the stoic mask his brother usually wore. His brother had spoken—in a shaking voice full of feeling, like a different person altogether—of having wanted to do things that were so unlike the good person he was. And worst of all, of having liked the feeling.

ACADEMY STANDARDS MUST HAVE LOWERED TO LET YOU LOT IN.

It was time for lunch. Hatter, Rhodes, and Drummer made their way to the Banquet Plaza, where Cook herself was dishing up some angler stew at the comfort stand.

"You're fitting in so well, young Madigan," she said to Hatter, "but you're still so skinny. Double portions for you!"

"Thanks! This is Rhodes and Drummer," he said.

"A pleasure to meet you!" Cook replied with that wide, happy smile of hers.

"Uh, yeah." Rhodes furrowed his brow. He took his food without another word, as did Drummer.

Hatter gave a small wave of farewell to Cook and followed his friends to a table.

"Hey, Madigan?" Rhodes said slowly.

"Yeah?" Hatter began shoveling food into his mouth.

"Look, I get how you were raised and everything, but you might not want to spend too much time associating with dirty sweatbands."

"Who?"

"Tenders. You already have a problem with your emotions, and the sweatbands are an example of how you don't want to be. You know?"

Hatter thought about it. It was true that Cook was always pretty passionate, and she didn't seem to mind letting anyone and everyone know exactly what she was feeling. But did that influence *his* behavior? Maybe. Probably. In fact, now that he thought about it, Weaver was always so completely open with him about everything she felt, and he'd always tried to do the same with her. Rhodes made a good point.

"Yeah, okay."

"Besides, sweatbands aren't really worth your time. They don't have much going on . . . up here." Rhodes tapped the side of his head.

That didn't seem true to Hatter. He again thought about Weaver, about how smart she was. But she wasn't going to be a tender, was she. She'd been chosen to apprentice with the alchemists. If she hadn't been smart, that wouldn't have been the case. She'd have had to be a tender. So yeah, again, maybe Rhodes made a good point.

"Well, well, well," an unfamiliar voice said. Hatter looked up to see a trio of older boys looking down at them. They wore the uniforms of upperclassmen. From Bond level through Tapers, the upperclassmen added a cutaway, thigh-length, flared coat over their cropped jackets, giving them not only authority and style, but abundant hidden pockets for weaponry.

The boy who'd spoken had his hat in hand, a blue band circling it. The other two wore their hats on their heads; both had orange bands. "Academy standards must have lowered to let you lot in."

Hatter's blood instantly began to boil. "First of all," he said, trying to control himself, "every Milliner has to attend the academy as a Cap, and second of all, I happen to be a Madigan, and he's the son of the Grand Milliner and—"

"Whoa! Emote much? Leash your attack dog, Rhodes. Whatever happened to a sense of humor?"

Rhodes laughed. "Madigan, this is West Trilby, a friend of mine. He's just joking." Rhodes stood and shook the boy's hand. "Those other two are Benedict Jingasa and Nigel Kufi."

The other two boys nodded at him, and he nodded back.

"Madigan? So Dalton's little brother then?" West asked. He was a tall, strong-looking boy, his hair shaved off except for a green strip running down the middle of his head. It was then that Hatter noticed the silver band, decorated with spades, wrapped around his arm. West was not only a Top Hat, a position of high respect and honor as well as status, but the Spade Top Hat—the cadet in charge of all other Spades. When Hatter became a Spade himself, West would be his Top Hat. He sat a little taller in his seat.

"Yes," he said.

"Heard about your combat skills from Rhodes. Sounds like you've definitely got the Madigan gene," Benedict said. He was the shortest of the three, with long bright orange hair that matched his hatband almost perfectly. Hatter noted that Benedict's eyes were of two different colors, gold and green. Hatter suppressed a smile. "I guess I do."

"Benedict's family lives next door to your old place on Breton Avenue," Rhodes said, gesturing for the upperclassmen to join them.

Hatter returned to eating, not because he was particularly hungry anymore, but because he wanted to hide the pain that had hit him square in the gut at the mention of Breton Avenue.

His old place. He hardly remembered it—he'd been so little. "That's a coincidence," he said as calmly as he could.

"Not really," Benedict replied, grabbing a biscuit off his plate and tossing it in his mouth. "It's where every Milliner family of a certain prestige lives."

Hatter took another bite of stew. "Yeah, and how does that work when your folks are on duty, away from home?"

"Well, we all look out for one another. So sometimes I'd stay with Nigel here when my parents were at war." Benedict gestured toward the third boy, the tallest and leanest with cropped dark hair and a storm of freckles across his nose and cheekbones. "Rhodes's mom works for Intelligence, so she's home a lot. She took care of us a fair bit. Everyone in the community works together."

"Sounds really nice," said Hatter.

"Yeah. I mean, we would have taken care of you guys too, you know." Nigel spoke for the first time, his voice thin and high, which did not match his round shape at all.

76

"Well, that wasn't my choice," Hatter replied.

"No, yeah, of course. But do you know why they took you away?" West's question seemed weighted with far more than just polite curiosity.

"No. I never asked."

"Yeah, and that's the right thing to do. I get it," Rhodes said, and Hatter was grateful for his support. "We're taught from a young age that we only need to know what people tell us. So why don't you shut up about it now, West?"

West glared at him for a moment but said nothing.

"Look, we need to head to class, but we wanted to make sure you were ready for tomorrow night," squeaked Nigel.

"What's tomorrow night?" asked Drummer, which surprised Hatter. He'd started to doubt that Drummer was capable of complete sentences.

West laughed. "Tomorrow night's initiation."

"For whom?" asked Hatter.

"For these two tweedledums. For you too."

"I still don't get it. What's this all for?"

"The Wellingtons," Benedict said.

"It's like a club," West explained. "Top students. We all did it as Caps. Very exclusive. Usually there's only one, two members per year. Sometimes even none. We three, we're it right now. Now that we've lost Dalton."

"Dalton was part of your club?" Hatter had never heard his brother mention a club before.

"Of course. He's a Madigan."

Hatter felt that familiar flush of pride and stared even harder at his stew. But he was pretty sure the other boys could see how thrilled this made him.

"What's the plan?" Rhodes asked.

"Oh, we can't tell you that," West replied with a mischievous grin. "Just be in the common area tomorrow at midnight. And dress warmly."

The three of them rose and left. Hatter looked at Rhodes, who smiled. "See, we're special." He took a giant bite of raisin-butterscotch cake covered with peanut butter, marshmallows, and gummy wads.

Hatter nodded. This was good. This was everything he had been hoping for. No, it was more than he'd been hoping for. These were his peers, Wonderlanders familiar with his family, whom he must have known as a small child. Never before, not even on his first day as an official cadet, had he felt such a keen sense of belonging.

LOOK, BUT DO NOT TOUCH.

That afternoon it was finally time for White Imagination class, where Hatter would learn to work with various caterpillar silks—how to tap into their power. He had seen Dalton's evolution over the years, how effortlessly he now used White Imagination for his purposes, and he had been more than a little envious.

Hatter was one of the few cadets who knew that Room 18 wasn't a room at all. Located at the end of a long, zigzagging tunnel in the southernmost part of the academy, Room 18 was actually a tent in what appeared to be a lush forest glade of permanent nighttime, despite its being on the second level inside the academy. Tiny flicker-moths flitted among tall blades of grass, their wings glowing red, orange, green, yellow, and blue. The tent itself was large and spacious, made of different-colored panels of silk. Yellow smoke seeped out between the stitches and seams, creating a mist in the glen. Inside the tent, Hatter found colorful cushions on the floor instead of desks and chairs. And in place of a tutor's desk, but larger, sat the instructor—a giant yellow caterpillar.

Hatter had never seen this instructor up close; his attempts to spy on the oversize larva having always been curiously thwarted. And even though this caterpillar was really just a projection manifested by the oracles who resided in the Valley of Mushrooms—all five of them communally projecting the single instructor—Hatter felt humbled and shy in his presence. The caterpillar barely fit inside the tent, his head pressing against the ceiling. Only his eyes moved as cadets entered and sat on the cushions, and Hatter wondered if Rhodes and the others felt the way he did—as if the caterpillar, despite what his eyes were doing, were watching only him.

Piles of wicker baskets surrounded the caterpillar like a nest. And though Hatter could not see the source of the smoke, it did seem that it was the caterpillar himself who was smoking. This much was confirmed when the creature let out a long sigh after the final cadet had taken her seat.

He gazed at the cadets and blinked. He blinked again.

He blinked a third time.

"Who are you?" His voice was soft, melodic.

One cadet was only too happy to offer a response. "Milliner cadets, sir!" Astra said, beaming.

The caterpillar nodded. He sat perfectly still, smoke swirling around his head and seeping out the top of the tent. His yellow hue seemed slightly orange now. Maybe it was a trick of the light.

"Imagination breathes life into all that is Wonderland." As the caterpillar said the word *breathe*, a stream of smoke left his mouth. "But its inhabitants find their own ways of controlling it. The royal family has it flowing through their veins. A mere thought can create wonders. And Milliners have it . . ." He paused again, waiting for something.

"In the fabric of the clothes and hats we make?" Newton tried.

"Yes. The fabric of the Milliner. Caterpillar silk. Different-colored threads from the caterpillar oracles. A precious gift from each, given when Wonderland was in its infancy. Threads, one could say, are the veins of clothing."

One could say that, thought Hatter, though he doubted very much that anyone did.

"The imaginative properties of caterpillar silk are exceedingly powerful. And you, you of the possible future, you alone have the ability to harness them in a fashion unlike anyone else in the queendom."

Awed silence.

"In this tent you shall learn of the properties of each color of caterpillar thread. And you will work with these threads. Imagination will flow within you."

The caterpillar was definitely orange. In fact, he was such a rich shade of orange he was almost red.

"Blue thread," said the caterpillar, and the lid of one of the baskets opened.

A single thread rose high into the air, as if it were dancing to the music of a snake charmer's instrument. It began to circle the caterpillar, floating. "Blue is the thread of vision. Blue sees all that is connected and understands what is to come. Orange thread." Another basket opened. A single orange thread rose into the air, joining the blue one in its course around the caterpillar. "Orange is strength. Green thread." And now green joined the orange and blue. "Green is growth and healing. Yellow thread." A stream of yellow joined the others. "Yellow is energy and heat. And then there is red. The heart thread. The thread of imagination itself."

All five threads circled around the caterpillar, weaving in and out through one another.

"We begin with the thread of strength, as we always do with Caps. Orange thread." In a moment that was like a quick intake of breath, every thread except for orange was sucked back into its basket. The orange thread rose above the cadets and divided into pieces, one piece for each of them, which settled curled up on the ground in front of their crossed legs.

"Look, but do not touch," said the caterpillar, who was now colored deep maroon.

Hatter stared at his thread. He didn't know what he expected would happen, but he waited hopefully.

"Observe the thread closely," the caterpillar instructed. "Look at its properties. See every small detail."

Hatter leaned so close to his thread that his nose almost touched it. He stared and stared, trying to see something special about its color or . . . something. Wasn't it glowing maybe, if ever so faintly? He almost seemed to taste the orangeness of his thread, a bittersweet tingling on his tongue. He stared harder, narrowing his focus. Everything melted away from him—everything except the tiny coil of orange on the ground.

A sudden ripple. Like a gust of wind had blown the thread. It slid several gwormmy-lengths, a messy line. Hatter looked up to note where the breeze had come from, only to see all his fellow cadets staring closely at their threads, which were still perfectly coiled.

Had he done that? Had he moved the thread?

"Nicely done, Hatter," said the caterpillar, who was now a rich shade of blue. The larva turned his head and stared toward the back of the tent. "That is all for today."

One by one, slowly, the cadets rose and shuffled out of the tent.

"That was fun," Rhodes said sarcastically as they made their way through the glen. "Ooh, the staring-at-thread class. My favorite."

Hatter nodded. "Yeah."

He supposed he'd have been just as frustrated as his friend if his own thread hadn't moved. But it had. And the thrill he'd felt . . . it was pure confidence, fearlessness, strength. He smiled to himself. He was getting it. He was becoming a Milliner.

13

TOO MUCH OF A MUCHNESS.

The rest of the day flew by so quickly that when Hatter went to bed, he could barely sleep for thinking about spiraling orange threads and his coming initiation into the Wellingtons. By the time he did fall asleep, he'd completely forgotten about his early-morning run, and was reminded of it only when he abruptly awoke to MM Clout towering over him in the dark.

The two quietly left the dormitory. Hatter began his jog, and once again the pain was almost instant. How could something as simple as running be so agonizing? And how could he be worse at it this morning compared to the last? When he'd made it three-quarters of the way around the academy, just as the suns were rising, he had to slow to a walk. And even then his feet felt like deadweights.

He stopped for a moment and bent over, panting, each inhalation like cold needles in his lungs. In a vain attempt to stretch out the pain, he stood and arched his back, staring at the towering academy to his left.

He was being watched from a window several stories up.

The tattooed boy.

They stared at each other for a moment. And then the kid vanished. Into thin air.

This was no residual nightmare. Hatter hadn't dreamed of the boy that night. But it couldn't be real either, could it?

He resumed his run, desperately hoping he might be fast enough to outrace the sinking feeling that chased him. He arrived back at his starting point only to discover that MM Clout had gone. Hatter returned to his bunk and collapsed.

He awoke a couple of hours later with the rest of the cadets and managed to convince himself that maybe he'd been so sleepy that he'd been in a dreaming-but-awake state when he'd seen the boy. It was enough of an explanation, at any rate, that he was able to carry on with his day, and in a pretty successful manner.

In Milliner Etiquette, when they were reviewing how to address royals, he came second only to Caledonia Alinari, a tall, short-haired blond girl with a fierce expression. She had known even the proper way to address a royal scribe ("Ahoy and good day"), which was pretty impressive.

Hatter had assumed his first Stealth Arts class would be loads more exciting than his History class, but it turned out to be terribly dull. There they were, in the infamous Wonderground—a vast room that could reweave itself into any place you desired it to be, whether the peak of the highest mountain, the heart of a dense forest, or one of the twelve deserts beyond space and time. And today it was an empty black room. And if that weren't bad enough, all they were asked to do there was sit perfectly still, without making a single sound, for the entire class.

Hatter ate lunch with Rhodes, Drummer, and the upper levels Benedict, West, and Nigel. Nigel and Benedict were Bond Clubs. And seeing as West was the Spades Top Hat, Hatter couldn't help but interrogate him about what it was like training as a Spade.

"You've got your sights set then," West said with a laugh, taking a sip of winglefruit juice.

"Yeah. I've spent my whole life being a spy, in a way, sneaking around the academy, watching cadets in class."

"Did you ever spy on the girls?" Nigel asked excitedly. "Do you know any secret entrances into the North Needle?"

"Uh, no," Hatter replied.

"Too bad." Nigel shook his head.

"There'll be plenty of sneaking around tonight," West said to Hatter. "We'll see how good you are."

For once, Hatter managed to keep his face neutral, showing nothing of what he felt. But he had little doubt: if there was one thing he excelled at, it was getting around the academy without being caught by tutors or MMs.

Weird: being in the Textillery as a cadet rather than high up on a roof beam with Weaver, looking down at the wealth of tools and fabrics. But here Hatter was, sitting at the long wooden table with the rest of the Caps.

If only Weaver could see me now! he kept thinking.

He tried to distract himself by closely examining his surroundings. Three walls of the Textillery were draped with rare silks of every color of the rainbow and a few others besides. The fourth wall was covered in weapons and armor, and it seemed as if the wall itself were glowing, the light from the windows high above reflecting off swords, daggers, J-blades, S-blades, and cuffs.

Hatter glanced up at the windows and felt a pang, missing Weaver, missing having someone with whom he could share his whirling thoughts.

Speaking of whirling thoughts . . . Hatter turned his head to look where he'd seen the tattooed boy a couple of days ago.

No one.

"Are we all met?" asked Tailor Quince, appearing from behind a silk tapestry detailing the entire history of King Nolan's grandfather. Tailor Quince was a small hunched man who wore tiny round spectacles at the end of his nose. His hair was long and gray, tied back in a knot. His beard was equally long and gray and also tied in a knot. The only thing Hatter knew about him was that he spoke little in his classes, and leaned in for quiet conversation with individual cadets, which of course in his "spy" days Hatter had never been able to hear from his perch in the rafters.

"Yes, sir!" boomed the Caps in response, all of them together in one room making for quite a presence.

Tailor Quince squinted and raised his hands. "Oh dear, no, no, no, no. That is too loud. Too much of a muchness. Don't do that again." He shuffled over to a large basket and handed it to Cadet Alinari, who was sitting to his right. "Take one; pass it along."

Caledonia reached into the basket and withdrew a plain doll, lacking a face. Just a simple sewn form of a Wonderlander, about a foot in height. She stared at it in confusion.

"Pass the basket along now, cadet."

Cadet Alinari passed the basket, and soon—

"Everyone have a doll?"

There was a moment when the Caps almost replied with a loud *Yes, sir!* but something stopped them. It was a sensation like what you might feel if you started to pull on a rope just as someone cut it in half. Instead, the cadets nodded yes.

"Good. Today you will fashion an outfit for your doll. No hat. I need to know your basic construction skill levels." Hatter glanced at Rhodes, who rolled his eyes; he evidently wasn't the only one who felt ridiculous playing with dolls.

"So, my little midsummer knights, you think playing with dolls is beneath your status as fierce warriors?" Tailor Quince asked. "Let me tell you a story. There once was a man who found the most powerful magic sword in all of Wonderland, the Vorpal Blade, but . . . he didn't know how to use a sword, so he used the mightiest weapon in the land as a doorstop." He paused for effect. The response from his students was confusion.

So he explained: "Thread is the most remarkable tool, but for those who don't know how to use it, it's a doorstop. Got it? To use a magic sword, you must first know how to use a regular sword. To manipulate mystical threads, you must first learn how to work with ordinary ones. Get going!"

The Caps were instantly on their feet, rushing about the room in search of the perfect fabrics and threads necessary for their work—all of them except Hatter. For the first time since he'd started classes, Hatter was truly nervous. A Millinery cadet's ability to craft wearable items was as important as the ability to craft weapons. He knew that the more skilled he was as a craftsman, the more White Imagination he'd be able to imbue into his clothes. And he was aware of how fierce the competition to collect caterpillar silk was for more advanced cadets, when they fashioned their Millinery frock coats and hatbands. Several students had been expelled from the academy for devious tactics in gathering thread—or for outright stealing.

Hatter's hands grew clammy. Unlike the other cadets, he hadn't been creating his own clothes since he was very young. Tutor Wren had often tried to teach him the most basic stitches, but he'd never mastered them; his skills remained woefully lacking. Because of this, the lessons taught in the Textillery were the one part of the academy curriculum that scared him.

He rose to join his fellow cadets sifting through the baskets of material. Other cadets had launched themselves into the mountain of ribbons in the far corner, while still others dangerously teetered at various levels of a tall tower of trunks, riffling through furs and scales.

Finally, Hatter found a simple black fabric that he thought would work well. He returned to his workstation and felt panic rise up inside him. *Now what?*

"A pattern," he heard Rhodes whisper.

Hatter looked around and saw cadets cutting shapes out of paper, which they would use to pattern their fabric.

From that point on he copied Rhodes, who quickly completed his work and left his station. Hatter tried to make his finished work look like his friend's, but it was an epic failure, his doll not nearly as neatly decked out. But at least it had a coat and pants.

"Time." Tailor Quince began making his rounds, starting at the opposite end of the table.

Rhodes reappeared at Hatter's side and gave him a wink. Hatter had no idea why. Then he examined Hatter's doll. Quickly, Rhodes began to sew some white fabric together. He then grabbed Hatter's doll and tore off the coat, replacing it with a white shirt. He picked apart the seams of the jacket and restitched it all together and did the same for the pants. He passed the doll back to Hatter. Hatter was about to object to Rhodes doing the work for him like that, but he heard some commotion coming from a few cadets down the table and turned to look.

"Sir, I fashioned pants. I did."

"Well, Cadet Ezer, your doll appears to be naked from the waist down."

Newton reached for the doll and held it carefully. "But . . . there were pants. I promise you."

"Don't be too concerned, Cadet Ezer, you did very well on the top half, especially all things considered—"

"No!" Newton interrupted. "No, not 'all things considered.' The jacket is perfect, the shirt flawless, and the pants were too."

"Too loud, too loud, Cadet Ezer. Where do you think you are? Don't worry about the trousers. You did a very good job for someone like you."

Newton stared straight ahead, not moving—almost, it seemed to Hatter, not breathing. He made the smallest of nods, and Tailor Quince continued on down the row.

"I've been looking forward to this," he said as he picked up Astra's doll. "It's been a long time since I've taught a Vost. What lovely work, what interesting color choices. You even made shoes. Very impressive."

Hatter had to admit he too was impressed with her work but less so with Astra's response, which was a large happy grin.

Tailor Quince made his way down to him and Rhodes, complimenting both of them on their skill. "But you lack creativity. And only with creativity can you harness White Imagination. Remember that."

Hatter and Rhodes nodded.

Tailor Quince returned to the front of the Textillery. "Class is dismissed. On your way out, check the list to see which group I have put you in."

A long, unfurled scroll materialized, tacked to the door.

"Good-bye." Tailor Quince turned around and exited through the same silk from which he had appeared.

Instantly the cadets rushed to the scroll.

"Good," said Rhodes, turning to Hatter with a smile. "We're in the same group. Drummer, how about you?"

Drummer peeled himself away from the scroll and nodded.

"Excellent. Madigan, you need to work on your skills, though. It's embarrassing."

"I know," Hatter replied, still staring at the scroll. Newton was standing in front of it, still as a statue. Then Cadet Alinari approached, and they exchanged a quiet word. She looked at the scroll and after a moment said something to him. Newton stormed off in a rage, clipping his shoulder on the doorjamb.

"I guess Newton's upset." Rhodes laughed as he, Drummer, and Hatter left the Textillery. "Hold out your hand, Madigan."

Hatter did. Something soft was slipped into it: a miniature pair of pants, perfectly stitched. He was taken with how intricate they were; they even had pockets. Quite frankly, they were beautiful. "Are these . . . ?"

Rhodes smirked.

"Why did you do that?"

"Because I felt like it. What's it matter? He's not going to make it to Brim, never mind graduation. He didn't even notice me sneak up and steal those things. Do you really want someone guarding Wonderland who can't tell when someone's right behind him?"

"Well, no . . . "

"Exactly. He'll be gone soon. He can't keep pace. Why not just speed up the process? In the long run, he'll probably be grateful he got cut so early."

"It still doesn't feel right."

"Well, that's your problem, isn't it, Madigan. Too much feeling. You've got to work on that. Think without feeling. Is it better for Newton to stay here and fail, or for him to be cut early so he can go find something he likes to do, and that he might be halfway decent at?"

Hatter thought for a moment. "I guess the second one."

"There you go."

DON'T YOU WANT TO READ YOUR STORY?

During his combat workshop in the HATBOX, Hatter didn't get hit once by the tattooed boy, despite inadvertently flinching when the kid first materialized and almost getting tackled as a result. At the last millisecond he dropped and rolled, and the boy went tumbling past. MM Haymaker commended Hatter on his defense.

In White Imagination class, Hatter got his orange thread to harden into a long, inflexible needle. The caterpillar said that he could at last touch it—the sole cadet in his class to be granted such a privilege. Hatter plucked the thread from the air and felt a *whoosh* flush over him. The power of orange thread, indeed.

At the end of class, as cadets were depositing their orange threads back in the basket, Hatter's mind leaped forward to that night. To his initiation into the Wellingtons. Whatever they'd be doing, he had to be impressive. He made as if to place his orange thread in the basket, but instead, with a flick of his fingers, he hid it up inside his shirtsleeve. He sensed the caterpillar watching him. But no—the instructor was facing the back of the tent.

Hatter felt a twinge of guilt. But he wasn't really stealing; more like borrowing. Borrowing some strength for a very important test this evening. He'd return the thread next class.

That night, as he lay silently under the covers waiting for some kind of sign from the Wellingtons, his stomach lurched. Why did they need to dress warmly? Would they be done with the initiation before his morning run with MM Clout? Why was he being forced to do a morning run in the first place? Was it because Clout recognized special potential in him, as he had in Dalton or . . . ?

He saw Rhodes slip out of bed. He did the same, pulling on his jacket. He double-checked that the orange thread was tucked safely in his pants pocket and joined Rhodes and Drummer as they snuck down the long aisle and out the door.

Benedict, West, and Nigel were waiting for them. Without a word they stepped out into the cold night.

"So," Hatter asked, his breath freezing in the air, "can you tell us where we're going now?"

There was a shared look among the upper-level cadets, and then West said, "We're going to the Archives."

Hatter's eyes grew wide before he had a chance to prevent them.

West laughed. "Wow, you're as easy to read as a book, Madigan. Anyone told you that?"

"Pretty much everyone," Rhodes said.

The Archives were a sacred cavern—not just to Milliners, but to all Wonderlanders. The academy had been built at its present location to fortify the Archives after the War of Red and White. The keepers of the Archives, known as the eeries, had been grateful and offered their services to the academy so that Wonderland might always have protectors. But the eeries were a mysterious and secretive bunch and never opened their doors except to "read" cadets and determine in which direction their life path should take them.

Some speculated that the eeries had formed from the silk of cocoons left behind by the first caterpillar oracles at the Beginning of All Things. Others said that the eeries consisted of nothing but smoke. Unlike the caterpillars, the eeries could not prophesy. They knew the past. They knew the present. They could only document what had already been and, based on that, make their determinations of what a Wonderlander should do—the true path of a Wonderlander, more often than not, being something that a Wonderlander himself could not see.

"But why are we going there?" Hatter asked, trying to sound casual.

"Don't you want to read your story? Don't you want to know where they plan on streaming you?" Nigel asked, his high-pitched voice bouncing off the outer walls.

"Sure. I guess. But I don't understand—the entrance is . . ." Hatter stopped. He was asking too many questions.

"There's another way in," West said. "Have some trust, Madigan."

They walked in silence now across the yard to the outer

western wall, which rose tall and formidable into the black sky—a barrier of giant gray bricks, each the size of a carriage.

"This isn't going to be as easy as strolling in the front door," West said. "You sure you guys are ready?"

Everyone nodded. West pushed hard against what looked like solid stone, but it swung away from his touch and opened out onto the cliff face of the Gray Peak. The boys slipped through the aperture one by one and stood looking down at the landscape. The gleaming towers of Wondertropolis could be seen in the distance, the city lights creating a halo in the night sky. And above it all, brighter than any other lights, glowed the Heart Crystal. It shone with a light both cold and warm, a light that was too bright to stare at and yet a comfort to the senses. Hatter had never been to the city. He had always wanted to go, though. Almost as much as he'd always wanted to be a Milliner.

"So it's all pretty straightforward. The cavern is just below us, and basically what you have to do is land *there*." West pointed down over the side of the cliff, and Hatter, Rhodes, and Drummer inched forward until they could see over the edge. The cliff face was long and rocky beneath them, the ground hidden by a swirling fog. The moonlight deftly tripped along the crevices and outcroppings, highlighting just how treacherous a wall lay below them.

"Uh, where?" Hatter asked, looking back at West.

West rolled his eyes and then closed them. He focused for a moment and then opened them again. "There."

Hatter turned to look again and saw a ledge highlighted by

the moonlight. It jutted out from the face of the cliff—approximately a hundred feet below them. "You want us to land on that?" He willed his voice not to quaver.

"Just visualize yourself landing there. It's not impossible. For a Wellington." Without warning, he jumped. Hatter watched wide-eyed as West landed as surefooted as a slithy tove, waved, and then disappeared into the cavern.

Benedict went next, casually stepping over the side of the cliff as if it were something he did every day. Nigel followed, jumping as if into a lake, even plugging his nose for some reason.

"Not all Milliners are born the same," Rhodes said, looking down at where the others had gone. "This jump is only for the best. You think any other Caps could do this?"

"I don't know," Hatter said.

"This is tradition for the best of the best. And that's us, right? So we have to go through it. And when we're Brims, we'll initiate the best new Caps."

Rhodes jumped.

Behind Hatter, a flat voice said, "I'm not doing that."

Hatter had forgotten about Drummer. "I think we have to."

Like a prisoner walking the plank of a ship, Drummer, with a sigh of resignation, walked off the cliff. Hatter looked over the side at where he was supposed to land. He closed his eyes and put his hands into his pockets, felt for the orange thread, and held it tightly between his fingers. Then he pictured himself successfully landing on the ledge. He imagined rough stone under his feet, the majestic view, the rushing wind echoing in the cavern behind him. He was overwhelmed by a feeling of lightness and ease, a brightness behind the eyes.

He opened his eyes and stepped to the cliff's edge, the tips of his boots sticking out into the air. He looked down, straight down, and imagined himself falling, a strong wind keeping him close to the craggy cliff wall. But not too close.

And he jumped.

Things didn't go quite as he'd imagined. He tried to envision a soft, graceful landing, but when the actual falling started and the wind began whipping around him, his mind raced and the calm focus he needed was gone. He was sure he'd break a leg, maybe more, but just before he slammed into the rocks, his coat billowed out and acted like a parachute, slowing him down. He landed, not gracefully but without breaking anything.

He'd made it. He'd actually done it.

"Was starting to think you'd left us," West said.

Hatter turned to see his friends waiting just inside the dark cavern. "Can't a guy take time to enjoy a view?"

The Wellingtons laughed.

"Come on," West said, "but keep it down."

The cavern grew darker as they wandered further into its depths. Finally, it became a narrow tunnel through which they had to walk in single file. No one said anything as the blackness engulfed them, and Hatter simply had to trust that West and his friends knew what they were doing. As he walked behind Rhodes, he heard the *creak* of rope rubbing against wood, and

then he understood. He sensed Rhodes stepping off stone and onto something before him, and Hatter slowed his walk to a crawl. Gwormmy-length by gwormmy-length he moved forward. The sound was different here. More hollow. There's a hole, realized Hatter. A large, deep, horrible hole.

And evidently a bridge that crossed it.

Hatter reached out blindly before him and held the thick rope railings with both hands. Concentrating, imagining his own continued safety, he stepped forward. Wood groaned underfoot and his body swung slightly to the right as his weight caused the bridge to compensate for his presence. Up ahead: a sharp *crack*; a desperate shout.

"What's going on?" West called out from the other side.

"Nigel!" Rhodes called back. "The boards broke beneath him!"

Hatter charged forward. He wanted to help. But it was so dark. If only he could see more clearly, just see . . .

Suddenly, he discerned a faint outline before him. It became stronger, and it was as if a small light had turned on. Just enough that Hatter was able to see distinct forms. Nigel was dangling from the bridge, holding on tight to a loose plank as Rhodes and Benedict tried to pull him up. That's when Hatter saw it. The plank Nigel was clinging to was sliding toward him. So were the two under Rhodes's feet. Hatter dove down and flattened himself on the boards, pinning them tight with his body.

"Madigan, what are you doing?" Rhodes asked in shock.

"Just get him up. Hurry. The boards are slipping."

If they hadn't realized the urgency before, they did now. Nigel was hauled up onto the bridge as it swung back and forth violently. Hatter held on for dear life, his legs sliding to the side, and his feet dangling over the chasm.

"Let's go!" Nigel said, getting to his feet. Hatter staggered up. They rushed across the bridge, avoiding the gap in the boards, and collapsed on the other side.

"How in Wonderland did you see those boards?" Rhodes was panting hard.

"The light," he replied, trying to stabilize his own breath.

"What light?" Benedict asked.

There was a pause.

"That really is some mighty imagination you have there, Madigan," West said in appreciation. "All right, let's move on."

Hatter was confused. Orange thread was meant to help him with strength, not vision. That was blue thread. How had he managed to see so well in the darkness with only orange thread as an aid?

He kept pace with the others as they waded through some unpleasant, smelly black goo. The tunnel eventually opened into a large cavernous room hollowed out of the mountain. The room was lit by a blue glow, though where it came from Hatter couldn't see, and its depths seemed immeasurable, as if the room stretched fully through the mountain and out the other side. Stalactites dripped down from the ceiling, shiny and wet, and stalagmites grew up from the floor, but stunted and flattened, used as supports for tables, or pillars on which dusty old books and folders of parchments teetered in tall towers.

Shelves carved out of the rock and piled high with more papers rose up so high that they vanished into darkness.

The Archives. This was where the eeries would read each student and determine whether he or she would continue at the Millinery or be sent away. This was where the Caps would learn which suit had been chosen for them.

But Hatter knew through conversations overheard in the academy halls that the eeries did such menial tasks unwillingly. He remembered one conversation between Tutors Orlage and Wren about some kind of stubborn dissent—eeries protesting that their business with cadets was taking away from their work.

"That's absurd," Orlage had complained. "It is because of the academy that they are given such freedoms and protected from the outside world, from enemies who would murder them for their knowledge."

Every story of every Wonderlander was here. Down to the smallest detail, all lives had been recorded by the eeries and were continuing to be recorded. Even this mischief of Hatter and his friends would feature in their stories. The good news was that the eeries were never aware of the meaning of their words as they wrote them. Only if they read their writings later did they comprehend. And they rarely read them. So it was likely that the eeries would never know that Hatter and his fellow cadets had broken into the Archives.

Hatter wandered to the middle of the room, where a large stone platform stood. On top of it were six desks, each fashioned out of particularly large stalagmites. This was where the eeries sat. This was where the eeries wrote—not with pen and ink, but with caterpillar thread. Each book was an embossed record. Hatter stepped up onto the platform. He felt a strange dizzying sensation, his whole body grew warm, and it felt as if his head were being pulled in one direction and his feet in the other.

"Madigan!" Rhodes whispered furiously, and Hatter jumped down off the platform.

Benedict vanished into a dark recess on the other side of the cave.

"Where's he going?" Hatter asked.

"We've been here once before," West said. He was leaning against a tower of papers that, oddly, had the smallest on the bottom and the largest on top. "He knows what he's looking for. Do you?"

"My story."

"Do you know what it looks like?" It was a rhetorical question, of course, said with a raised eyebrow.

"It's a small book, bound in red leather, with a gold star with seven points embossed on the front," replied Hatter.

West and Rhodes stared at him in shock, and if Hatter could have stared at himself, he would have done the same. Where in Wonderland had that answer come from?

"Okay," West said slowly. "Well. Good. Now find it. But remember, read it where you find it. Do not move it."

Hatter took a long slow look around the cave. "Why?"

"I don't know. That's what I've been told."

Hatter scanned the shelves. He could see his story, the book of his life, perfectly in his mind's eye, but where it was he had no idea. And the more he thought about it, the less he was able to see the leather-bound tome.

Stop thinking about it so hard. Think about something else.

Rhodes and West had gone off to read their own stories. He was alone, and he worked his way through the dark into another, smaller cave. This one had a light, a single flickering candle standing on top of a small round wooden table. Not only was every wall of this cave obscured by books—so was the ceiling. Hatter leaned back so he could stare at the spines of the books above him. And then he saw it. A red spine that he knew belonged to his story.

But how exactly could he read it if he wasn't allowed to remove it? With sudden determination, he climbed up onto the little table and reached for the book, pulling it slowly out and down toward himself. He glanced at the cover, running his fingers over the gold star, and then jumped off the table. Leaning against it, his heart pumping fast, he stared at the cover once more. There was no real reason a Wonderlander shouldn't read his or her own story. This wasn't an oracle or a prophecy. It was a historical document that chronicled what had already happened, not what was to come. But it was still something that wasn't done.

But Hatter wanted to read his story. He wanted to know. *Needed* to know. He had to know the part of his life he could remember only in flashes here and there. The part where he went from having parents to not having parents.

Hatter opened the book.

The candle went out.

In the dim blue glow that haunted the rest of the Archives, Hatter stared at the first page of his story.

It was blank.

KEEP CLIMBING!

The first page was blank.

So was the second.

And the third.

He flipped faster and faster through the pages till all was a white blur.

Nothing. Every page completely and totally blank.

A loud, dull *thud* sounded from somewhere in the larger cavern, as if a boulder had become dislodged and fallen from a great height. Hatter closed the book and shoved it inside his vest, and then ran out to see the others at the mouth of the tunnel.

"What's going on?" he asked, not liking the panicked looks on their faces.

"Not sure," West said, "but I think whatever security the eeries have on this place has just been activated."

Hatter looked up into the darkness overhead. He heard what might've been the shushing of river rapids, faint but growing louder. He wasn't the only one who heard it.

"I'm not waiting to find out what *that* is," Rhodes said, and sprinted into the tunnel, followed quickly by Benedict, West, and Nigel.

Only Hatter and Drummer were left, heads tilted up, listening.

"Wings," Drummer said in that monotone of his.

Yes, it was obvious now, the distinct sound of flapping. More than one set of wings was coming toward them through the darkness.

"Hundreds," Drummer said. "Thousands."

He dove into the tunnel and Hatter ran after him. There was a sudden gust of wind at his back, as if the flapping wings had entered the tunnel in pursuit. At the bridge, Hatter and Drummer didn't slow down; they launched themselves out onto the groaning wooden planks. The rope railings burned Hatter's hands as he hurried, unaware of how dangerously the bridge swayed. He remembered the missing board just in time and called out a warning, he and Drummer leaping over the open space and rushing onto solid ground again, only to pick up speed.

Rhodes and the Wellingtons were at the mouth of the cave, moonlight shining on the ledge where they had all landed to reach this sacred place.

"Let's go!" West ordered as Drummer and Hatter joined them. West started to climb the mountain, picking his way up the steep, unfriendly face of the cliff.

"Seriously?" Hatter said.

"Did you think we were going to fly?" Nigel shouted over the noise of flapping wings and the wind rushing at them from all sides.

Surreptitiously taking the orange thread from his pocket and tying it around his right index finger, Hatter climbed with the rest of them—Rhodes, West, Benedict, Nigel, and Drummer, all clambering up the jagged rocks, carefully finding hand- and footholds.

A high-pitched squeal echoed out of the cave, making the entire mountain vibrate, like gnashing teeth.

Imagine yourself surefooted as a noffy goat, Hatter instructed himself.

He reached out and, with his right hand, grabbed a protrusion of rock above his head. He wedged the toe-end of his right boot into a crevice at the level of his waist, and hauled himself up. Left hand now on a spiky knob of rock, left foot struggling for purchase, again he heaved himself up, just as—

A winged creature with the face of a wolf and the talons of an eagle burst from the cave below. Its leathery wings easily spanned ten feet across. Others of its kind swarmed out into the sky. Drummer had been right; there were hundreds of them—meat eaters with fangs the size of swords. Blind, they navigated their environment using echolocation, their shrieks mapping the landscape as sound waves bounced off surfaces near and far, tree, cliff, and Wonderlander.

"Keep climbing!" Rhodes yelled.

Hatter's arms ached, his shoulder sockets ached, his calves

ached. Everything ached. He was almost halfway to the top of the cliff, but it might as well have been in the planet's stratosphere, it seemed so distant.

One of the beasts attacked the cliff a spirit-dane's length to Hatter's left; deadly splinters of rock fell clattering down the mountainside. Hatter's right hand lost its grip, his feet slipped from beneath him, and his body swung out into open air. Only the fingertips of his left hand kept him from falling into the fog below, tumbling down through that damp whiteness to fatal ground. He threw his right hand forward, found a granite lip wide enough to grab. His feet worked themselves into cracks, and Hatter held himself flat and still against the uncaring rock, breathing hard.

A crash above sent shards of quartz and limestone hailing down on him. He held fast, waited, started to climb again. But the winged beasts were everywhere, shrieking, manic-jawed, trying to locate their prey. Repeatedly, they threw themselves against the cliff, dislodging whole chunks of it, and now a boulder bounced toward Hatter in a welter of shards and dust.

He threw himself sideways.

His feet landed on a narrow outcropping. His fingertips pressed down on jutting stone. But then a prickly wing hit him hard and he fell—down and down into a sea of fog.

Time seemed to slow. How calm he was now that he was falling to his death. But something happened as he plummeted through the mist. Time sped up again. The rushing wind. The cold and wet. The ground now visible and rapidly approaching. He panicked.

Imagine a branch catching my vest, a miraculously located trampoline to land on, any—!

Something pierced his left shoulder. This was it, the brutal explosion of pain as he hit the ground, his mind and body at the moment of their obliteration.

But no, he was moving skyward, being carried.

His eyelids grew heavy. He managed to turn his head. He saw a flapping shadow above him, heard a shrill cry, and then all went black.

Y

Moments. Just moments. In and out. And blackness. The Wellingtons surrounding him. Floating. No. Not floating, being carried. Blackness. The tattooed boy staring down at him. Blackness. Benedict with a bandage. Pain. Searing pain. Blackness.

Y

Hatter awoke in his bunk. He tried to prop himself up, muttering, "Sorry I'm late, MM Clout."

"He's clearly still out of it. Hey, Madigan. It's me, West," whispered a familiar voice.

Hatter's vision focused. The Wellingtons and his new classmates were staring down at him with concern. "What's going on?"

"We were hoping you could tell us," Rhodes said. "We

found you way down along the inside of the wall, almost at the South Needle. You were unconscious and had this crazy hole in your shoulder."

Oh, right. Hatter reached up to his wound and felt fabric.

"I patched you up," Benedict said.

"Thanks." It still hurt, though, which he wasn't about to admit. "Uh, I'm pretty sure one of those beasts saved me. Or it accidentally stuck me with its talon and then happened to drop me off on the safe side of the wall." Both sounded equally unlikely. And yet . . .

"Crazy," Nigel said.

"I guess." Hatter suddenly remembered his story, the blank book of his life. He wasn't wearing his academy jacket. Had Rhodes or any of the others seen it? Was the book even still in his jacket pocket or had it fallen out at some point? "You guys should go. I'm all right now."

"Yeah, okay." West smiled broadly. "Welcome to the Wellingtons, Madigan. You and Rhodes and Drummer all made it." And with Nigel and Benedict, he snuck stealthily out of the Caps dormitory.

"Seriously," Hatter said to Rhodes and Drummer. "I'm okay. Go to bed."

Alone, he instantly fell asleep, not waking until someone shook him by the shoulder and he yelped with pain.

"Time to get up," Rhodes said.

"And you had to grab my shoulder to wake me?" Hatter said, reeling.

"Oh. Totally forgot. Sorry."

Light flooded the room. Cadets were putting the final touches on their bunks in preparation for inspection. Hatter scrambled to his feet and dressed as quickly as he could with an injured shoulder. Rhodes and Drummer made his bed. As he put on his jacket, he felt something hard in the inner pocket. His book. So it hadn't fallen out, after all. But how was he ever going to return it without anyone knowing? Why, really, had he even stolen it in the first place?

Speaking of stealing . . .

Hatter reached into his pants pocket. Nothing. Then he remembered: he'd tied the thread to his finger. But his hands were bare.

He'd lost the thread.

MM Clout stomped into the room, his typically grumpy self, showing no sign of unusual displeasure with Hatter for having missed their early-morning workout. In fact, Clout acted as if he had no knowledge of any such workouts at all.

16

NO ONE THINKS YOU BELONG HERE.

T he next day, Hatter was grateful for the deskbound listening required of him in his tutor classes. The classes were boring, but at least they didn't aggravate his wound.

Tutor Mars was lecturing on the historical importance of each suit. "I've been teaching here long enough to know that certain suits have a more glamorous appeal to Caps than others. And yes, I can understand the apparent thrill of becoming a spy or a member of the military. But the value that the Diamonds and Hearts bring to Wonderland cannot be overstated. The Spades would not know where to spy, the Clubs not know where to attack, if not for the Diamonds' defensive strategies that protect our land. And without Hearts to protect the royal family, I cringe to even think what would happen to Wonderland. The highest honor a cadet can achieve is to be named the queen's personal bodyguard."

True, thought Hatter. But there was only one such role, and it was now filled by his brother.

"I know you'll say that is only one position. But you should think of the Hearts as an elite force under the palace's command. Not very different from the Clubs when you think about it."

MM Mars was making it sound pretty good to be a Heart, and Hatter *had* seen how much Dalton enjoyed being one. But he wanted to do his own thing, forge his own path.

"You are a short while away from the moment when you will be read by the eeries and streamed into a suit. This is a time-honored tradition gifted to each Milliner by a mystical and ancient race. The eeries have been following your life story since you were born. They know you better than you know yourself."

Hatter's hand was in the air before he realized he had raised it. Rhodes furrowed his brow at him.

"Cadet Madigan. Did you want to tell us something about Dalton and his experience as a Heart?" asked Tutor Mars.

"No. I mean, sure, he really likes it. I just wanted to ask about the eeries and the reading."

Tutor Mars stared at him for a moment, and then finally said, "Yes?"

"What if they don't have a story for you?"

"I don't understand."

"What if they haven't written your story?"

"That's not something that happens, so there really isn't an answer to such an odd and puzzling question," replied Tutor Mars, looking at him through squinted eyes.

"Oh. Okay," said Hatter. That certainly made him feel like a misfit: being the only Wonderlander with no story.

"Now, of course, not all of you will be streamed," Mars continued. "Some of you will find that your calling is outside of the Millinery Academy. We all have our destinies in Wonderland, whatever they may be. It's nothing to be ashamed of."

Hatter tried to avoid Rhodes after class, but he wasn't fast enough out of the room.

"That was kind of weird there, Madigan," Rhodes quipped, locking step with him in the hall. "I never knew you could do such a good impression of a Vost. But I wouldn't do it again, if I were you. Stuff like that just makes you look really bad."

Hatter ignored him, kept walking.

Rhodes grabbed him by the arm and stopped him. "Hey, I'm trying to help," he said. "You're my friend, and I don't want you to make a fool of yourself."

Of course. Hatter was beginning to understand. It was all about Rhodes and his reputation. He sighed and rolled his eyes. Rhodes took a step closer. "Don't give me attitude, Madigan. You want to hang out with the top cadets, you've got to act like one. Not like some stupid baby who needs to ask questions."

"I'm not going to do it again," he said quietly, noticing a small crowd had formed.

"Yeah? You think you can control those outbursts of yours?"

Hatter glanced around. Everyone was staring. This was horrible. He didn't need everyone thinking that he didn't belong here. All because he'd asked a dumb question. A blur of turquoise passed through his line of vision. He wrenched his arm away from Rhodes and turned.

"Hey, Astra!" he called out. Astra stopped and bounced back toward him.

"Hi, Hatter! What's up?"

This had to work; it just had to. Though even before he said anything, a small knot formed in his gut. "Just wondering what you thought of Tutor Mars's class . . . if you really believed all that stuff about it not being shameful to be kicked out of the academy."

"Oh, yeah, sure. I think it's fine."

Hatter saw the eyes of the cadets who had been staring at him a few moments ago now turn and stare at Astra. It was working. "Good. Because I think you're going to make a great tailor someday. I might even come by and get you to make me a suit when I've graduated."

"Oh. Well, I don't think I'm going to be a tailor, but you could ask my parents!" Astra said with a smile.

Rhodes smirked at Astra. Hatter ought to have felt relieved seeing Rhodes's attention switch from him to her. But that smile just made the knot in his stomach tighter. Hatter stared at Astra, unable to remember what he wanted to say next.

"Come on, Astra," Rhodes said. "Everyone knows you're not making it to Brims. You're a mess." He grinned at Hatter, and Hatter gave him a feeble smile back. The plan had worked, but maybe it hadn't been such a good plan.

"That's not true," Astra said. Her smile faltered, and Hatter swore he could see her lower lip quiver. The knot in his gut got so tight it seemed to be preventing him from breathing properly.

"Seriously?" Rhodes continued. "How can you even think that? Everyone knows that a Vost never makes it to Brims."

"I will," she said quietly.

Hatter could see how upset she was getting, which was all the more upsetting considering her usual unflappably happy demeanor. But Rhodes was his friend again, and Hatter just couldn't stop him. That would defeat the purpose, and then he would have made Astra upset for no reason. Right?

No, no, this was wrong. He should stop him. Somehow.

"Rhodes—" he started, his voice catching at the back of his throat.

Rhodes waved him off and continued talking. "Okay,"— Rhodes raised his arm in the air—"how about this: if you don't think Astra is making it to Brims, put your hand up." The cadets in the hallway looked at one another. Rhodes looked at Hatter, and Hatter felt trapped. If he didn't raise his hand, he'd become Rhodes's target again. If he did, though . . . Hatter noticed a few hands were already in the air. Well, if he wasn't the first one, if he was merely following what everyone else was doing, maybe that was okay. He raised his hand slowly. A few more cadets raised their hands, then more, then more, until all the cadets in the hallway had their hands in the air. All, Hatter noticed, except Caledonia Alinari, who had just turned the corner and was staring at Rhodes and Hatter with a stern expression on her face.

"See! No one thinks you belong here, Astra. You should

just go home now—why make the eeries waste time reading you?"

A tear fell down Astra's cheek, her big eyes wide and shining. Caledonia grabbed her by the arm, surprising everyone, but especially Astra, who yelped.

"Come on. Let's get out of here." Caledonia threw Hatter a scowl before escorting Astra from the hall. The rest of the cadets continued on their way, and Hatter and Rhodes were left standing together.

"See how delusional she is?" Rhodes said.

Hatter felt horrible. He felt like a coward, and he didn't know what was worse: Astra's tear or Cadet Alinari's scowl.

"And hey, sorry about earlier. You're totally one of us. I shouldn't have said all that," Rhodes added.

Hatter nodded.

Oh good.

He was one of "us" again.

Why did that not feel particularly comforting?

17

TONIGHT WE BATTLE IT OUT FOR THE SPADES!

For the first time, Hatter's morning run wasn't a punishment. It was a reprieve. He'd been troubled by the Astra incident since it happened. Running, he had no chance to think about anything but his breathing and the pain in his shoulder—the struggle to *keep going*. He made it all around the academy without stopping, though he did glance up when he passed the window where he'd seen the tattooed boy. But there was no one. Maybe it really had been his imagination.

Fortunately, too, Stealth Arts was his first class of the day, and Astra wasn't in it. And in White Imagination class, which he did share with her, he was too afraid that the caterpillar would ask him about the missing orange thread to notice much else. As it turned out, his concern was misplaced, since the caterpillar simply stated, "Arrogance should not be mistaken for bravery," and then sent small spirals of blue thread flying at the cadets for the remainder of the period.

But what helped him push the whole thing out of his head completely was an announcement made during dinner. It had probably been a strategic move to make the announcement then, considering how excited the general student population was at the news. Even at an institution that valued discipline and stoicism, it was hard for cadets to hold back their excitement. A Top Hat duel. The first of the year. Someone had challenged West for his position as Spades Top Hat.

After dinner, and even though attendance was optional, the whole student body and every tutor and MM filed into the Wonderground. Hatter even saw Sir Isaac Shimmer sitting in his pajamas up at the top of the grandstand; for some reason he looked nervous, as if the outcome of the fight actually mattered to him. Well, maybe it did—maybe he and one of the Master Milliners had a bet going, as was often the case.

The Wonderground had taken on the form of a large spade-shaped stadium with a sandy arena in the middle. Even though the Wonderground was inside the academy, the stadium appeared as if it were outdoors and open to the night sky, and Hatter marveled at the imagination needed to achieve this. He knew that under his feet were caterpillar thread and pools of White Imagination that allowed the Wonderground to reweave into different settings, but the stadium seemed as immovable as the great Gray Cliffs on which the academy sat.

Hatter climbed the grandstand with Rhodes and slipped into one of the saved seats next to Nigel and Benedict. They were in a prime location, with front-row views of the action. Hatter looked up at the sky—a giant spade mapped out in stars.

The back of his chair had decorative spades carved into it.

"Who challenged West?" Hatter asked.

"A Brim, name of Dogberry," Benedict said.

"A *Brim?*" Rhodes asked, astonished. "When was the last time that happened?"

"It happens plenty. Cadets trying to show off, challenging upper levels," Benedict explained. "Except there's rarely any follow-through. They usually get too scared and pull out of the contest. Except of course with Dalton." Benedict gave Hatter a small nod, and Hatter responded likewise.

Dalton had been the youngest Top Hat in the academy's history—a newly streamed Brim Heart who had challenged and beaten a Peak. This success had made him a target, and he was challenged by several cadets every year. It got to the point where a Cobbler finally just ambushed him in a hallway. Grand Milliner Falcon had to put a stop to such doings and expelled the Cobbler. The surprise attack had certainly helped Dalton hone his superior fighting skills, though.

It was something to aspire to. But Hatter wasn't sure he could do it—challenge someone when he made it to Brims. As a Brim, he'd have only just begun training with a hat. How could he possibly be ready for a duel by then? But Dalton had always been ready. For anything.

"Welcome to the first Top Hat duel of the season," announced a disembodied voice that echoed around the Wonderground. The cadets sat quietly, although an excited, brief clapping could be heard somewhere to Hatter's left. He felt sure it was Astra.

"Tonight we battle it out for the Spades!"

Again the solitary clapping quickly petering out into silence.

"The challenger, from Brims—Cadet Dogberry Shake!"

Dogberry entered the arena through a tunnel under the stands. He was pretty much the opposite of formidable—tiny, with a mass of curly blond hair and very pale skin. His hat, too tall for his body, teetered about, ready to topple over. The boy looked stunned. His face was expressionless, and he walked slowly to his starting position as if he really didn't want to be there, as if he were about ready to turn around and run.

"And defending his title as Spades Top Hat is Taper Cadet West Trilby!"

The general level of excitement in the room rose, though of course no one made a sound. Especially not the anonymous clapper. In fact, Hatter could almost hear the clapper not clapping. He could tell, though, that it wasn't just Spades who supported the charismatic West; he seemed quite well liked in general. He entered the arena with determination and all due seriousness, stopped for a moment to take in the crowd, and then whipped off his hat and gave a low bow. The silence became even more supportive.

"The rules are simple. Whoever gives up first, loses. No underhanded moves and no injury that may lead to permanent damage. A general expectation of good form is . . . expected." The amplified voice paused for a moment. "Begin!"

The two cadets eyed each other across the sandy arena. It seemed quite clear West was waiting for Dogberry to make the first move. Which is precisely what happened. Dogberry whipped his hat off his head and sent it flying toward West, who ducked easily out of the way and stood up with a disappointed shake of his head. Dogberry charged at West, and West stepped to the side just as Dogberry's hat came flying back toward its owner and hit Dogberry in the face. The boy fell backward onto the ground. The silence from the crowd was highly amused.

West waited as Dogberry stood up, placed his hat back on his head, and drew his J-blade. West unsheathed his own blade, and the two approached each other. Dogberry lunged, his weapon raised high above his head, but West parried easily enough, spinning and swinging his blade to within half a gwormmy-length of Dogberry's stomach, holding it still. Dogberry looked down and stared at it very calmly for a cadet who would have had his guts spilled all over the Wonderground had West not restrained himself. Dogberry tossed his blade away. West sheathed his.

It didn't seem as if Dogberry had much understanding of his own weapons.

"How does someone reach Brim Spades and not know how to use a J-blade?" Hatter whispered.

"Hand-to-hand's next, I bet," Rhodes said.

West and Dogberry circled each other in the center of the arena, holding their fists in front of their faces. Dogberry tried a left hook, and West ducked. He tried two uppercuts, one right after the other, and West jumped back.

"Bo-ring," Rhodes said.

Dogberry launched himself at West, grabbing him and holding him tight in a weird-looking hug. West cried out and wrenched away, reaching for his cheek. "He bit me!"

"Foul!" the disembodied voice of the announcer called.

The two boys began to retreat to their spots, but suddenly Dogberry turned around and charged West. He jumped onto West's back, and West, taken completely by surprise, fell face-first into the dirt. A loud *crack* accompanied the fall. Dogberry grabbed West's hat and threw it to the side of the ring with one hand and with the other grabbed West's mohawk, pulled his head up, and slammed his face into the ground.

"Foul!" the announcer called again.

Dogberry rose and climbed off West. When West started to stand, Dogberry kicked him in the side, causing him to roll onto his back. Then Dogberry was on top of him again, this time straight-out punching his face. West was clawing at Dogberry, but it didn't seem to do anything but encourage the boy.

"Foul, foul!"

Dogberry kept punching, and West's face was getting slick with his own blood. In a blur, a figure jumped into the arena; it was Caledonia.

"Cadet Alinari, remove yourself from the ring!" the amplified voice ordered.

Caledonia sprinted across the sand, grabbed Dogberry by his collar, yanked him off West, and threw him to the ground. "Bad form!" she said.

One of the referees, a Peak named Busby, was making his way over to remove Caledonia when Dogberry swept his foot across the dirt, catching her ankle. Caledonia fell hard on her back. He then leaped on top of her and started punching her face. She blocked several blows and got him in the gut. Dogberry whipped off his hat and threw it behind him, hitting Busby in the stomach and sending him flying backward.

Dogberry focused again on Caledonia.

"Watch it!" Astra called out, and Caledonia turned her head just in time. A pocket U-blade pinned her ear to the ground. She screamed in pain.

Suddenly a hat came flying at Dogberry, hitting him squarely in the back of the head with such force that the boy was knocked unconscious. Silence fell over the crowd, and only West's moaning could be heard. MM Haymaker leaped down into the arena and approached West. MM Clout ran over to check on Caledonia.

MM Haymaker knelt down and examined West closely. "Healers!" she called. "Immediately!"

The alarm rang out, three loud chimes.

Benedict jumped over the barrier into the ring and hurried to West's side.

"Cadet Jingasa, stay back," Haymaker ordered.

Benedict stopped short, silent as he stared down at his friend. There was a lot of blood. It mingled with the sand beneath West, forming dark muddy clumps.

There was a flurry of green as the healers rushed into the arena, all wearing their signature green berets. Hatter watched as their leader, Commander Divina, crouched down and cradled West's head in her hands. She was still for a moment, and then she made a quick gesture. Hatter saw the emerald ribbon that encircled her beret unravel into a single green glowing thread of caterpillar silk. Green thread, the thread of healing and growth, was a vital tool for all Milliner medics. The filament floated loose in the air, shining in the light. Then the end of the thread became firm and sharp, and the commander forced it like a needle into West's skin. She began stitching up the open wound. When she turned to bark orders at one of her healers, Hatter saw that the entire side of her face was scarred and burned and sutured together with green threads—now so dark they were practically black. Hatter remembered the story about her that Cook had once whispered to him. The commander had almost been killed in battle by an explosion. She had saved herself by using the green thread to close her own wounds, and the thread remained there to this day. Not because it was necessary, but as a reminder to everyone of the kind of person they were dealing with.

When the commander finished her stitching, she produced a small green pod from her pocket. She placed it carefully on West's forehead, and instantly thin green vines grew out of it, draping and winding their way gently around his body until he was completely covered except for his face. A healer slipped his hands under West's shoulders, and the body rose, stiff as a board, and floated in the air. MM Clout helped Caledonia limp to the door, and the commander along with her healers escorted West's body out of the arena, leaving behind a dark wet patch on the ground—and of course the unconscious

Dogberry, whom they had only briefly glanced at. He was stirring now, and quickly the tutors and MMs took control of the
cadets.

"Everyone back to the Needles!" announced Head Tutor
Orlage.

The cadets rose and began to leave the grandstand. Hatter
too, though he watched as Dogberry sat up. The boy rubbed his
head and looked around with a dazed expression. He saw the
blood on the ground and stared wide-eyed at MM Haymaker.
Hatter just managed to hear him say, "Where am I?" before
Hatter was engulfed by the wave of students heading for the
exit. It pushed him along until he was swept out the doors and
directly into the tattooed boy.

Hatter stood, stunned, just staring at him. The boy returned
the look for a moment and then said, "You have to come with
me now." He turned and rushed off in the opposite direction
from the flow of students.

Hatter watched the boy's retreating back. No longer would
he pretend, no longer would he lie to himself about what he
was, in fact, seeing. He felt an intense need to know what was
going on.

The boy turned. "Now!"

And Hatter followed him.

18

HE'S ABOUT TO JUMP.

The tattooed boy was standing by a large hole in the wall, an entrance to the seams that Hatter had discovered only a few lunar cycles ago. The opening appeared in the wall when you tickled under the chin of the knight statue standing next to it.

"Come quickly!" The boy ducked into the seams, and Hatter followed, the aperture closing up immediately behind them.

Hatter wished he had a bit of blue caterpillar thread to help him see in the darkness. Sure, he knew the seams well enough, but there were so many options, so many twists and turns and byways leading off in numerous directions. If he could see, it'd be easier to understand the route the boy was taking.

He reached out and touched the wall of the seam. The fabric was smooth, if a little frayed. Closing his eyes, he ran his fingers along the wall, imagining that he was empowered by any blue threads he touched. Without knowing quite why,

Hatter stopped on a spot. Then he focused hard. Once again that wave of confidence washed over him. He opened his eyes, and suddenly he was able to see in the dark, to see the figure of the boy running down the seam far ahead of him.

Hatter followed, his heart pumping fast. The seam delved deeper into the interior of the academy. He turned another corner and saw slatted light a short distance ahead. The boy was there, standing next to a rectangular vent that opened into the Hall of Mirrors.

"He's about to jump." The boy pointed.

Sir Isaac Shimmer was standing before an ornate glass, staring hard into it. It wasn't just any looking glass but one connected to the Crystal Continuum, the means by which many Wonderlanders traveled through the queendom, entering through one glass and emerging from another. Hatter himself, in quiet moments, had snuck out to the Hall of Mirrors and stared into them, so tempted to explore the rest of Wonderland. To leave the academy and have an adventure. The only time he'd been brave enough to give the continuum a try had been after a particularly vicious argument with Dalton, when his older brother had accused Hatter of being a coward. In an attempt to prove him wrong, Hatter had rushed to the Hall of Mirrors and jumped through the closest looking glass. It had taken him into the large domed library in the Tutor Corps training facility, and he'd been instantly punished by Tutor Wren (whom he'd interrupted trying to mediate a debate between a dictionary and a novel).

Hatter had forgotten that not every looking glass in the

Hall of Mirrors was connected to the Crystal Continuum, that some were part of a closed-circuit system used within the academy itself. Upper-level cadets were encouraged to practice portal running within the safety of the institution.

He hadn't again ventured into a looking-glass portal, although he had made a point of memorizing which mirrors in the hall were part of the academy's closed-circuit system, which were directly connected to specific destinations, and which connected to the main avenues of the Crystal Continuum itself, allowing a traveler access to many destinations, including the farthest reaches of Wonderland.

The looking glass that held Shimmer's attention connected to the Crystal Continuum.

"Where is he going?" Hatter asked in a whisper.

"Home," the boy answered. "Boarderland."

Shimmer was from Boarderland? Would the Millinery knowingly employ a Boarderlander? The neighboring country wasn't exactly Wonderland's enemy, but it was no ally either. It was populated by many different tribes—some peaceful, most violent—and ruled over by a decadent king.

Wait a minute. The boy had said *home* with such longing and melancholy. Hatter turned to him, studied him, and realized:

"Those markings on your head and neck," he said. "Those are tribal tattoos, aren't they? From Boarderland."

The boy hadn't meant Shimmer at all. He'd been talking about his own home. Except how could a creation of the HATBOX have a home anywhere except *in* the HATBOX?

"He's gone," the boy said.

Hatter looked; Shimmer was indeed gone. Hatter pulled free the vent grating, jumped down into the hall, and ran to the looking glass that the HATBOX inventor had just entered. He saw swirling light, but nothing that could tell him if Shimmer was in fact headed to Boarderland.

Hatter returned to the vent and crawled back into the academy's seam, to where he'd left the boy, but—

The boy had vanished.

HOW STUPID DO YOU THINK WE ARE?

W hy hadn't he asked the boy his name? Or why he kept appearing at odd times, without warning? And what did Shimmer have to do with anything? Wasn't the guy allowed to visit other places if he wanted? Even Boarderland? There was no law against it.

Hatter returned to his dormitory.

"I'll kill him," Rhodes was telling Drummer, giving free play to his emotions. He paced the aisle, hands balled into fists, jaw clenched. The room was abuzz, Caps standing and sitting in small clumps, breathlessly talking about what had just happened. Which was when Hatter remembered the Top Hat duel between West and Dogberry.

"Me too," said Drummer in a show of solidarity, though he seemed his normal blank self.

"It's all very strange," Newton said.

"And how could you know, blind boy?" Rhodes snapped.

Newton let out an exasperated sigh. "I have my description bug." He pointed to his ear, and for the first time Hatter noticed a small blue glow coming from inside. "And anyway, what Dogberry said after was weird. When he asked where he was."

Hatter turned to him, thinking back to just before he'd run into the tattooed boy. "That *was* weird, wasn't it?"

Rhodes stopped pacing. He glared at Newton. "Just shut up, okay?"

Newton shrugged and lay back on top of his covers, folding his hands across his stomach.

Rhodes came up and sat close to Hatter. "We can't let him get away with what he did to West."

"MM Haymaker and your father will punish him," said Hatter, shifting away from Rhodes slightly.

"The worst he can get is expulsion, and that's not near punishment enough. Anyway, we can't let a Wellington be treated like that and then do nothing."

As if summoned by Rhodes's anger, Nigel and Benedict appeared at the door of the dormitory. "Madigan. Rhodes. Drummer. Come on."

The boys got to their feet and followed the upperclassmen out of the South Needle.

"Where are we going?" Hatter asked.

"The Healing Room," Benedict said.

"To check on West?" That would be way better than whatever Rhodes had in mind.

"No," Nigel said.

It was after curfew. They entered the deathly silent academy hall through the south entrance. The lights had been dimmed, and the glowing orbs floating above them flickered with a single candle each.

"We have to sneak past the admin offices. There's no other way," Nigel whispered.

"There is," Hatter replied. "And it's safer, at least as far as not getting caught goes. Follow me."

Back at the entrance, Hatter pulled aside the tapestry that flanked it on the left (the one depicting the Chess War of Deep Blue in surprisingly graphic detail). Behind it was the flat wall of the academy. Hatter blew on the spot and, just as it happened for him in so many other locations, the thread fell apart, revealing an opening to a dark passage that Hatter ducked into first, followed by the others. He led the way, stopping to explain that there were steps ahead, or a drop, or that they needed to bend low. Eventually they made it to their destination, and Hatter pushed on the ceiling, opening a wooden trapdoor above them. He lifted himself through to the other side, stepping out of the seat of a bench just outside the Healing Room. He held the trapdoor open for the others as they climbed out, each stunned as to where the journey had taken them, and then closed it behind them.

"You're going to make a great Spade," Benedict said, impressed.

Hatter's heart did a little jig.

The special quiet that greeted them in the room could be found in only one other place—the top of Empty Mountain, a treacherous peak that had claimed the lives of many adventurers. It was speculated that the quiet was actually a collection of final breaths. It was a heavy quiet. It enveloped the boys as they walked through the room, making them a little sleepy. Long, gauzy, pale-green fabrics hung from the high ceiling, separating the patients. The room was filled with a luminous jade glow. Pulsing green caterpillar thread was everywhere, running through the ceiling and walls like veins. Thicker, braided green strands emerged from the walls and wrapped around patients' arms.

"Found West," whispered Benedict, near the far end of the room. They joined him at the foot of a plush white bed with a soft white duvet cover and pillows piled everywhere. West was sound asleep. He looked bad. Really bad. The Healers had done a great job fixing him up, but his face was covered in what looked like one large purple-and-black bruise.

Benedict stared, shaking his head slowly and biting the insides of his cheeks. "Anyone seen Dogberry?" he asked quietly, barely calm enough to speak.

"He wasn't hurt badly enough to be here," Hatter said.

"Oh, he's here somewhere," Nigel said. "I heard MM Haymaker say something about 'for his own protection.'"

They wandered up and down the rows of beds, but there were only three other cadets to be found, none of them Dogberry. Hatter was a bit surprised to see the other cadets and the degree of their injuries. One cadet had glowing green stitches across his chest and a deep bite taken out of his shoulder. Hatter could only guess what had happened there.

He glanced to his left and saw a small and almost

imperceptible door. It had no handle and was the same shade of white as the walls. He walked up to it and pushed. It opened onto a small room. It looked like a storage room maybe, with tins of salve and glass jars filled with swirling colors stacked on high shelves. In the middle of the room, in what was clearly a temporary setup, was a cot. And on it, sleeping, was Dogberry.

Hatter stared at the boy and thought back to what Newton had said. It had seemed so strange, all of it. Especially at the end, when Dogberry had acted so confused. As if he didn't know what he'd done. But maybe he'd been faking.

"Good work," Rhodes said at his shoulder. "Guys, he's over here!"

Dogberry stirred, opened his eyes. The rest of the Wellingtons were in the doorway, looking at him. He jumped up to his feet, standing behind the cot and keeping it between them and him. He raised his hands in a gesture of surrender, knowing why the Wellingtons had come.

"Look," he said, "I don't know what happened. I don't know why I can't remember, and I'm really, really sorry about Cadet Trilby. He's my Top Hat. I respect him more than any-body. He's amazing."

"Which is probably why you thought it'd be impressive if you beat him," Benedict said, stepping past Hatter toward the cot.

Hatter had an impulse to grab Benedict and stop him, but he didn't. He just kind of stood there, his arms limp at his sides.

"I don't even remember challenging him," Dogberry whined. "I don't want to be a Top Hat—I never have!"

"How stupid do you think we are?" Nigel asked.

"Guys . . . please," Dogberry said. But Benedict was not having any of it. He grabbed the cot and shoved it to the side. Dogberry ran to his left, but Benedict grabbed him easily by his lapel, hoisted him up, and slammed him against the wall. The shelves shook, and the liquid in the glass jars sloshed around.

Dogberry flailed at Benedict in some kind of defensive move, but it was a pretty pathetic attempt. Benedict threw him to the ground and kicked him in the ribs.

Hatter held his breath in shock. This wasn't right. This wasn't fair. This was no way to even the score.

Nigel jumped into the fray and lifted Dogberry to his feet, throwing him against one of the shelves. Dogberry hit it hard, and several glass bottles crashed to the floor, spilling green and blue liquids everywhere. Dogberry keeled over, and Hatter could see sticky red blood dripping from the back of his head.

He wanted to tell his friends to stop it. He wanted to do something, anything. Benedict forced Dogberry upright and punched him in the face. Why didn't Dogberry fight back? He had the talent; he'd done it in the Wonderground.

Dogberry collapsed to the floor, shaking and crying.

Benedict stood over him and shook his head. "You're a pathetic coward."

"Can I have a go?" Rhodes asked, approaching.

"Then me," Drummer said.

"Nah, it's enough. Let's get out of here," Benedict replied. He turned and made his way back to the exit, followed by Nigel.

Rhodes stayed where he was, staring at Dogberry. He leaned down and said, "You better hope I never get you alone. Got it?"

If Dogberry nodded, Hatter didn't see it. Rhodes stood and spit on him. Hatter's stomach clenched. Finally Rhodes turned away, and they all left the room, Hatter the last one, closing the door behind him after taking a final look at the bleeding Dogberry.

They left the Healing Room and made their way back to the South Needle using Hatter's secret route. Everyone was silent, and as they parted ways in the common area, only a few nods were exchanged.

Hatter lay in bed feeling anxious, his stomach tight and aching. He thought about everything that had happened. Thought about Dogberry, broken and bleeding. He sat up. Maybe he really did deserve it. Maybe it *was* justice. But what if something happened to him overnight? What if one of his wounds got infected? That wouldn't be good—he might even die.

Hatter slipped out from under his covers and snuck out of the dormitory.

He was soon back in the Healing Room, this time by himself.

Dogberry lay just as they had left him: on the floor, surrounded by shards of broken glass. It looked as if he had passed out. Hatter knelt down and shook him, trying to wake him.

Dogberry moved a little and opened his eyes. He saw Hatter and recoiled in fear.

"It's okay. I'm not here to hurt you," Hatter said quickly. He helped Dogberry to his cot, noticing a small piece of glass protruding from the back of his head.

"I'll see what I can do here." Hatter had no particular healing knowledge, but he had to try something. He looked around the storage room and found a cabinet with several sets of drawers. He searched through them until he found some bandages and a whole bunch of little bottles with clear liquid. "Is this anything useful?" he asked, showing one of the bottles to Dogberry.

With half-closed eyes, Dogberry looked up. "Yeah, that's asepticol. They used that on me when they brought me here," he said softly.

"Perfect." Hatter set to work cleaning Dogberry's cuts, which, with the help of the asepticol, began to heal instantly. He then examined the piece of glass closely and decided the only thing he could do was pull it out. Hatter leaned in and gently pinched hold of the slippery glass covered in Dogberry's blood.

"And what exactly do you think you're doing, Cadet Madigan?"

I'VE BEEN AT THE ACADEMY A GOOD LONG WHILE. I KNOW EVERYTHING.

Wishing he could make himself invisible, Hatter turned as slowly as a thorgul wisp to face Tutor Wren, who glared at him, arms folded across his chest.

"I'm waiting," the tutor said.

"Please, sir," said Dogberry, "he came back to help me."

"Back? To help you? We need to work on your storytelling abilities, Dogberry. From the beginning, if you please."

So Dogberry explained. He told of being woken up, and of his beating. He said that Hatter had been present at the beating but hadn't participated in it, and he refused to give the names of the perpetrators. He explained how Hatter had returned to help fix him up. And then he stopped explaining, his eyelids heavy.

"Let me have a look at your head," said Tutor Wren. With one quick sweep of a hand, he removed the glass and stepped back. "Tend to the wound, Madigan."

143

Hatter did and saw the wound start to heal instantaneously. "Now, Dogberry, get some rest. Madigan, with me."

Out in the hall, the tutor demanded to know who had beaten up Dogberry, but Hatter wasn't about to snitch on his friends.

"Hatter," Tutor Wren said, his voice softening. "You don't have to tell me. I believe I know. I realize that you're excited to be at the academy. And from what I hear from your other teachers, and from what I've observed in my own class, you are living up to your potential. But I would prefer it if you did not spend your time with the Wellingtons."

Hatter's surprise must have shown on his face.

"I've been at the academy a good long while," Tutor Wren said. "I know everything. Which I suppose also means that I know I don't know everything. But still, I know everything."

"Well, they're my friends. They like me," Hatter said.

"They seem to, yes. But they are selfish boys and you are not. I don't want to see you become someone you aren't."

"Dalton was one of them."

"Dalton is a wonderful Milliner, a good brother to you, but he was one of the selfish ones."

Fists clenched, Hatter opened his mouth to defend his brother.

"I'm sorry to say it to you, but Dalton has always been full of self-love. It's what has gotten him ahead. It's what makes him so sure of himself. A good quality, now that he has learned how to temper it. But he made mistakes when he was younger. We all do."

Hatter had trouble imagining Tutor Wren as young. It was almost as impossible to believe as Dalton not being perfect. He wasn't sure he completely trusted Tutor Wren's assessment of his brother. Or at least, he didn't really want to. What kind of mistakes had Dalton made? He pushed the question out of his mind. It was one too many things to think about after a night like he'd just had.

"Now then," Tutor Wren said, "I believe Dogberry when he says you were not part of the beating, although the fact that you did not stop your friends disappoints me. And you came to help him afterward, which was a kindness, although had you chosen inappropriate medicines, you might have made his wounds worse. You will have detention until I determine you no longer need it."

"But Tutor Wren—"

"No. You are extremely fortunate that this is the only punishment I am giving you. Even now I'm worried it isn't enough."

Hatter shook his head and sighed.

"Yes?" Tutor Wren arched a pale eyebrow.

"It's nothing."

"Such a sigh is never nothing."

"It's just . . . I came back to help because I felt bad. Everyone's been warning me that I feel too much, that shows of emotions are unacceptable for a Milliner. But I can't seem to stop. And now I'm being punished. Again. For feeling. I hate that I can't control myself."

He felt so vulnerable saying this, but there was something about Tutor Wren that made it impossible for Hatter to keep

145

these thoughts to himself. The tutor always had this effect on him.

"Ah, I see." Tutor Wren was quiet a moment. "Well, Hatter, you did something wrong, but it was not feeling things. You felt the right thing; you felt empathy and concern for a fellow Wonderlander. And that is very good. It was your actions that were faulty."

"But if I just didn't feel anything," Hatter almost whispered, "then I wouldn't ever have any trouble."

"Again, this time you got in trouble for your actions. In the past you've gotten in trouble for your feelings. They are not one and the same. And besides,"—Tutor Wren glanced down the hall, but he and Hatter were quite alone—"some of us don't always agree with how emotions are handled here."

That shocked Hatter. "Really?"

"Emotions are part of being a living creature, and they can be very useful. Controlling and containing all emotion has not always been a mandate at the academy. Things have changed since your parents' generation, including the addition of that line to the Code of Honor. Some of us don't think such changes are necessarily for the better. But enough." Tutor Wren pulled out his white-gold pocket watch and consulted it. "It's almost lights out, past time for you to return to the South Needle."

Hatter felt overwhelmed; so much was going on in his brain.

Rhodes was waiting for him back at the dormitory

"Where have *you* been?" he asked in a furious whisper.

"I went to check on Dogberry, Tutor Wren caught me, and now I have detention for basically forever," Hatter replied, trying to sound just as furious.

"Dogberry? Why would you . . . ? Did you tell Wren about us? Did Dogberry?"

"Dogberry didn't say anything, and what kind of friend do you think I am?"

Rhodes studied him with a raised eyebrow.

"I'm going to bed now," Hatter said, "because even though I never wanted to beat up Dogberry and didn't throw a single punch, I'm the one getting punished for it."

A short time later, Hatter lay fuming under his bunk's thin blanket. He'd just been trying to do a good thing. Why should he be punished for *that*? How was that fair?

WHY DON'T YOU MIND YOUR OWN BUSINESS?

The next day, after his last class, Hatter made his way to the academy's lowest level, to a series of rooms that ran parallel to the kitchens and the tenders' sleeping quarters. At a door marked *DT*, he knocked. No one answered. He eased the door open and saw a pile of boxes in a corner of the room, some overturned chairs against a wall. And Cadet Alinari. Caledonia. She sat, back straight, hands on her desk, determinedly facing forward. Hatter was surprised. She didn't seem the type to get detention. But then, he wasn't usually the type to get it either.

He sat next to her. "Hi."

"Don't talk to me."

Hatter looked around for a tutor or any kind of authority figure. "Why not? Are we not allowed to talk here? It's my first time getting detention."

Cadet Alinari scowled at him. "Are you suggesting I get detention a lot?"

"No. I just . . . don't know the rules."

Caledonia faced front again. "I don't want you to talk to me because I don't like you."

"Why not?"

"Don't talk to me."

The door was flung open, and Astra bounded into the room. She made eye contact with Hatter and smiled for pure joy. "You! I'm sorry you're here, but isn't it fun that you are!"

Hatter got up and moved to a desk as distant from Caledonia as he could find. "Not really," he muttered.

"Why do you do that?" Caledonia asked as Astra sat down next to her.

"Do what?" Astra beamed.

"Act so nice to him. After what he did to you."

"Oh, he didn't mean it! He was trying to impress Grand Milliner Victus's son," she replied, waving away the idea.

"That's not true!" Hatter turned to Caledonia. "Why don't you mind your own business?"

"Don't talk to me."

The door opened again, and Tutor Ampersand entered. Her hair hung so long it touched the floor and swept in a train behind her. A large purple birthmark encircled her right eye. She sat behind the small desk at the front of the room and looked at the cadets.

"We're missing one of you," she said, as if suspicious they were hiding someone.

"Who?" Astra asked.

Tutor Ampersand looked at her and shook her head. "You really don't ever want out of detention do you, Cadet Vost?"

Astra laughed. "Of course I want out!"

"Then you need to stop asking questions. I don't know what will drive it home. Another week for you." The tutor opened her book and made a mark in it.

Astra shrugged.

The door opened for a third time and in walked Newton, slowly getting the lay of the room with the help of his cane.

"Cadet Ezer, you're late," Tutor Ampersand said, tapping her pocket watch as if in confirmation.

"I'm sorry," he said, and reached out, feeling for the back of a chair. When his hand found one, he sat himself down carefully.

"Yes, just as you were after you mistakenly made up the Bonds' bunks instead of the Brims'. Another week for you," replied Tutor Ampersand. "Now that everyone is here, this is how it works. You will do your own homework, and you will not help one another or speak with one another. You will sit in one spot, and you will not move until the end of detention. Very simple. Am I clear?"

"Yes, Tutor Ampersand," they replied in unison.

Detention after that became rather boring, and Hatter was grateful. It wasn't fair. It wasn't fair that Caledonia wanted to make him the bad guy. He wasn't a bad guy. Even Astra wasn't mad at him anymore. He was the one who had gone to help Dogberry.

Whatever, it didn't matter. He was here to sit quietly and get this stupid detention thing over with.

A ball of paper landed in front of his nose.

"You're one of us now," it said, and there was a picture of a grinning cat drawn in the corner. Hatter looked up, and Astra gave him a little wave.

Just get this stupid detention over with.

22

YOU HAVE A HERO COMPLEX.

Suit-streaming time was a few weeks away and lessons became more intense, combat exercises in the HATBOX calibrated to such an aggressive level that at least half a dozen cadets per session were sent to the Healing Room. White Imagination classes were also getting more dangerous— although it was a psychological danger rather than a physical one. Cadets were now working with all but red thread, touching and manipulating the other colors. Several cadets had burst into tears attempting to harness their power. The stress must have been getting to some of Hatter's fellow Caps; many of them had fainted at least once in the HATBOX, while more than a few fainted *every time* they entered it, as if even the prospect of yet more combat training was too much to bear.

"Never in my life have I encountered such a pathetic group of cadets," MM Haymaker declared when Twist fell to the floor one morning before a single maneuver had been demonstrated. "You're as fragile as a house made of playing cards!"

Hatter and Rhodes exchanged a glance. It definitely felt good to be a top cadet. Or almost top.

The problem for Hatter was Textillery class—his least favorite since, thanks to Rhodes, he was in a group that far exceeded his skill level. They had begun crafting the hats with which they would train as Brims. "Madigan, you're pretty terrible at this," Rhodes said, pulling Hatter's lumpy top hat off its mold.

"Never said I wasn't," Hatter replied with a sigh, taking the hat in his hands. This was his third attempt to mold the felt onto the wooden form. Somehow he couldn't get all the lumps out of it.

"Let me do it," Rhodes said.

Hatter couldn't believe how easily it came to Rhodes, and he was really impressed when, later that week, he had a felt hat, perfectly shaped, awaiting only the silk lining.

"Good luck," Rhodes said as Hatter unrolled the silk and stared at it apprehensively. Hatter was pretty sure luck would be the only way he'd manage to make this work. He cut and recut several shapes that didn't remotely fit the inside of his hat before the bell rang for lunch.

Hatter still took his meals with his fellow Wellingtons. Rhodes had told them about Hatter's loyalty, and they had been appreciative. And when West finally returned to classes a few days later and joined them at the table, he'd exchanged a hearty handshake with Hatter.

"Heard what you did, or rather, didn't do. You're a good friend, Madigan," he'd said.

That compliment alone seemed to make up for the horribleness of his ongoing detention.

It wasn't that there was anything particularly awful about spending time in that underground room. It was just the feeling that everyone, except Astra, hated him. Hatter didn't like being hated. And he certainly didn't like being hated by Caledonia. He also didn't like feeling left out. He'd watch the three of them pass notes, Caledonia scribbling something onto a page and floating it to Newton, who ran his forefinger over it. Hatter had observed that Newton had a small metal cap connected to his finger with blue caterpillar thread and that it glowed—as did an implant in his ear—when he moved it across the page; somehow, the cap on Newton's finger was reading the note into his ear. Which was pretty cool.

Hatter would see Newton smile and then start tapping on the paper, composing sentences onto it in some kind of code. The paper would float across the room, and it was Caledonia's turn to smile. Then it would be sent off to Astra. And so on.

It was never sent to Hatter.

This general pattern of morning run, classes, detention, and evening exercises, and morning run, classes, detention, and evening exercises constituted Hatter's life, and it started to take its toll on him. In MM Haymaker's combat workshop, he kept hoping to be partnered again with the tattooed boy. Ever

155

since their adventure in the Hall of Mirrors, Hatter had been waiting for something, anything, that would explain why the boy had taken him there in the first place. And then, when the tattooed boy finally *did* materialize in front of him and they began grappling, Hatter whispered fiercely into his ear, "What do you want from me?"

The boy said nothing back.

In White Imagination class, although he was always in top form, invariably Hatter's performance was compared to Dalton's. And in Tutor Wren's class all he felt was deep shame.

Even meals had a note of discomfort for him. Rhodes had taken to picking on one of Cook's tenders, a boy a couple of years older than them. If the boy was too messy with his service, Rhodes would complain. If he was too neat, Rhodes would complain. There was pretty much nothing the boy could do to please him, and Cook would look at Hatter with an expression that implied he was somehow to blame.

"Watch what you're doing!" Rhodes was once again yelling at the tender.

"I'm sorry," the boy replied, withdrawing the ladle quickly.

"You spilled all over my arm!"

"But you pulled your tray back just as I—"

"Just get me a clean tray and a fresh serving," Rhodes snapped. The boy scurried away.

"Why are you so mean to him?" asked Hatter, exhausted and not in the mood to play nice.

Rhodes looked at him with a fury that normally scared

Hatter but today just annoyed him. *Get over yourself,* thought Hatter.

"Because how is he going to learn to do anything properly if we let him get away with all these mistakes?"

"Maybe you don't need to be everyone's teacher," Hatter said as the boy returned with a new tray piled high with food.

"Excuse me?" Rhodes said, taking the tray but still staring right at Hatter.

"Never mind," replied Hatter, feeling that familiar fear—he had made a target of himself.

Rhodes didn't say anything else, and Hatter thought maybe he'd let the issue drop as they joined the rest of the Wellingtons at their table. But he'd thought wrong.

"So Madigan here thinks I shouldn't be telling a sweatband that he screwed up when he spills a bunch of stew on my arm," Rhodes announced as they sat down.

"That's not what I meant," Hatter said.

"Tenders don't take pride in their work anymore," Benedict said. "My mother's gone through at least four sweatbands this past year alone."

"Well, maybe that says something about how she treats them," Hatter said. Why did he keep speaking without thinking? Wasn't that something he was supposed to have improved on since beginning his formal training? Somehow he was getting worse at not keeping his mouth shut.

"What?" Benedict's expression was as cold as his tone.

"Uh, I just . . . I knew a lot of tenders when I was growing up, and they always worked really hard. But maybe they didn't work as hard as the tenders who were here way before my time. I don't know," Hatter replied.

"Exactly," Benedict said slowly, still squinting at him.

"Yeah, so look, I've got to go. Tutor Wren wanted to talk to me before class," Hatter lied, standing up and moving away from the table before anyone could say more.

He suffered through his afternoon classes in a virtual fog. Feeling so out of place. The sensation reminded him of being a little kid again, arriving at the academy, walking down the halls, watching as tutors and Master Milliners squinted at him and judged him. Then it was time for detention, and Hatter was almost grateful to disappear down into the subterranean depths of the academy where he was most comfortable. Where he had grown up.

And then there was the tattooed boy. Again.

"Who are you and what's your name?" Hatter blurted out.

"Arlo," the boy answered. "Follow me."

He'd probably be late for detention, but Hatter followed Arlo into a short seam that connected two parallel hallways. As they jumped out of what looked like a large drainpipe, Hatter heard voices around a corner. One sounded like Shimmer. Arlo was obsessed with Shimmer, it seemed. But why Shimmer would be down in this part of the academy made little sense to Hatter. The other voice was altogether different and spoke in an accent that was strangely familiar. In fact, it sounded a bit like Arlo's.

"Almost every time we've tried, the cadet fainted before

we could fully take possession," the voice said. "Something's wrong and you need to fix it."

"It worked on that Dogberry kid—the rest of you should be able to do it too," Shimmer replied.

"Just fix it already."

There was silence then, and Hatter decided to peek around the corner. "He's coming this way!" he whispered, seeing Shimmer, alone, walking toward him.

Arlo vanished. What a convenient trick that was.

"Oh hello, Sir Isaac!" Hatter said.

"Hello, cadet." Shimmer barely glanced at him, didn't slow his stride in the least. "What are you doing down here?"

"Detention, I'm afraid, sir."

Then Shimmer was gone and Hatter examined the empty hallway. Who'd been talking with Shimmer? Where did he go? What did that reference to fainting mean? What did Dogberry have to do with anything?

Arlo didn't return, so Hatter slipped back into the seam and arrived at detention. He saw Caledonia and Tutor Ampersand standing in the doorway. They seemed to be in some kind of argument, and Hatter didn't know exactly where to look or go. So he just stood and watched them.

"You have a hero complex, young lady," Tutor Ampersand said.

"That's not true!" Caledonia's voice was high and wavering.

"How dare you disagree with me! That's another week on top of the week you just earned."

"No one was helping him!"

"He's not a 'he.' He's a hologram. And that's yet another week for continuing to debate the subject. And Madigan! What are you staring at?" Tutor Ampersand turned abruptly and looked at Hatter.

"Nothing. I just was waiting till I could go into detention," he replied as calmly as he could, though his heart was beating fast. The mention of the hologram, of helping a hologram who seemed to be much more than that . . . But he couldn't ask Caledonia about it, could he? She hated him.

"Get in, the both of you!" Tutor Ampersand ordered, and Hatter and Caledonia quickly marched into the room.

Hatter sat in his usual spot. Tutor Ampersand opened her book and was instantly engrossed, her ears angled back, stiff. Note-passing time had begun, and for the first time Hatter gave it a shot.

What happened with the hologram? Why did he need help? Did he ask you to follow him? he wrote. As he had done in his very first imagination class, when he made his orange thread move as if by a sudden wind, he visualized a convenient breeze carrying his note to Caledonia's desk. It fell right in front of her. She read the note with a frown, then crumpled it into a ball and threw it away.

Hatter felt even more alone than usual. He stayed behind until after the others left, then stepped out into the hallway. Something grabbed his arm and he turned around.

He expected—hoped—to see Caledonia. But when he turned, he saw a boy. He wasn't a cadet. Nor was he Arlo. Down the left side of his face, in almost a perfectly straight line, was a scar. It went directly through his left eye, leaving the iris a milky white. He wore a cap on his head, heavy boots on his feet, and dark tweed trousers held up by suspenders. He looked altogether rough. And he scowled at Hatter.

"Why were you spying on me?" he asked, and Hatter recognized the voice he'd heard speaking with Shimmer.

"Well, I do want to be a Spade after all," Hatter answered, wrenching his jacket out of the boy's grip.

"Stay out of it, Wonderlander," the boy said, and then disappeared. Just like that.

Hatter stood in the empty hall. Something was definitely going on. Arlo, Dogberry, fainting cadets, the scarred kid—they were connected somehow. Shimmer too. He had to investigate.

Or no. No. That wasn't right. What had Tutor Ampersand said to Caledonia? About playing the hero? Cadets didn't investigate things. Cadets followed orders and went to classes and didn't allow anything to distract them.

He had to stay focused on his studies and his training, and forget everything else. That was what a good cadet would do . . .

YOUR PARENTS WOULD BE ASHAMED.

Cadet Madigan was starting to enjoy his morning run under MM Clout's watchful eye—the periods of steady physical exertion, when he was all breath and pumping limbs and could be alone with his thoughts. These thoughts always centered on Arlo, who seemed sad but also cautiously hopeful; and timid, as if he were afraid of upsetting someone capable of causing him great harm while also propelled by an urgent need that left him little choice but to risk it.

Questions needed answering, that was for sure, and Hatter thought he saw Arlo everywhere—in Wonderground, in the South Needle, and in the Banquet Plaza at lunch, just before Rhodes started loudly bragging about how he'd gotten the last tarty tart. Walking to the Wellingtons' table, he sang the praises of his tasty treat. A tender chased after him with a glass of winglefruit juice. Rhodes had left the juice in the food line, setting it on the counter as he'd made room on his tray for the last wondercrumpet, which he said would pair nicely with the last tarty tart. The tender called out Rhodes's name, Rhodes abruptly turned, and the tender knocked into him, spilling the winglefruit juice all over him and his tray.

A suspenseful silence descended as Rhodes took in the mess that covered his person and the tender, who stood frozen, the empty glass shaking in his hand.

The next thing happened so quickly Hatter didn't register the action until the tender was on the floor, blood streaming from his nose, Rhodes kicking him in the ribs. Hatter grabbed Rhodes around the middle and pulled him away from the tender. It wasn't easy. Rhodes flailed in his arms and pushed and twisted until he'd pried himself loose. Hatter had seen many kinds of fire in Rhodes's eyes before now, but this was the first time he'd seen anything quite so dangerous.

"What's wrong with you, Madigan?" he yelled, spit flying out of his mouth.

"What's wrong with *you*?" Hatter yelled back, his heart jumping, warning him that no good could come of this. "It was an accident!"

"So what? We're their betters! They serve us! They need to be reminded of their place!"

"If we're their 'betters,' whatever that means, then we need to behave better. We're supposed to protect the citizens of Wonderland. Not hurt them."

"You're just soft because you were raised with them!"

"I'm not soft."

"You're nothing like your brother, Madigan. Every teeny-tiny feeling you have, you think you have to share it with everyone—like we even care. You've spent too much time living with dirty sweatbands. You should be one of them. You don't deserve to be a Milliner. Your parents would be ashamed."

Hatter punched him in the face. Hard. He put all his anger and loneliness into that punch.

He punched big-time.

Rhodes lay on the ground next to the tender, who just stared up at Hatter, wide-eyed.

"Big mistake, Madigan," Rhodes mumbled. "Big mistake."

Maybe it was, but Hatter felt pretty good about it.

WISH I COULD HAVE DONE IT MYSELF.

"**M**ore detention for you, I'm afraid," Tutor Wren said, alone with Hatter in his office. "Because of that altercation of yours in the Banquet Plaza."

Hatter already had detention indefinitely, so he didn't much mind. Besides, he detected a gleam in Tutor Wren's eyes, as if the old fellow wasn't exactly displeased. Or not as displeased as he should've been.

Something shifted in the academy. Now, as Hatter walked the halls between classes, cadets said hi to him. Or in the Banquet Plaza, in line for food, they would start talking to him about how weird it was that Tutor Mars got so excited over boring stuff like the kinds of soil that could be found in different parts of Wonderland, or how MM Haymaker could probably—what did he, Hatter, think?—defeat an entire army of Black Imagination warriors on her own.

But nowhere was the shift more evident than in detention. The day of the "altercation," like always, Hatter sat waiting for Tutor Ampersand to arrive. Like always, Astra entered and gave him a happy hello. Unlike always, Caledonia gave up her usual seat for the desk in front of him.

"I saw what you did," she said, turning toward him.

"Yeah?"

"Wish I could have done it myself," she said with a smile.

"I bet you were on your way over, though." Hatter hoped she would take it as a compliment, not teasing.

"She was, she was!" Astra said excitedly.

"She was trying to play it cool," Newton said from his seat.

"So is that it, then?" Caledonia asked Hatter.

"Is what it?"

"You and Rhodes. You and the Wellingtons?"

Hatter's stomach lurched. He'd kind of assumed that there was no coming back from this with Rhodes, but the Wellingtons . . . yeah, he supposed it was over with them too.

"I guess so." He wanted to cry. He wanted to cry so badly, but he managed not to.

"I'm . . . sorry," Caledonia said softly.

"You are?" Hatter was kind of surprised.

"They were your friends. They might be horrible people, but they were your friends."

"Hey, come on, West is okay. And Drummer? He doesn't do much of anything really—"

"He doesn't do much of anything, and that's the problem. But yeah, West is okay, I guess," Caledonia replied. "Look. You did the right thing."

"I like them," he said, his voice almost too quiet to be heard.

"I don't know why," Caledonia scoffed.

"Because . . . because they liked me. And they knew my family, and they grew up in my old neighborhood, and . . ." Nope, he really had to stop talking now if he was going to manage the whole not-crying thing.

"Hey, Hatter," Newton said. "I grew up in your old neighborhood too, with all those guys. That *should* make me one of them, right? But they've never included me. In fact, they go out of their way to harass me. You know why? Because I scare them. They don't like that there's something wrong with me."

"There's nothing wrong with you!" said Astra.

Newton shook his head and continued. "They're cowards, Hatter. And I bet you wouldn't have hung out with them if you'd grown up in that neighborhood."

"You don't know."

"I do," Astra said. "I told you, our parents were good friends, and you and I would have been good friends, I just know it. Your parents did not hang out with the Victuses or the Benedicts."

"Stop it!" shouted Hatter suddenly. He saw Caledonia give Astra a look.

"What's wrong?" she asked.

"You all act like you know my parents better than I knew my parents. You all act like you know me better than I know me. You don't know me at all. None of you knows me at all." Hatter felt hot tears burn in his eyes. "Just shut up, all of you, just shut up and—"

The door opened, and as Tutor Ampersand entered the room, Caledonia and Astra returned to their seats.

Hatter bowed his head and stared at the desk. He blinked, and a single tear fell and made a little pool on the tan-colored wood. *No. No. No. No.*

No.

He took a deep breath and exhaled slowly. And the tears retreated.

A piece of paper floated down onto his desk, the corner of which dipped into the small pool and soaked up the tear.

You're going to be okay, it said.

The piece of paper slowly got more and more wet until it couldn't soak up any more.

YOU DON'T DESERVE TO BE A MILLINER.

Hatter felt as if it were his first day of classes all over again—every day, the same feelings of isolation. This despite the fact that more cadets tried to include him in their hangouts and conversation than ever before. Not Rhodes, though. Rhodes refused to talk to him, harassed him, made him a target.

At inspection one morning, just after Hatter finished making his bed and stood ready at its foot, and MM Clout was working his way up the aisle, Rhodes rushed over and yanked off the covers and pulled Hatter's clothes from the shelves. Hatter stared in shock, and it took him a moment to realize he had only seconds to get things back in order before MM Clout got to him. He was still tucking in his covers when he heard the familiar roar, "Cadet Madigan!"

Hatter stopped dead, halfway bent over, his hand underneath his mattress. He shot to attention and turned to face his superior. "Yes, sir!"

"One week until streaming, and you don't know how to be

prepared for inspection? You know what this means," said MM Clout.

"Yes, sir! Making the beds of other cadets, sir!"

"No!" MM Clout approached Hatter and looked down at him. "Who do you think you are, Cadet Madigan? We have higher expectations for a cadet like you, so your insubordination deserves a larger punishment. You will meet me tomorrow morning before dawn out in the yard, and every morning before streaming. Clearly you need extra training in cadet discipline."

Hatter stared at MM Clout. He didn't understand. They already met in the yard every morning before dawn. Was the Master Milliner only pretending to punish him? Why wasn't he punishing him for real?

"Yes, sir! Tomorrow morning before dawn, sir!"

MM Clout moved on to Newton, and Hatter glanced over at Rhodes who gave him a smirk. *Joke's on him*, thought Hatter, though it was little comfort.

When he wasn't being a target, Rhodes and Drummer refused to talk with him at all (not that the loss of Drummer's fascinating conversation affected Hatter too badly), and even though other Caps let him sit with them at meals, Hatter repeatedly glanced over at the Wellingtons, wondering what they were talking about so happily.

"You're watching them again, aren't you?" Newton said when Hatter didn't answer some question he'd just asked.

"What? Oh. No. Yes," Hatter said lamely.

"Just ignore them," Astra said.

Hatter tried, but it was difficult. Especially when Benedict passed his table and laughed. "You've really gone up in the world there, Madigan."

"What is with their obsession with status?" Newton said with a shake of his head.

"I think they just want what's best for Wonderland," Hatter replied.

Newton laughed. "Oh yes, that makes so much sense."

Hatter was feeling defensive now. "No, it does. We are being trained to be the protectors of Wonderland. We are responsible for all its citizens. We can't be emotional; we can't take things personally. Someone like—"

"No, please go on," Newton said. "Someone like . . . me?"

"You have certain . . . challenges . . . in protecting . . ." Hatter couldn't keep going. He felt so stupid.

"I do, don't I? And clearly the most important thing about a Milliner is that we can fight, right?"

"Well, yes."

Newton just shook his head and sighed.

"You know, it would be nice if once in a while you didn't talk to me like I was a total tweedledum," Hatter said.

"Stop acting like one," Newton replied, a similar edge to his voice.

"Play nice." Caledonia sat down to join them. "Also, aren't you late for class?"

Hatter and Newton jumped to their feet.

"If you help me, I can avoid being late," Newton whispered.

Hatter didn't know what that meant until Newton extended his arm.

"Oh, sure." Hatter guided Newton quickly through the Banquet Plaza to the exit, the Wellingtons laughing at him as they passed. "How do you handle it?" he asked Newton when they were out of the plaza, walking quickly down the hall toward the Textillery. "Everyone laughing at you, I mean."

"You mean that doesn't happen to everyone?"

"Uh . . ."

Newton smirked. "You really don't have much of a sense of humor. How can someone who feels every little emotion the way you do not find things funny?"

"I've never found there to be much to laugh about."

"Oh, I don't know. Life's complicated," Newton said, "but that doesn't mean it isn't also silly."

Hatter glanced at Newton. He really didn't know what to make of him. He was . . . strange.

They arrived at the Textillery just in time and parted ways, heading to opposite ends of the room. Hatter suddenly realized that he had to sit in his old spot next to Rhodes. He slid into his chair, keeping his attention directly in front of him.

Tailor Quince entered the room, followed by his assistants. "Today is your last day to finish your practice hat," he announced. "This hat is the one you will use in combat training, the one you will imbue with White Imagination, and . . . yes. You know the importance of your hat. You must be finished by the end of class. You will leave your hats in your spots, and I shall examine them. By tomorrow you will know how well you did, and you will be able to take your hat with you for your streaming ceremony. Everyone understand?"

"Yes, sir!" the cadets called out, in their excitement forgetting that Tailor Quince hated loud noises.

He reacted as if in great pain and waved at them with his arms. "Nod, cadets, just . . . nod," he said.

During class, Hatter struggled with his silk lining. He just couldn't get it the right shape, and every time he tried to glue it into the hat, he made a mess. He pulled off the latest silk piece, all sticky and covered in glue.

"Pathetic," Rhodes said quietly.

Hatter got up to cut some more silk. Astra was standing nearby, examining various ribbons for her hatband.

"You look perfectly miserable," she said with a laugh.

"I'm not going to finish in time," Hatter muttered in reply. "I haven't even made a lining."

"Can I help?"

Hatter looked at her and realized that if there was anyone else in his group aside from Rhodes who could show him what to do, it was Astra. Why hadn't he seen it before?

"Uh, well, I can't seem to cut the right shape."

"It's just using measurements. Let me give you the formula." She grabbed Hatter's hand and wrote on it with the chalk they used to mark up the fabric. "And here's another little trick. Don't put the glue on the silk, put it on the hat!"

Hatter nodded and stared at the formula. It made sense. He could do this. He could do this before the end of class. "Thanks," he said, and Astra beamed.

175

Hatter cut some new silk and returned to the table. Then he drew a new pattern and cut it. It fit! It didn't look great, but it fit! He then carefully glued it to the inside, and with only a couple of minutes to spare he was done. His hat didn't have a band, and the inside was definitely less than perfect, but it was done. And *he'd* done it—no one else.

"Time," said Tailor Quince, and all the cadets stopped their work and placed their hats at their workstations.

Hatter let his sense of accomplishment carry him through the day. Rhodes and the Wellingtons—what did he care? Even when Nigel bodychecked him in the hallway, he was able to hold down his anger and keep calm. It was about becoming a Milliner, he told himself. All the rest of it, all the stupid drama with other cadets, didn't matter. He was going to become the best.

To become the best: he'd almost forgotten that promise to himself.

Hatter met MM Clout in the yard before dawn. The Master Milliner seemed grouchier than usual. Without waiting to be told, Hatter started his run.

"What in Wonderland are you doing, cadet?" MM Clout yelled after him.

Hatter stopped and turned to look at MM Clout. "I was running, sir," he replied, confused.

"And who asked you to run, cadet?"

"No, one, sir. I just thought—"

"You're a cadet! You're not meant to think! Now, fifty push-ups, go!"

Hatter was down on the cold ground instantly and understood: now that he was being punished, he'd have to do a different morning workout. Though, considering he was being made to do all the usual things he did at the evening workout, and that he was done way before the suns rose, it didn't seem that terrible a punishment. And now that the wound in his shoulder had pretty much completely healed, push-ups were a breeze.

At inspection Hatter kept a firm eye on Rhodes and Drummer, ready to tackle them if they tried to mess with his bunk. But they didn't do anything. Rhodes just gave him that same smug smile. Hatter really wanted to wallop that stupid face again and took small satisfaction at seeing how the bruise around Rhodes's eye was still very purple.

Instead he took out all his aggression during his combat workshop, and he even got a rare compliment from MM Haymaker at the end of class. "Good to see you finally channeling those emotions of yours."

It might have taken him what felt like forever, but he was slowly figuring out how to focus his feelings. In a way, this whole business with Rhodes was a good thing.

"Will you read the list for me?" asked Newton as they headed to the Textillery, along with pretty much every other Cap, at their lunch break.

177

"Okay. But can't you read the list for yourself, with that finger thing?" Hatter asked.

"Sure. But I like making you do stuff because you feel so guilty," Newton replied. Once again, Hatter just stared at Newton. Even though he knew it was a joke, he also knew it wasn't a joke. Well, maybe he deserved it, but he hadn't actually been all that mean to Newton himself. He'd just never stopped Rhodes when he had been.

Which was pretty bad.

They stood and waited in line for their turn at the long list, and Hatter scanned for his name and Newton's.

"You got a pass 'with exceptional promise,'" read Hatter.

Newton beamed. "Fantastic! And you?"

Hatter looked down the list of names. He couldn't find his anywhere. He didn't understand. His hat, even though the inside was kind of a mess, wasn't that bad. It was definitely better than Twist's, who had somehow made his completely square. He read lower and lower and lower down the list until he came to the very end. There he saw it: *Hatter Madigan—did not complete*.

He stared at the words and swallowed hard.

"Hey, Hatter, is everything okay?" Newton asked.

"Yeah. Is everything okay?" an all-too-familiar voice asked. Rhodes shoved him to the side and looked at the list.

"Second to a Vost," Rhodes said. "Of course." He turned and looked at Hatter. "Hate getting second place. I guess it's better than last place though, am I right?"

Hatter immediately understood. "What did you do to my hat?"

"You didn't make a hat."

"What. Did. You. Do?" Hatter could barely get the words out. So much for channeling his emotions into his class work. Right now he wanted to channel his emotions into Rhodes's face.

"Look, maybe the mercury's gone to your head or something, but all I remember is watching you try to make a hat over and over and not being able to."

"That's not true. I made a hat."

Rhodes took a step toward him. "No, *I* made a hat. You didn't make anything. You don't deserve to be a Milliner."

"Please. You think no one deserves to be a Milliner. If you had your way, you'd be the only cadet at the academy," said Newton.

"Say that to my face, blind boy!" Rhodes said, whipping around.

"You know very well I can't see where it is," replied Newton. His self-mockery surprised Rhodes, who stood dumbfounded. "Thank goodness, really. I imagine you look just as ugly as your voice sounds."

"I'll kill you. I'll . . . kill you!" Rhodes sputtered, clenching his fists.

"We're being a little dramatic, aren't we? And very unoriginal."

"And before you can put an end to Newton, you'll have me

to deal with first," Hatter told Rhodes. "And I'm ready, if you are. Let's see what you can do."

Rhodes feinted, but Hatter didn't react. He waited with the patience of an upperclassman well trained in combat strategy. Rhodes unballed his fists, said something under his breath, and stalked off.

"I'll be in the Textillery, stating my case to Tailor Quince," Hatter said to Newton.

He pushed open the heavy double doors and entered the empty room. The quiet reminded him of the morning of his very first day of classes, sitting with Weaver and saying good-bye. Wow, he really wished he could talk with her right about now.

"Tailor Quince!" His voice echoed high up into the rafters. "Tailor Quince, I need to speak with you!"

Nothing.

"Tailor Quince!" *Please*, he thought. *Please answer.*

Hatter had the sudden sensation that someone was standing behind him, and he turned, prepared to plead his case with the head tailor.

Staring back at him was Arlo. "I need to talk to you."

"Funny," Hatter said. "I've been wanting to say the same thing to you."

"Meet me up there"—Arlo pointed at the rafters as he faded to nothing—"in the window alcove where you used to meet your friend."

Finally. No longer would Hatter be mysteriously ushered around the academy by a figment that shouldn't have been able to leave the HATBOX. He would get answers.

26

I WANT TO BE FREE OF THE MACHINE.

Hatter dashed across to the far end of the Textillery and slipped behind a silk tapestry depicting the first hat ever made in Wonderland—basically a small triangular cloth that rested on top of a Milliner's head. The seam behind the tapestry led to steps, and in a matter of moments Hatter was in the rafters. He paused to look around. So much had happened since the last time he was here; it felt like a lifetime ago.

As soon as he reached the alcove where he used to sit with Weaver, Arlo materialized and said, "I, and others with me, are trapped. We need your help to be free."

Hatter nodded, thoughtful. "A little more information would be good," he said. "I mean, who—no, *what*—are you? I was told that you and the other sparring partners are made by the HATBOX, but *you* keep appearing outside of it. And that other kid too. The one with the scar on his face."

"Benjamin," Arlo said. "He's like me, but not. He doesn't want to be free."

"Yeah, but I don't understand how you're able to be here with me now, outside the HATBOX, when you're a *part* of it, and so . . . I figure you're something more, right? But what, exactly?"

"It's hard to explain. I'll try. I was a Boarderlander, an orphan, and I lived in a quite unpleasant home with others like me. Dr. Shimmer came and took us away, to a much nicer home. Clean, with good food. But then it got strange." Arlo looked down, working to hold back tears. "My friends disappeared one by one. Dr. Shimmer said they had been adopted, and I wanted to believe him. But sometimes at night, I couldn't sleep, I heard so much crying. So one time I snuck out of bed and followed the cries, and I saw him. Dr. Shimmer was plugging my friends into the machine. I didn't know exactly what I was witnessing until he did it to me, but the machine vacuumed up my friends' souls, and afterward Dr. Shimmer discarded their bodies like empty husks."

"No way," Hatter said, more to himself than to Arlo. "That's too . . . unbelievable. You're telling me that what Master Milliner Haymaker called holograms are really disembodied souls?"

"I don't know if everything projected by the HATBOX comes from the souls of once-living creatures, but that's how it is for me and others. Dr. Shimmer took *my* soul when he caught me watching him that night. In the HATBOX, I can have a body, but only for as long as the sparring program is allowed to run. Outside the HATBOX, well, shake my hand."

Hatter reached out; his hand passed through Arlo's. And yet how many times, when he and Arlo sparred, had the kid felt as solid as a flesh-and-blood Boarderlander?

"For a while, I had no control over when I appeared," Arlo went on, "and it only ever happened within the HATBOX itself. It would just suddenly happen, and there'd be a cadet, and I would feel compelled to fight. And then it would be over and I'd disappear back into the workings of the HATBOX. It took a long time for me to learn how to control myself—to be able to move when and where I wanted to. It took me a long time to realize I even wanted to control myself. But I practiced: before, when Doctor Shimmer was still testing everything, and then more when we were moved here. I've been teaching others, but it's hard."

"But if all of this is true," Hatter said, trying to understand, "why does the machine need souls? Does it have something to do with the combination of science and imagination that enables the HATBOX to function? Are the souls necessary for the imagination part of it? Like maybe Shimmer imbues the 'holograms' with souls' imaginations because it helps them— the holograms, I mean—perform in the HATBOX?"

"All I know," Arlo said, "is that we are part of the machine, and we are also part of one another, and we are also ourselves. And we are supposed to possess cadets."

"What?"

"We are programmed to go after the youngest, weakest ones and take up residence inside their bodies. But I don't want to

183

possess anyone. I want to be free of the machine even if it means . . . that there's nothing. But I believe there *is* something, waiting for me, and that I will meet my parents and be surrounded by the love I didn't have when I was alive. Please. I don't want to be a slave to the HATBOX and Dr. Shimmer anymore. My friends and I need your help to turn off the machine. It's the only way we can be free."

"But why do you need a cadet to help you? Why me?"

"Turning off the machine requires two fully substantial beings—Dr. Shimmer and another. It requires being outside the HATBOX's fields of power. And when I am outside the HATBOX—"

"You have no physical substance."

"I can manifest and converse, but nothing more. As to your other question: Why you? I had wanted your friend to help at first, but then she left and didn't come back. And since she's your friend, I thought that maybe you were as kind as she is."

"You're talking about Weaver?" Hatter asked.

"I don't know. The girl you used to speak with here, a long while ago. I thought you should be trained for the gauntlet, hoping that I could soon convince you to help me. But sometimes you weren't kind, so just in case you weren't going to help me, I also spoke with the other cadet, the one who saved the boy in that fight. But now I see I was wrong, and that you are kind. I'm sorry I made the mistake."

"Trained for the gauntlet? You haven't—"

"The man who yells at you every morning is easy to possess.

He has a very simple mind. So one of my friends has been train-ing you through him in the mornings."

Hatter was completely and totally flabbergasted. "You mean all this time, that hasn't been MM Clout?"

"For your training, no. For everything else, yes. And of course that was him this morning, which caused some confusion."

Hatter leaned his head back on the cold glass of the win-dow, thoughtful. "Why don't a couple of you just possess a cadet and Shimmer, and turn off the machine yourselves?"

"We must take possession of bodies when they are in the HATBOX. It's true that, once we are in possession, we have physical substance outside the HATBOX, but all souls in the machine have knowledge of each and every possession. If one of us tries to turn off the machine, the others will know of it and fight back. The others already know of the MM Clout possession, although they don't yet understand its purpose. They think my friend is showing off. Shimmer is too strong of mind for us to possess him."

"What others?"

"The souls who don't want to be free," Arlo explained. "Like Benjamin, the scarred boy you saw. They are not my friends and don't want to be free. They want to possess cadets. They don't care what they do so long as they can have bodies again. They will grow in those bodies, and train at the acad-emy, and after they graduate, they will fight for Dr. Shimmer, to overthrow Wonderland's queen and make him the ruler instead."

Hatter felt as if his thoughts were spilling out of his ears, there were so many. Organizing them seemed an impossible task. "And the stuff about fainting that we overheard Benjamin discussing with Dr. Shimmer?"

"It happens sometimes when a soul tries to take possession of a body. It happened with Cadet Shake before one of Benjamin's followers was able to fully possess him."

Dogberry had been possessed? That explained why he'd behaved the way he had during the Top Hat duel. And why he couldn't remember what he'd done.

Hatter turned to Arlo, but the boy had erased himself as if he'd never been.

THE PROCEDURE IS SIMPLE.

Hatter told Newton that he hadn't found Tailor Quince in the Textillery and then fell silent. It was amazing how little the whole hat thing mattered to him since he'd spoken with Arlo. A part of him wanted to tell Newton about the tattooed boy from Boarderland, but another part wasn't sure that he should. He still didn't know Cadet Ezer that well. Newton, however, didn't fail to notice how silent and preoccupied Hatter was, and he mistakenly believed the reason had everything to do with the missing hat.

"I've been thinking," Newton said as they walked to the streaming ceremony at the Wonderground. "You don't have to worry. The eeries know all our stories, and they'll know you made a hat. I don't think it'll affect your being streamed into the Spades."

Hatter hadn't even considered what the eeries might know about his hat. Hopefully, Newton was right. Then again, the eeries didn't seem to have written his story. And even if the eeries knew everyone's story—everyone's but *his*—they would know Dogberry's. They'd know if Dogberry had been possessed. They'd know about MM Clout too. From them maybe, he could confirm that Arlo's story was true. But what then?

The Wonderground had been transformed into a lavish theater of blue and gold. Onstage, flanking a nondescript wooden door, sat MM Haymaker and Tutor Orlage. The door stood on its own, not attached to any walls. On the far sides of the stage, hanging from the flies, were four long banners, each depicting the symbol of a suit: Hearts and Diamonds on the left, Clubs and Spades on the right. Under each banner sat that suit's Top Hat.

The Caps entered single file into the Wonderground—all of them except Hatter wearing their newly constructed headgear. Hatter's head was bare, but he carried his story, the blank book, in his pocket. Seeing West, Top Hat for the Spades, on the stage, he went from excitement to sadness in a moment, remembering yet again that he was no longer a Wellington. What would happen when he became a Spade? West seemed like an okay Wonderlander, especially compared to Rhodes and the other Wellingtons. But he was still one of their group. Even worse, what if Rhodes also became a Spade? Would Hatter spend the rest of his time at the academy dealing with the kid's annoying games and nasty attitude? The mere thought of it was exhausting.

Once all cadets were seated, MM Haymaker rose and took center stage. "The procedure is simple," she announced in a loud, clear voice. "You hear your name; you come up and pass through the door. When you return from streaming, you will either sign the register with your Top Hat and then return to your seat, or—if you haven't made it to the next level—you will be asked to leave."

MM Haymaker returned to her seat.

"Cadet Fez!" announced the same disembodied voice that had been heard at the Top Hat duel.

Cadet Fez rose from his seat down near the front and climbed the stairs to the door. He glanced at MM Haymaker, and then opened the door. Hatter strained to see what was on the other side, but it looked as if it were just the back wall of the stage. Cadet Fez stepped through and closed the door behind him. Almost immediately, the door opened and he reappeared. He turned slowly and walked over to where the Top Hat for the Clubs was sitting and, with a tremulous hand, signed the register. Then he stood upright and returned to his seat.

"Cadet Topi!" the disembodied voice boomed.

The cadet made her way over to the door and walked through it, only to return in the blink of a spirit-dane's eye. Hatter had heard about this from his brother: how a cadet, visiting the eeries, might feel as if he were with them for a lunar hour or more, but no time would pass in Wonderland at all.

"While we wait, why don't you describe for me—in very specific detail—what the Wonderground looks like," Newton said.

"Okay," Hatter replied, and leaned over to whisper the description to him.

Meanwhile, the cadets were streamed one by one, in and out through the door. Several were cut from the academy and—no longer needing to maintain any kind of stoic dignity, as they were no longer cadets—left the Wonderground in tears. One boy slammed the door behind him so hard that the banners shook. Hatter couldn't help but feel bad for them, watching fellow Caps as they were escorted from the Wonderground to pack up their belongings and wait for their disappointed parents. In the past, seeing cadets expelled, he'd always felt a sense of pride that the academy was so exclusive. He'd always been pretty confident of his own place, but now doubt crept over him. What if he didn't make the cut?

But many familiar faces made it to Brims. Rhodes became a Spade and West stood to give him a firm handshake when he signed the register. Drummer was streamed into the Clubs, which made sense considering his general fighting abilities— they lacked finesse but were impressive nonetheless. Caledonia was also streamed into Clubs, which wasn't much of a surprise to Hatter; she was a military type if he'd ever seen one. She gave her Top Hat such a firm handshake that when she left the stage, the Top Hat shook out her hand from the pain.

"Cadet Madigan!" bellowed the voice.

"Ever wonder who that is?" Newton said as Hatter stood and adjusted his vest.

"Who? The voice?"

190

"Yeah, I mean does the person work here, or did they record their voice a long time ago?"

"I . . . have no idea." This wasn't really where Hatter's mind was at present. But how could Newton know how distracted he was?

"Good luck."

"Thanks."

Hatter walked down to the stage, feeling naked with his bare head. He climbed up and passed West. And then he opened the door.

IT'S NOT ABOUT WHAT YOU WANT, BUT WHAT YOU ARE.

He was in a small, round room, dark and empty except for a glowing pool of water in its center. He approached the pool, and though the water was as transparent as air, he couldn't see any details under its surface, not how deep it went, nothing. The surface rippled, but there was no breeze.

"Step into the pool," a voice said. Had the other cadets done this? And if so, had they spent enough time with the eeries that they'd completely dried off before returning to the Wonderground?

Bracing himself for cold and wet, Hatter dropped into the pool. Something pulled on his leg and he shot downward. Once under the surface Hatter realized he wasn't surrounded by water but by that same rippling light. He was falling down a hole, and falling deep. He glanced at his feet, expecting to see something holding fast to his ankles, but nothing was there. What he did notice was the ground coming up to meet him at an extraordinary speed.

He didn't have time to imagine his way out of the situation before he found himself standing upright on a stone floor.
He was in a cavern he easily recognized: the Archives. The
place looked exactly the same as when he'd visited it with the
Wellingtons, just not as dark because of the wealth of candles
now placed throughout. As if to remind him of that night of
trespass, his shoulder flared with pain, which was strange, since
the wound had healed.

A whisper: his name. Hatter turned around sharply. The
three eeries stood atop three large stalagmites. They were
draped head to toe in a strange fabric Hatter had never seen
before. Their cloaks almost perfectly matched the texture and
color of the stone they stood on, so that it was difficult to
see where the stalagmites ended and they began. When the
candlelight flickered in the figures' direction, suddenly a thin,
almost skeletal hand or shoulder could be seen, as if the fabric
had vanished in the light.

Shadows, Hatter understood suddenly. They were wearing
shadows.

"Approach," the whisper said. Hatter wasn't sure if the
eeries were whispering, or if they'd sent a whisper as their
emissary. He approached. When he reached the foot of the
platform, he had a sense memory of standing on it, his body
being pulled in two directions, and he stopped short.

"Step up onto the rock," the whisper said.

Hatter took a deep breath and stepped onto the platform,
but the strange sensation that he'd felt last time didn't come.

The eeries faced him. Up close he could see that the shadows they were wearing hung on their forms like wet sheets, clinging to their hollowed cheeks and bony frames, and dripping onto the floor. Some shadow oozed in his direction, and Hatter took a small step to the side.

"Hatter Madigan," the whisper asked, "why did you take your story?"

All breath seemed to leave his body, as if he'd been punched in the gut.

"Why did you take your story?" the whisper asked again.

"I—I—" stammered Hatter.

The eerie standing in the center tilted its head slightly to the left. It seemed to be a little confused as to why Hatter wasn't answering. Hatter himself was more than a little confused.

"I don't know. I took it because—because—"

"Because it was empty."

Hatter swallowed hard. "Yes."

There was a stillness now that seemed more still than the stillness before. Hatter was officially holding his breath. No one said anything. No one did anything. He wanted to ask. He had to ask. He needed to ask.

"Why is it empty?" both the whisper and Hatter asked at the same time.

"Jinx," the whisper said.

"Why are you asking me? You're the ones who write the stories." Hatter was starting to get irritated with the eeries.

"You are the one who lives the story."

"But . . . I have lived my story. I am living my story. It has a beginning, and currently I'm in the middle, and eventually—" He stopped short.

"Eventually, it will have an end," the whisper finished.

"Yes," Hatter said quietly.

"Do you have the story?"

"Yes."

Hatter pulled it from his vest pocket and offered it back to the eeries. None of them attempted to reach for it. Instead, it floated out of his hands into the air toward them and opened itself to the first page.

"Fascinating," the whisper said. The book closed and fell with a *thump* to the platform. "Hatter Madigan. You are a cadet with great potential."

Well, at least that sounded pretty good.

"Potential to excel and potential to be your own downfall."

Oh. Hatter stared at the book, unceremoniously dropped at his feet. "Which is it?" he asked softly.

"We don't know. We don't know your story. You shall be streamed into the Hearts, and in time perhaps the truth will be revealed."

Hearts? No. Not Hearts. "I don't want to be a Heart," he said before he could think.

"It's not about what you want, but what you are."

"But you don't even know me. You know nothing about me. You said so yourselves!"

"You lack self-control," the whisper said.

Hatter couldn't take it anymore. He kicked the book hard,

and it flew off the platform and skidded across the cavern floor. "I know!" he yelled. "I know! Everyone can stop saying it! I'm working on it!"

He stormed off the platform and back toward the entrance. He paused. Walked back and picked up his story. "Since you don't need this, I guess I'll keep it!"

He marched over to the entrance and realized only then that there was no way he could storm out of the cavern. He looked up. Just a stone ceiling. No sign of a pool of water anywhere.

"Hatter," the whisper said.

Hatter turned and found himself face-to-face with one of the eeries.

"Yes?" he asked quietly.

The eerie reached up. The shadow fell from its arm, revealing a white, thin hand—bone or white skin, it was very difficult to tell. The eerie placed its hand on Hatter's cheek. Suddenly he felt that pulling sensation from before. He wanted to pry himself away from the eerie, but he couldn't.

"You have a story," it said. "It is just not for us to tell."

"But why me? What's wrong with me?" Tears welled in Hatter's eyes. He hated himself. He hated himself for being so emotional. He hated himself for not having a story.

"You are not the first; you will not be the last. Nothing is wrong with you. You are simply unusual."

He was starting to feel nauseated; the pulling had turned into a kind of corkscrew twisting. "But how can I just go on, not knowing, not understanding? Who are the others who don't have stories? Is there a connection among us?"

"I don't know. Only you do."

That made no sense. Thoughts swirled in his brain. The nausea was definitely taking hold. He closed his eyes and saw Arlo's face.

"Who is that?" asked the eerie.

"That's Arlo," Hatter replied, somehow understanding the question.

"He is here, and he is not."

Sure. Sounded about right. "Dogberry," Hatter said, opening his eyes.

"Cadet Shake has been sent home."

The eerie removed its hand from Hatter's cheek. Hatter collapsed to the floor. The nausea vanished, but he felt completely winded, like he'd just run around the academy five times. He looked up; the eerie was again standing with its group on the platform. Hatter rose slowly to his feet. He noticed something red out of the corner of his eye and saw a heart-shaped patch on his vest lapel. He looked at the book in his hands.

"Here," he said, holding it out in front of him.

"Keep it," the whisper said.

And then Hatter felt the sensation of being whisked up toward the stone ceiling, except he never hit it. He instead rose up into the pale-blue light, higher and higher, toward the pool, toward the academy, toward a future he didn't want, holding in his hands a past that didn't exist.

29

IT'S WHAT I WANTED!

On the Wonderground stage, Hatter turned automatically toward West but then remembered: *Hearts. Stupid Hearts.* He about-faced and walked toward the Hearts Top Hat—a Taper girl, tall, with black hair shaved at the sides and a long ponytail. He signed his name in the register; the black ink seeped into the paper and turned gold.

As Hatter returned to his seat, he heard Rhodes snort. "Hearts! You'll make a good doorman someday."

"Your father was a bodyguard," Hatter snapped back.

"My father began as a Spade, and you know it. And now he's a Spade again. Claiming that it's a Milliner's highest honor to be a royal bodyguard is just something they have to say, otherwise no one would want to do it."

Hatter started to get up, to pummel Rhodes, but—

"He's not worth it," Newton said in that calm, steady voice of his.

Hatter thought Rhodes was the definition of *worth it*, but he unclenched his fists and faced forward, staring at nothing. Sure, it was a relief to have made it to Brims, but why did it have to be as a Heart? He didn't want to follow Dalton's path, no matter how proud he was of his brother. He wanted to make his own path. But without a story, how could he know what his path was supposed to be? The eeries hadn't been even close to helpful about *that*, had they? His hands again became fists.

"Cadet Ezer!"

Rhodes and Drummer snickered as Newton picked his way toward the stage. It was slow going, since he'd never before been in this particular Wonderground configuration. MM Haymaker got up to help him, but Newton asked her to return to her seat. He walked with careful determination onto the stage and, without erring a single step, up to the door. It was impressive that he'd found it so easily, and Hatter then realized that when Newton had asked him what the room looked like, it hadn't just been for curiosity's sake. He'd been plotting his course.

Newton passed through the door, almost immediately returned, and this time accepted the help that MM Haymaker offered. He walked over to the Diamonds Top Hat and signed the register. Then he returned to his seat next to Hatter.

"You made it!" Hatter said when Newton was again next to him.

"Much to the surprise of your former friends, no doubt."

A wash of shame passed over Hatter. He'd been just like his former friends. But if the eeries had deemed Newton good enough, who was he to question the kid's worth as a Milliner? "Diamonds," he said. "A strategist. That makes sense."

"Because I'm useless in combat?"

"Because you're really smart."

"I'll pretend to believe you." But Newton smiled.

Astra was the last cadet to visit the eeries, bounding up onto the stage and through the door. She reappeared half a moment later, positively beaming. Which was weird, since a Vost never made it past Caps. But on her lapel was a patch signifying her suit as a Brim. She'd made it.

"Spades!" Caledonia's voice sang out.

Cadet Alinari jumped onstage and lifted her friend off the floor in a big hug.

"It's what I wanted!" Astra said, laughing loudly and repeatedly looking at her lapel, as if to make sure the Spades emblem on it was real.

Hatter sat, conflicted. He couldn't believe it. Astra, a Spade? But not him? Okay, it had been wrong to assume she'd get cut from the academy, and he did feel guilty for having made that assumption, but still . . . Astra was so un-Spadelike in every way. No, not only un-Spadelike: un-cadetlike.

"Yes, yes—we'll be quiet," Caledonia singsonged, as Tutor Orlage made to get up. She held her finger to her lips and took Astra's arm in hers. The two practically skipped to West, who apparently couldn't help but smile at the sight. Astra signed the register with a flourish, and the two girls left the stage, still grinning like crazy. Hatter was surprised they hadn't been given extra detention then and there for such a display. He supposed that, just this once, there was some leniency on emotional outbursts.

Tutor Orlage walked to center stage. "Congratulations, Brims. You will now be given your room assignments. These will be your roommates for the duration of your stay at the academy. A cadet's roommate is always from a different suit to promote cooperation between the suits and also to make sure you don't cheat on your homework." That was it. No other ceremony. But Hatter understood. They had simply done what was expected of them. Why praise them for making it to the next level? Tutor Orlage unfurled a long scroll of paper and began reading out room assignments.

"We're together," Newton said to Hatter.

"How do you know?"

"It makes sense."

It didn't make sense to Hatter, but he supposed if they kept the unique order of the alphabet from the dormitory, it was a possibility. Sure enough, he heard his name accompanied by Newton's. He also heard Rhodes scoff quietly at his back, and Hatter wondered for the first time why no one ever criticized the kid for such obvious expressions of emotion.

"Congratulations," he said, as he and Newton joined Astra and Caledonia in the yard. Hatter's next words were difficult for him to find, freighted as they were with his own disappointment, but he thought that he should say them. He tried to believe them. Astra had accomplished something important, even if he didn't understand how. "You'll make an excellent Spade."

Astra guffawed, still surprised at her success. "And the Hearts are lucky to have *you*!"

Hatter winced.

"If I weren't a Diamond Brim and didn't know better, Astra," Newton said, "you'd be the first person I told my secrets to. You'll make an excellent spy."

"It's probably going to be rough," Caledonia warned, "with Rhodes also being a Spade."

"I'll keep an eye on Rhodes," Hatter said.

"Yeah"—Newton was already cracking himself up—"you keep an eye on him and I'll keep an ear."

HAVE YOU NOTICED ANYTHING STRANGE GOING ON AT THE ACADEMY?

T heir room in the South Needle was on the top floor, and Newton was as excited about this as Hatter.

"I would have thought you'd be the opposite," Hatter said. "Usually, Caps and anyone else not used to the high, open spaces of the Needle or riding on swifties . . . it all makes them pretty nervous."

"You forget that I've had a lot of practice. I've been on every floor many times, having to make up all those Brim bunks."

The swifties moved up and down on powerful electromagnetic currents generated by yellow caterpillar thread, and they were guided invisibly by blue-thread configurations that tapped into the riders' consciousness to determine the desired floors. Hatter himself had become an expert swifty rider long before he was a Cap, while still just a ward of the academy, by virtue of his many stealth missions to the Needle. Standing on a transparent platform that rose and fell with great speed, no railings to keep him from falling off, no handholds to steady himself:

it was almost as cool as fighting card soldiers in the HATBOX.

He and Newton boarded a west swifty and were playing games even before they reached the third floor, putting their weight first on one edge and then another. Riders couldn't exactly surf the air on a swifty—the channels of travel were too rigid—but they could pretend. Standing on its back edge, Hatter and Newton rode theirs at a tilt, front edge uppermost, as if they were popping a wheelie. Up and up and up and up they went, making a Wonderpark ride out of an everyday means of transport until—

The swifty stopped at the top floor.

"You do the honors," Hatter said outside their room.

Newton felt for the doorknob and turned it. The door swung back on its hinges. The room was small, barely big enough to fit two bunks, two small desks, and a single wardrobe. Opposite the front door, a window took up the entire wall. Hatter held Newton's arm and together they crossed the threshold.

"Okay," Hatter said, "so there are two beds, left and right. Which do you want?"

"I don't care. The left, I guess."

Hatter turned Newton so that he faced his bed. Newton took a single step and reached out, felt the length and breadth of his bed with both hands.

"Just past the head of your bed there's a desk and chair," Hatter told him. "Your side of the room is exactly the same as mine, and it's about three paces from your bed to mine. Past our desks is a window. A big one."

Newton went slowly to his desk and examined it with his hands. "What else?"

"A wardrobe for our stuff. We have to share. It's back here by the door, but on my side. You want me to show you?"

"No." Newton felt his way back toward Hatter, fingers running along his bed till he reached the foot of it, then extending his arms to keep from knocking into anything as he measured again how many paces it was from his bed to the door. "Not much room."

"Cozy."

When he found the wardrobe, Newton briefly traced his hands along its front, opened it, and touched the clothes inside.

"They unpacked for us."

Hatter stepped up for a closer look. Something was missing. He checked the top shelf, got down on his knees, and felt every gwormmy-length of the wardrobe's floor. It was definitely missing. But it *couldn't* be missing. It had to be there; it just had to be.

"What's wrong?" Newton asked.

"My father's hat. It's not here."

"Okay, don't panic. Where did you last see it?"

"What does that matter? They moved all our stuff."

"Just answer the question: Where did you last see it?"

"Under my bed."

"So look under your bed."

Hatter was there in an instant, crouching down, reaching under—

"Find it?"

"Yes."

Newton held out his hand. "Can I hold it?"

Hatter brought the hat into the open. It struck him as more worn than ever, frayed almost to the point of disintegration. A sad hat. He passed it to Newton.

"This silk," Newton said, his fingers carefully examining the hat's brim, crown, and what was left of its lining, "it's so soft. I've never felt anything like it. And the structure—it's solid and true. The shape . . . I'm surprised anyone could make a hat so symmetrical even with the molds in the Textillery. It's as close to a perfect specimen as I've ever encountered."

"It's falling apart," Hatter said quietly.

"That can be fixed."

"It doesn't seem to have any imagination imbued in it."

"I think you're wrong."

"Wait," Hatter said, "are you able to tell just by touch if gear has imagination in it?"

"It's something I'm working on," Newton replied with a smile.

"Cool."

His father's hat again in his hands, Hatter closed his eyes and tried to experience it, to understand it, the way that Newton had. He ran his fingers over its brim, crown, and lining. The silk *was* really soft—almost like liquid. A liquid that Hatter's fingers dipped into, sending out little ripples. He opened his eyes and stowed the hat back under his bed.

"So what's the view out our window like?" Newton asked.

It seemed as if all of Wonderland—awash in impressive sunlight, one golden orb almost directly above the other—were stretched out below. The gleaming towers of Wondertropolis rose up in the middle distance, basking in the glow of the Heart Crystal. Off to one side, at a greater distance, were the Volcanic Plains, and beyond them the Valley of Mushrooms. To the south, Mount Isolation and Forever Forest shadowed the horizon. Only Outerwilderbeastia and the Chessboard Desert couldn't be seen. Hatter described all of this to his friend, who sat quietly and listened.

"Hey, uh . . . Newton?" Hatter said. "Have you noticed anything strange going on at the academy?"

Newton thought a moment. "Dogberry, of course," he said. "That was strange. And at first I thought it odd that so many cadets were fainting in the HATBOX, but I guess that's just normal for Caps—the stress and everything. Why're you asking?"

"I don't know. Just because of Dogberry, I guess."

Should he tell Newton all he'd learned from Arlo? He hadn't been asked to keep the knowledge strictly to himself, had he? But would Newton even believe him? It wasn't as if souls trapped in machines or possessing cadets' bodies were common chitchat. And what if Newton told a tutor or a Master Milliner that Cadet Madigan had gone batty from the stress of training? Would he be able to help Arlo then?

"Just think," Newton said. "That was the last graduation ceremony we'll be part of until we graduate as Milliners. From here, each of us rises from Brim to Cobbler and beyond at our own pace."

"Or not," Hatter said.

"Bet you a lunar cycle's supply of tarty tarts that I get to Cobbler level before you."

"You're on."

Thunk! Two multifaceted crystals tumbled into the message hoard—a receptacle embedded in the wall—by the door.

"Our Brim schedules?" Newton said. "They don't waste time, do they?"

He and Hatter slotted the gems into the crystal-readers on their desks. Class schedules appeared on their desktop screens. Reading what his coming days were to be filled with, Hatter felt hollow. It wasn't as if he didn't get to continue his combat training, but his Milliner Etiquette class had been split into three separate sections, each with a unique focus on serving at the palace. There was even a subsection on dancing!

"I don't know if I can do this," Hatter said to himself.

"Of course you can," Newton replied, drawing his finger across his schedule and nodding as he listened to it. He gave one last nod and turned in Hatter's direction. "Why are you a Milliner?"

"Well . . . I mean, I was born one."

"Yes, but why do you care? Why did you work so hard in your Cap classes?"

"To become a Spade."

"Honestly, Hatter, sometimes you are just too stubborn for your own good. I know the reason, and I'm not even you."

"Well, if you're so clever, Mr. Strategist, why don't you tell me?"

"You want to serve and protect Wonderland. That's why you finally cracked with Rhodes. He's been a jerk to everyone, but it was only when he turned on someone who wasn't a cadet, but just a plain old Wonderlander, that you walloped him. You're a Heart now, and you'll get to live and work around the palace. It might not *sound* as exciting as being a Spade to you, but it does to me. You'll be close to the most powerful Wonderlanders in the queendom. And anyway, a Milliner's life isn't about what you want for yourself. It's about something bigger. And you get that. Deep down."

Hatter wasn't sure that was true, but it was as good an excuse as any. It was something he could maybe pretend to think was true. He glanced at the clock above the door. He had to hurry if he didn't want to be late for his first class as a Brim Heart.

He ran out of the room and onto a swifty, jumped off before it stopped at the ground floor, and then hurried past the large group of new Caps entering the Needle. They seemed so young, so awed by their surroundings. Had he looked like that on his first day as a cadet? Unbelievable.

Hatter entered the academy proper and stopped. He could take a shortcut through the seams that would help him get to the other side of the building in time for class. He pulled back a tapestry—the same one from that fateful night when they had all snuck into the Healing Room—and climbed into the dark seam inside the walls. This time he turned in the opposite direction and headed into a tunnel that angled downward. He rounded corner after corner. The tunnel became steeper, propelling him forward so quickly that he had to run. And then he was tumbling, the decline so steep he couldn't stop himself. He missed the turnoff to his exit but couldn't stop. It felt as if he were tumbling through the entire academy and would come out the other side, if not clear across Wonderland.

Suddenly the tunnel flattened, and he skidded to a stop. He looked around. So much for making up for lost time. He was turning to go back up the steep incline when he heard voices.

He turned, paused. He really should get to class.

Instead, he took a left and crawled along a narrow tunnel toward the sound of the voices, feeling dirt under his hands. He glanced up and saw rock and mud. *Definitely not in the academy anymore.* He kept crawling, and the ground beneath him got as hard as stone. He turned a corner, and there was light. Carefully he approached the small vent and looked through it into a room where a tangled mass of brightly glowing yellow caterpillar thread covered the ceiling. The yellow thread transmitted power while circuits of blue thread transmitted information in glowing sapphire pulses, speeding this way and that like little blue vehicles traveling along the busy roads of Wondertropolis. They were azure shooting stars. They were tiny turquoise snakes. They moved so quickly that he looked, only to have the light disappear. The whole picture was one of constant colorful movement, and the shadows cast by the cables changed into a thousand different pictures. There were bright flashes of lightning too. Sometimes, a zigzag of light would explode from the end of one cable and launch itself over to the start of another, raining droplets of light down onto the ground below. It looked magical, but it was science: thread tech.

Hatter knew where he was now: underneath the HATBOX. And the miraculous contraption he was looking at must be what Arlo had called "the machine," the holo-generator and program controller for the HATBOX.

Standing in the midst of the caterpillar thread and pulsing lights was Sir Isaac Shimmer—wearing, as ever, pajamas.

"An entire group of Caps streamed and not one single possession that's taken hold," the doctor was mumbling. "So many failed attempts. All those students collapsing. Always knew it was a long-term game. No, the training, the waiting for the cadets to move through all eight levels—*that* I knew would take a long time. But not *this*. And why do the power levels keep dipping? Must be a loose connection somewhere. Has to be. But I've checked. Check again, Shimmer. Stop whining."

Sir Isaac sat down in the middle of the room, his legs crossed. He took one sparking filament of yellow thread in his left hand, another in his right, and closed his eyes. The light in the room began to travel down the cables and into him and then out beneath him along the cables on the floor. It was as if Shimmer were sitting at the base of a waterfall with all the light flowing through him. It was mesmerizing to watch, but

Hatter was suddenly jarred back to his senses by the distant echoing charm of the class bell.

His shortcut had turned into the longest cut ever. And he was about to be late for his first Heart class ever. Not good.

As quickly as he could, he scuttled backward until he was again in the tunnel. With great effort he climbed up the steep slope. Back in the seams, he made his way to the exit. Muddy and exhausted, he bolted outside, down the path, and through the antechamber of the HATBOX. He ran over and pulled open the door and all the Brim Hearts turned to look at him.

"Detention, Cadet Madigan," MM Tornado said.

THERE IS NO SUCH THING AS BAD FORM WHEN YOU'RE A HEART.

MM Tornado had been an intimidating presence to Hatter ever since he first arrived at the academy. There was just something about her that inspired fear. She was a small wiry woman, all muscle and no nonsense. She had a severe purple bob that never seemed to grow or vary in length. She never smiled and barely spoke. It seemed as if she had no interest in being friendly with anyone, not even her fellow MMs.

She watched Hatter as he took his position with the rest of the Brim Hearts, directing a particularly icy eye at his dirty shoes. He stood at attention and waited for her to turn on the HATBOX, barely able to contain himself. He was about to see his sparring partner Arlo for the first time since their talk in the Textillery alcove. And after what he'd just seen and heard in the machine room, he was ready to help.

"Begin!" MM Tornado said, and the sparring partners appeared.

But it wasn't Arlo who materialized in front of Hatter; it was Benjamin—the Boarderlander with the scar on his face. He charged at Hatter with such speed and ferocity that Hatter instinctively, reflexively, jumped to the side, knocking into Twist, who had just thrown a roundhouse at his own sparring partner. Hatter started to apologize when he felt a pain in his lower back and went flying to the ground. "Bad form!" he called out, pushing himself up and spinning around.

"What was that, Cadet Madigan?" MM Tornado's voice cut through the violence. The sparring partners vanished as she marched toward him.

"Uh—uh—" Hatter stammered.

"I asked you a question, cadet. What did you just say?" She wasn't much taller than him, but her presence still overpowered him. It didn't help that he felt kind of woozy.

"I said, 'Bad form,' ma'am!"

"And what was the purpose of saying such a thing?"

Hatter didn't know how to answer. Surely it was obvious. Kicking someone while his back was turned was not the proper way to fight.

"My partner, he . . . he attacked me from behind. It was bad form."

MM Tornado took a step closer and squinted even harder at him, so much so that Hatter thought maybe she'd closed her eyes.

"What does form have to do with anything?" she asked.

"Well, uh, it has to do with everything. With Milliner

etiquette and honor and . . ." He stopped. He still couldn't quite understand her point.

"And you think an assassin from Boarderland is going to care about honor and etiquette, do you?" she asked. Her eyes widened, and for the first time he noticed they were the same color as her hair, and that inside the deep violet of her pupils were jagged flashes of gold. They were terrifyingly intense to look into.

Boarderland. The land where orphans were emptied of their souls and their bodies were cast off as so much trash. No, it was probable that good form didn't matter to Boarderlanders.

"No, ma'am!" Hatter said.

MM Tornado stared at him for a moment longer and then turned around and marched into the middle of the room.

"No, indeed! I know everyone thinks Heart is the softest of suits. The easiest to pass and conquer. But know this: you are not the military; you are not spies; and you are not strategists. As royal bodyguards, you are *all* of these things. There is not an enemy code of behavior you can rely on, no so-called rules of engagement. There is no one you can trust, no one's honor on which you can rely, no matter their pedigree. You must anticipate and counter all possible schemes against the royal family. You must be ready to fight at a moment's notice, both within the palace and without. To protect the queen, you may be sent on deadly missions far away or you may remain within the palace walls, where you should not assume that, just because there is luxury, there is no risk of violence. The queen's enemies—and thus, yours—are everywhere. To be a Heart is to be ready for everything. And to know that 'everything' includes those things you have no idea how to prepare for. If you think that graduating as a Heart will be anything less than the hardest, most demanding program here at the Millinery, you are sorely mistaken. So . . . if someone kicks you from behind, you get up and punch him in the face. There is no such thing as bad form when you're a Heart. There is only winning and losing. Actually, no—losing isn't an option. Is that clear?"

"Yes, ma'am!" the Brim Hearts called out, Hatter's voice rising above the rest.

The sparring partners rematerialized. Benjamin charged at Hatter, but he was ready. He knelt down, ramming his shoulder into the kid's stomach and flipping him onto the ground. Benjamin kipped up onto his feet and aimed a kick at Hatter's gut. But Hatter grabbed his foot and twisted it. Benjamin collapsed facedown on the floor, and Hatter was on him, a knee in his back, a fistful of the kid's hair in his hand, about to slam his head again and again against the hard tile . . .

And then he was on his feet, backing quickly away. Almost running. Out the door of the HATBOX and into the antechamber. He stood there, his breathing labored, his pulse racing.

"What in Wonderland was that, Cadet Madigan?" MM Tornado said, marching after him. "No one leaves my class without permission."

"I don't know. I'm sorry, ma'am. I'm sorry I did that."

"Did what?"

"Grabbed my sparring partner's hair and almost smashed his face like that."

"It wasn't a particularly elegant move, nor probably the wisest option to choose, but I don't see why you're apologizing for it."

Hatter stared into those fierce eyes of hers and didn't know quite what to say. Could he tell her that it had been the same move a possessed Dogberry had used on West in the Top Hat duel? And that he was afraid he too might be possessed? Why else had he felt dizzy? He'd almost fainted. Maybe one of Benjamin's followers had gotten inside him. How did a person know if he were possessed or not?

"Are you done with this nonsense?" MM Tornado asked, folding her arms across her chest.

Hatter managed to nod, and he followed her back into the HATBOX. Cadets were still fighting, but as MM Tornado reappeared, the holograms vanished, and the cadets stopped and stood at attention.

"It would seem," MM Tornado declared, "that a return to basics is required. Your lack of technique and inventiveness is shocking. I'm putting off basic hat training for a few weeks. Let's pretend you are all scared little Caps and go over punches and kicks."

Hatter was grateful to MM Tornado for humiliating the whole class that way. It took the attention off him, and all the Brim Hearts were now determined to prove that they were better fighters than Caps. It helped him too to take his mind off his fears and just focus on his skills.

Tutor Wren was still Hatter's History teacher, and as Hatter entered the room, the tutor directed a small, approving nod his way, which he answered with a slight nod of his own. He was starting to understand why someone might want to be a Heart. Yes, it felt odd having his entire future suddenly mapped out for him, a future that he hadn't wanted. It had been fine, back when he anticipated being a Spade, but the thought that he was now supposed to become something else? Something that was so *not* what he'd always dreamed for himself? It helped to see Tutor Wren, who sincerely enjoyed teaching the history of the Heart suit and what it meant to be a royal bodyguard.

Hatter took a seat next to Twist, who gave him that same shy smile he'd given him in combat class. He wasn't sure why that smile kept happening, but he tried to smile back.

"Brim Hearts," Tutor Wren said. He was not sitting behind his desk but standing in a far corner, gazing up at a teetering tower of books, his back to the cadets. Hatter waited for him to say something else. Anything else. There was a too-long silence.

"Has he fallen asleep?" Twist whispered in an earnest voice.

Hatter shook his head. He stared at Tutor Wren's motionless back. Then again . . .

"Hearts!" Tutor Wren abruptly turned and faced them.

"The oldest suit, a suit from before the academy was founded. Before a military was needed. Before Wonderland even had enemies. The royal bodyguards have existed for as long as there have been royals. No suit requires more patience, more keen observation, and more deadly skills. There is a long list of famous Milliners who have served as the queen's bodyguard, and we shall discuss them today. But there is also a list of illustrious Milliners who were part of the royal bodyguard corps and were important despite never having the highest honor. Our own MM Clout was a member of the royal bodyguards and won many commendations for his service."

And is probably one of the most bitter Master Milliners at the academy, Hatter thought. *Aside from the Grand Milliner.*

"Let us begin with Opus Vandermeer, the very first queen's bodyguard and the genius behind the Vandermeer Proposition, one of the deadliest moves one can make with a J-blade."

After class, Hatter found himself walking to lunch with Twist at his side. It was a bit like having a puppy, and he finally couldn't handle it anymore. He stopped and turned to Twist. "What?" he asked, completely exasperated.

"What do you mean, *what?*" Twist looked terrified.

"What do you want from me? Why do you keep smiling at me? It's . . . weird."

"I'm sorry," Twist said, his face falling. "I just . . . you taking on Rhodes was really amazing. He's been telling me what to do since we were little, and I just never could stand up to him. You're an inspiration."

Hatter stared at Twist. "Uh, okay."

"Would you mind being my friend?" Twist asked with a slight squeak. "I know you have your friends, but since we're both Hearts, we could talk sometimes."

"Sure." Hatter shifted uncomfortably.

"You're going to make a great bodyguard someday," Twist said. "You just are so clearly meant to be a Heart, the way you protected that tender and stuff."

It's a compliment, Hatter told himself. "Thanks," Hatter said. "I'm going to go to lunch now."

What an exhausting morning.

32

HERE'S HOPING IT'S NOT TOO WEIRD.

The day continued in a similarly exhausting fashion. First he had lunch with his new gang of detention misfits, each of them going on and on about their training. The worst was having to listen to Astra talk about her Spades Stealth class. Then he had to endure Milliner Etiquette 203, otherwise known as dance class.

"A bodyguard must be able to rescue a royal even if the peril is one of reputation and not of life or death. For instance, no royal should be left without a dance partner," said MM Bliss. "Now, pair off!"

The Master Milliner tapped his cane on the floor, and everyone awkwardly sought out a dance partner. Hatter was lucky that Cadet Lin came right for him, though he barely knew her. It turned out she was already a very good dancer, and she helped him to not look completely foolish.

A happy interval came in the late afternoon, with White Imagination 200, when the caterpillar singled out Hatter for particular praise. Cadets were now harnessing the imagination of various threads to instill its power in other objects, and evidently no Brim in any suit had managed, in the past several generations, to imbue a mirror with his or her own face as a toddler on the first try. As Hatter had. He'd succeeded where even Dalton had failed.

Last but not least was his Textillery class. Hatter couldn't help but feel rage swell up inside when he entered the work-room, remembering what Rhodes had done with his hat. Not that Hatter even knew the specifics, but it was gone, and it was Rhodes's fault, and that was enough. That was the one good thing about not being a Spade: not having to look at Rhodes's smug face.

"Today we begin fashioning basic weapons," Tailor Quince said in his usual quiet voice. "Your goal in time will be to man-ufacture the Milliner's ultimate weapon: his pack, backpack, satchel—whatever you'd like to call it—the thing he wears over two shoulders. I once suggested 'bag of magnificence,' but I was outvoted. A Milliner's pack contains all the weapons in his arsenal but is also made from caterpillar silk, thus infusing it with White Imagination so that it can function with but a thought. It can propel you into the air; it can fight your foes for you while you take on others. It is the ultimate weapon. But all weapons are fashioned using the same basic techniques, so you need to learn those techniques first. And that's why in Brims we teach you how to fashion the C-blade—the simplest of blades to construct, but that doesn't mean it is simple to do. Let's begin by learning how to fasten metal pieces together."

The basket was passed around and everyone in the class took two rectangular pieces of metal. What followed were basic welding instructions that almost immediately went over Hatter's head. He focused so hard, tried to listen carefully, and watched as Tailor Quince showed them every single step. But by the end of the class he had not managed to make the two pieces stick.

On his way to detention, Hatter felt pretty low. How was he ever going to be able to make a weapon when he couldn't make the simplest thing? The eeries had gotten it wrong; he wasn't meant to be a Heart. Arlo had gotten it wrong too, had picked the wrong cadet. How was Hatter supposed to help a bunch of trapped souls when he couldn't keep his own hat safe or fuse two pieces of metal, and didn't have the strength of will to keep from becoming possessed—which, by this time, is what he'd convinced himself had happened to him in the HATBOX?

Hatter was brought out of his thoughts by the sight of his fellow detainees standing in a clump in front of the locked detention room door.

"What's going on?" he asked.

"No idea," Newton replied.

"Detention has been moved—come with me to the tutors' lounge!" announced Tutor Ampersand, who had somehow materialized behind them. "You're to give it a thorough cleaning. Come on!"

Caledonia flashed Hatter a look he understood well. The tutors were odd creatures. A species not quite Wonderlander and not quite animal, and pretty secretive. Strange beings that had strange habits, and Hatter could only wonder what exactly they'd find in the lounge.

"Here's hoping it's not too weird," Caledonia whispered as they followed Tutor Ampersand.

"Oh, I'm hoping it is!" Astra said with a smile.

33

YOU MEAN THAT'S NOT ON PURPOSE?

The tutors' lounge was at the center of the east wing of tutor classrooms. There was no hallway, no door. It was just somewhere in the middle of it all, where really there wasn't a middle in the first place.

To access it, you had to go up to the top of the academy and walk along a narrow bridge until you came to a large floating cube with a square hole cut in the top. An old wooden ladder missing at least five steps reached down from the bridge into the cube, and on climbing down it you were at last in the tutor lounge. Each wall, as well as the floor, of the large square room was covered in books, and each wall of books was covered in yet another, and another, so that the inside of the room was far smaller than the outside. Standing atop the floor of books were several worn plush couches, each with patches of colors that did not remotely match. Except for the couch in the north-east corner. In that couch lived the dormouse, and so instead

227

of patches he had some finely crafted windows and—at its base—a tiny elegant door.

When the four cadets climbed down into the room, they stopped in their tracks. It was not the tutors sitting in the far corner drinking parsnip tea that shocked them. Nor Tutor Mars reclining so far back in a chair that his head dangled lower than his legs. Nor Tutor Vim who was smoking a glass pipe full of whirling smoke of green and purple, his ears floppy and pointing in two completely separate directions. It was the general level of disorganization: books absolutely everywhere, scrolls unfurled across the breadth of the room. Every shelf was filled, every cubby packed. Dusting seemed quite impossible.

"Oh, how cute!" Astra exclaimed as a dust bunny hopped past, leaving a trail of white in his wake. The creature stopped and looked at Astra, twitching his whiskers. His eyes widened in fear and he exploded in a cloud of particles.

"Oh no!" Astra said, bringing her hand to her mouth.

"Don't worry, Cadet Vost," Tutor Ampersand said, climbing down the ladder and joining them. "The bits will find each other, and he'll be himself again. Dust bunnies are awfully sensitive. If they're afraid that someone is about to clean their habitat . . . *poof!*"

Astra nodded, but Hatter couldn't help but inwardly roll his eyes. Detention had officially become a very silly thing.

"Don't worry about cleaning. Think of it more as organizing. We use the standard alphabet here in the tutor lounge, thank you very much," instructed Tutor Ampersand. "Q to P." She gestured toward the center of the room, but Hatter couldn't tell which books needed to be put away and which were already where they belonged.

"What should *I* do?" Newton asked.

"Well . . ." Tutor Ampersand had clearly not thought this punishment through at all. "You could . . ." She snapped her fingers. "Yes! You could listen to the latest version of Tutor Vim's speech he's giving to the Wonderland High Council on the varied and surprising uses of mold."

"And give him feedback?" Newton asked slowly.

"Oh goodness no. No, just listen. He likes to read it out loud several times before he has to present it."

Newton nodded, and Hatter wasn't entirely sure if he'd lucked out in his assignment or if he had been given the worse one. He watched Newton carefully negotiate the piles of books and the uneven floor with his cane until he reached Tutor Vim.

"You two," Tutor Ampersand said to Hatter and Caledonia, "get to work. Start here!" She pointed to what looked like a coffee table made of books.

"You mean that's not on purpose?" Caledonia asked.

Tutor Ampersand sighed and wandered over to sit in quiet conference with Tutor Riggle, her train of hair sweeping a path in the dust as she did.

"That would be a no, then," Hatter said. The two of them made their way to the coffee table and began to dismantle it. Then they carried large piles of books over to the shelves and stared at the tightly packed rows bursting before them.

"This is impossible," Caledonia said.

But they began shoving books in between the ones already on the shelves—sometimes it worked when a book was kind enough to scooch over a little bit. But others were stubborn, not remotely interested in being helpful. Some of them even made themselves thicker, adding a couple pages here and there.

"Uh, Hatter," Caledonia said softly.

"Yeah?"

"I don't know if you remember, but a while ago you asked me about that hologram boy . . ."

"Arlo!"

"So you know him?" Caledonia whispered in amazement.

"I do. He used to be my sparring partner."

"He's in the Textillery. He showed up during my weapons class while we were all getting ready to leave. He's staying up in the rafters. He said you'd be able to get up there somehow. Something bad's happening, or is about to happen."

"I know."

"So you'll go see him? You'll help?"

"Yes."

Caledonia smiled brightly just as Astra staggered by with a pile of books teetering high above her head.

"Astra, he's in!"

"I told you he would be." Her cheerful voice was slightly muffled behind all the books. She continued her treacherous journey across the room, the pile of books swaying this way and that way, and then a third way not often spoken of.

"What's everybody so excited about?" Newton asked, coming up to Hatter and Caledonia.

It seemed unfair to keep him out of the loop. Hatter related everything Arlo had told him about the machine, the trapped souls, Arlo's wish to be set free, Dogberry's possession, and Dr. Shimmer's plot to possess an army of cadets and have them train in the academy until they were ready to help him overthrow the queen. Caledonia listened without any show of surprise, which confirmed for Hatter that she'd heard it all from Arlo.

"We'll go after evening exercises," he said. "The four of us. We'll meet Arlo in the Textillery and find out what exactly we have to do to shut off the machine and set the souls free. After evening classes we'll have the best chance of not being missed."

"Sounds like a plan," Caledonia said.

HOW DO WE TURN OFF THE MACHINE?

Hatter could discern a couple of advantages to the way the Millinery Academy was run as opposed to other Wonderland institutions. For one, most of the cadets themselves valued discipline just as much as their instructors and didn't need to be watched over all the time. It was why the Wellingtons were able to sneak about with relative ease as they did. For another, the Master Milliners lived off campus and only tutors lived in the academy itself. Cadets weren't nearly as frightened of tutors as they were of Master Milliners, so being caught by one was not usually a big deal, though Hatter's run-in with Tutor Wren in the Healing Room had definitely changed his opinion on that subject.

So it wasn't impossible for Hatter and Newton to sneak out of the South Needle that evening to speak with Arlo in the Textillery, but it was difficult to escape the prying eyes of fellow cadets, especially the eyes of cadets who actively and completely despised them. For the first time since the streaming,

Hatter was very aware of Rhodes's attention as he sat at one of the tables in the common area, sore and sweaty from the evening workout.

"Why does he keep staring at me like that?" Hatter asked Newton. "Why can't he leave me alone?"

Newton shrugged. "I assume he's decided you are his mortal enemy now."

Hatter glared back at Rhodes, who was sitting with the other Wellingtons over at the couches. Rhodes said something to his friends, and then all of them turned to look at Hatter, talking to one another and laughing. Hatter felt heat rising up in him. He couldn't get into a confrontation, not now. He had to sneak out with Newton, meet the girls, and be invisible, not the center of attention in another Rhodes/Madigan showdown.

"Hi, Madigan!" Twist said. "Can I sit with you?"

Hatter looked up and saw his new friend looking at him with a smile. He must have had some kind of weird expression on his face because Twist's expression turned to one of concern.

"What? What is it?" Twist asked.

Hatter turned to see Rhodes standing up, making his way over to him, flanked by Nigel and Drummer. Twist followed his look. "Oh," he said. He clenched his fists.

Hatter saw him do it and said softly, "Don't make a scene. Newton and I are trying to sneak out, and we don't need the extra attention." He immediately realized he probably shouldn't have said that to Twist, and judging by Newton's startled expression, Newton agreed.

But Twist didn't ask why. Didn't probe. "I'll take care of it,"

234

he said, not sounding entirely sure of himself. Before Hatter could say anything, Twist had walked off to intercept Rhodes and the others. "What do you want?" he asked loudly, his voice cracking as it often did.

Rhodes rolled his eyes. "Get out of the way, Twist."

"Back off!" Twist said, a bit more confidence in his voice.

Rhodes's focus finally switched, and he stared at Twist in surprise. Then he grabbed the boy by the shoulders and pushed him to the side.

Twist stumbled for a moment but rushed back in front of Rhodes again. "Don't push me!"

"You don't want to fight me, Twist," Rhodes said with a laugh. Nigel laughed too. Drummer just stood there, looking as if he were sleeping with his eyes open.

"Sure I do." And with that, Twist sent a fast and sudden jab at Rhodes's jaw.

Rhodes staggered backward and brought his hand to his face, massaging his jaw. "Oh, you've asked for it now!"

The other cadets had gathered around, and after the fight broke out, more and more joined in, taking sides, until there was an all-out brawl, where it didn't seem anyone knew exactly why punches were being thrown.

"Should we help him?" Hatter watched as Twist was raised high into the air by a massive Peak. As he asked it, Twist smiled at Hatter and mouthed the word *Go!* just before he was brought back down into the crowd and disappeared.

"Quick! Let's move!" Hatter said, and helped Newton rush across to the doors as fast as possible and into the yard. They met the girls a moment later, and Hatter led them into the academy's seams ("These passages are amazing!" Astra gushed) and up to the rafters in the high-ceilinged Textillery.

As often happened when he came up here, he was thinking of Weaver, of how weird it was that a good friend could be somewhere doing something that he knew nothing about. He hoped she was okay.

"The possessions are beginning," Arlo said, fidgeting mightily, when Hatter and his friends reached him in the alcove.

"I guess Shimmer fixed whatever was glitchy with the machine," Hatter said. And then, after Arlo's evident surprise, he added: "I saw him in the machine room, remembered what we heard him talking about with Benjamin, and put one and one together. I want to help you, Arlo." He gestured at his friends. "We all do. Not sure how much good *I'll* be to you, though. I'm so weak, souls that are only supposed to infiltrate Caps got briefly into me, a Brim, the last time I was in the HATBOX."

"What do you mean?"

Hatter described the flush of anger he'd felt when sparring with Benjamin, and how he'd been about to smash the kid's head into the floor, either in imitation of or homage to what Dogberry had done to Cadet Trilby during the Top Hat duel.

"Did you faint?" Arlo asked.

"No."

"Then you weren't possessed. You are not weak, Hatter. You're strong. It's another reason I came to you."

236

"I have a question," Caledonia said. "Kind of important. How do we turn off the machine?

"We need Shimmer, right?" Hatter asked.

Arlo did his best impression of a bobble head. "Yes. You saw him with the machine? With the caterpillar circuits and everything? Did you see him plug himself into the machine?"

"I did, yeah."

"He plugs himself into it to run certain programs. Shutdown is one of them. He has to be plugged into the machine for the gauntlet to even be able to show up in the HATBOX arena, and you can't get to the power crystals without running the gauntlet. If you remove the power crystals from the lid of the HATBOX arena, the whole system shuts down."

"Shimmer will never agree to it," Caledonia said. "Do we think he's going to willingly hook himself up to his precious invention so that somebody can go and turn it off and ruin his plan for Wonderland domination?"

"It does sound doubtful," Newton said.

A sudden wash of bitterness swept over Hatter. What did it matter how much he and his friends wanted to help Arlo? They were barely even Brims, not even close to mature Milliners. What could they possibly do?

"I think we need to talk with the Grand Milliner about this," Astra said.

Hatter nodded. "I agree."

"He won't believe it," Caledonia said, contemptuous. "Tutor Ampersand didn't believe me when I tried to warn her."

"But the Grand Milliner is different," Astra persisted. "If anything happens to the academy or any of its cadets, he's responsible."

"I don't like that idea," Caledonia said, folding her arms across her chest.

"How about we ask Arlo what he thinks?" Newton suggested.

Everyone turned and looked at Arlo.

"Yes, I think the Grand Milliner should be told," he said after a moment's consideration, "if it doesn't take too long. But couldn't we, in the meantime, work on a way to trick Shimmer into plugging himself into the machine?"

They could. And they would.

YOU ARE A FOOTNOTE IN OUR HISTORY.

They stood in front of the Grand Milliner's office door and stared up at it.

"That is a *big* door," Astra said.

It rose thirty feet above them. It looked like a tree, and there was a good reason for this: it *was* a tree. More precisely, it was the trunk of a tree. Or rather, half of the trunk of a hollowed-out tree, bark and all, attached to the walls of the academy with massive hinges. A mighty butterscotch oak, it had been felled long before such trees had become rare. This one had grown to ten feet across; it was small for a butterscotch oak but large for a door.

"Do we knock?" Caledonia asked.

"I think we just go in." Hatter reached for the giant brass knob and pushed. The door gave way easily and opened into the foyer of Grand Milliner Victus's office. It was a dark and gloomy place, lit by hanging lanterns on two walls and one candle standing on the secretary's desk. The whole room was paneled with mahogany.

The door slammed shut behind them. The light of the candle on the desk flickered.

"Can I help you?" asked a small, thin voice.

"Uh . . . yeah." Hatter looked around. "We need to see the Grand Milliner."

"Do you have an appointment?" The sound of pages turning could be heard. Caledonia walked up to the desk. She motioned to Hatter and the others.

Hatter took Newton's elbow, and they all approached. A small lizard sat on the desktop in front of a day planner. He wore a pair of round glasses that made his eyes look comically huge.

"Hi there!" Astra said with a smile. "I'm Cadet Vost!"

The lizard looked at her with a blank expression. "I'm Bilifred Von-Scail." He paused. "But you can call me Bill."

"Nice to meet you, Bill! So to answer your question, we don't have an appointment, but it's urgent that we see the Grand Milliner right away. We'd never come here without an appointment otherwise."

"I see," replied Bill. He looked down at the day planner, in which not a single meeting was scheduled, and stared at it for a good long while before raising his head. This time his expression seemed far more distraught.

Hatter was starting to find this rather annoying. It couldn't be that hard getting past Bill to see the Grand Milliner, could it? Couldn't they just grab Bill and toss him into a drawer or something?

"What if we book an appointment right now?" Astra's voice was softer. "Would that be better?"

Bill stared at her through those glasses of his and then blinked once. Then he nodded and grabbed a large pen. It was a normal-size pen really—it just seemed large relative to Bill. "When would you like an appointment?"

"Now!" Hatter snapped. Bill's eyes grew even wider, and the pen slipped from his grasp. "I mean, this time today would be great if that's possible."

"That time is available, yes," Bill replied, picking up the pen again. "You may have a seat."

Hatter sighed audibly and led Newton to a row of chairs leaning up against the far wall, below one of the hanging lights. The girls joined them, and they all had just sat down as: "Cadet Vost!"

Astra stood up. "Yes?"

"The Grand Milliner will see you and your friends now," Bill said.

The rest of them rose, and they all walked up to the desk, where Bill stood staring at them. "Yes?"

"Which way do we go?" Hatter asked.

"Which way do you want to go?"

"Whatever way takes us to his office."

"Very well!" Bill said, and he jumped onto a giant green button on his desk. Suddenly the floor gave way beneath them,

241

and Hatter and the rest found themselves sliding at great speed down a plunging dark tunnel.

"Is this fun?" Newton asked loudly over Astra's screams. "I'm not sure this is fun."

"I don't know if it's supposed to be, but it definitely is ridiculous," Hatter replied, turning his head back to look at him. Newton nodded in response.

Almost as soon as it had begun, the sliding stopped, and the four of them were ejected in a heap onto the ground.

"What the—?" Grand Milliner Victus jumped out of his chair, startled. "Oh, for silk's sake! Why does Bill insist on— get up, all of you. How undignified. Really."

The four cadets scrambled to their feet. Victus's office was even darker than his foyer. The walls had the same mahogany paneling, but the floor was covered in a soft, dark-maroon carpet, which had definitely helped protect them from their fall. Thick maroon curtains hid any windows there might have been; not a sliver of light seeped through them.

"There's a hallway and a staircase and a door," Victus said, sitting back down behind a desk so large it took up almost the entire width of the office. "Who in Wonderland invented such an absurd entrance, I'll never know."

"Actually, sir, it was Grand Milliner Glass, who was known to be fond of ladders and chutes and also thought it saved her time when—"

"A Vost. I should have known it would be a Vost. Come here, all of you. What in the brillig do you want?" Victus asked.

242

Then he saw Hatter. "Cadet Madigan," he said as if the sylla-
bles were foul-tasting.

"Yes, sir." Hatter stood as tall and as straight as he could.

"And who else besides the Vost girl? Ah, Cadet Alinari,
I see. And Cadet Ezer. Quite the motley crew. What do you
want?" The last was delivered bluntly, like tearing a piece of
thread with your teeth.

"Sir, we have something very important to tell you," Astra
said, all in a rush. "The HATBOX contains the souls of dead
Boarderlanders who want to be free, but Sir Isaac Shimmer can
control most of them and is forcing them to possess cadets—
the souls are part of his HATBOX programs somehow—and
after the possessed cadets finish training here, he's going to use
them to take over Wonderland, so the HATBOX needs to be
turned off and—"

Grand Milliner Victus held up a hand to silence her, and
stood in angry disbelief, his mouth aslant, his jaw clenched,
words gathering within him like a subterranean force about to
blow.

"What kind of prank is this?" he shouted. "Out! All of you!
Out, out, out! Now!"

Hatter and his friends hurried to leave, couldn't reach the
door fast enough.

"Not you, Madigan."

Hatter braved a quick, tight smile for his friends and turned
back to the Grand Milliner's desk. He heard the sound of
the door opening and closing. He was alone with the Grand

Milliner, suddenly aware of a loud ticking from somewhere in a corner.

"Cadet Madigan," Victus said, tenting his fingers and resting his chin on them. "I'm surprised to still see you here, studying at the academy."

That stung. "This is where I belong, sir."

The Grand Milliner leaned forward. "I never thought I'd say this to a Madigan: you belong in the tenders' quarters."

Hatter knew that Grand Milliner Victus was tough, at times downright scary, and that the Wonderlander could be blunter than a pommel. He tried not to take it personally, to treat the insult as some kind of test of his self-control. Though it was an odd time for such a test, considering the Grand Milliner's own outburst a moment earlier.

"You think you're better than everyone, Madigan. Just like the rest of your family. But the difference is that you *are* the outcast. You lack discipline, you let your emotions get the better of you, and you choose to spend your free time with some of the most useless cadets in the academy's history."

"Sir," Hatter tried, "you might not like me, but—"

"Don't flatter yourself. I don't care enough about you to dislike you. Now your parents, I hated. And your brother, I actively despise. Because they at least greatly affect the course of our wonderful land. You are irrelevant to me. You are irrelevant to the academy. And you will be irrelevant to Wonderland. You are a footnote in our history. Not even that—you are a sentence that was deleted because it was extraneous to the story."

244

Hatter struggled to maintain his composure. What if the Grand Milliner was right? He was and always would be an outcast. After all, he had no story to speak of. No words on any page. He held himself as rigid as Wonderland steel, found words.

"But sir, what Astra said . . . if you'll come with me, you can hear from some of the trapped souls yourself—"

"You think you and your friends can trick me into believing something so truly absurd about the HATBOX? To play into your little game to make you all feel like you matter? Enough! Leave now and don't insult me with your infantile pranks!"

Hatter turned on his heels and stormed out of the Grand Milliner's office, slamming the door behind him.

He stood in the darkened hall before the carpeted staircase that led up to the foyer. His heart was racing, his breath puffing out furiously, and he could feel hot tears welling up. Had Victus always disliked him this much? Had he always disliked his family?

It kind of made sense—why the Grand Milliner would hate Dalton. He might see Dalton as having stolen his job from him. And what had Rhodes said at the streaming? Something about how being a Heart was a demotion? So Victus had been something else first. He had been forced into becoming the queen's bodyguard. Being fired from something he hadn't even wanted must have really, really hurt. If Hatter understood anything, it was how powerful emotions were. But what was it about his parents? What had they done? What was their history with

245

Victus? Hatter felt tears rise. He knew so little about them.

He dried his eyes, wiped his cheeks, and started up the stairs, wondering what he'd tell his friends when they asked what Victus had wanted. And they would definitely ask. It wasn't every day that the Grand Milliner met with a Brim alone in his office. But he wasn't about to repeat any of Victus's hateful words.

$$\Upsilon$$

"So?" Newton asked.

"Victus doesn't believe us," Hatter mumbled.

"I warned you," Caledonia said.

"Looks like we're too late," Astra said, because they had just entered the Banquet Plaza, which was empty of cadets. Tenders busied themselves cleaning trays and dishes, wiping down tables.

"Wait here." Hatter made his way over to Cook who was breaking down one of the food stands. "Hi, Cook!" he said.

Cook looked up and smiled brightly at him.

"I don't suppose there's anything left to eat?"

Cook looked over Hatter's shoulder at the others. "Glad to see you've made some really nice new friends," she said. "Not like those old ones."

Hatter felt his stomach sink. It hurt to think that Cook had been disappointed in his choices as a cadet. Though it hadn't occurred to him until this moment that he cared what she thought of him. This, of course, just made Hatter feel worse. Everything was conspiring to prove the Grand Milliner's point. He wasn't meant to be a Milliner. He was a lowly tender.

"Go on and sit," Cook said. "I'll bring you all a little something."

Hatter thanked her and in short order, he and Newton and Caledonia and Astra were sitting before a plate piled high with sandwiches. They dug in and ate in silence for a moment.

"I wonder," Newton said. "Do you think it's that the Grand Milliner doesn't believe us, or do you think he won't help us because he does?"

"That doesn't make sense," Astra said.

"Doesn't it? It's known that the Grand Milliner isn't happy about being fired as the queen's bodyguard. Maybe he wants to punish the Queen of Hearts? Maybe he's the one who wants to raise an army to overthrow her, and he's using Shimmer to do it?"

Hatter stared at his plate, thinking about his conversation with the Grand Milliner and his time with Rhodes. It definitely seemed like that family didn't have much respect for the cadets at the academy. In fact, the Grand Milliner seemed to hate being in charge of the academy in the first place. Hatter himself would *always* love the academy and all it represented, no matter what became of him. And if, by helping Arlo, he exposed Grand Milliner Victus for what he obviously was— evil—then he'd do everything he could to help. Even as a soon-to-be tender.

"Newton might have a point," Hatter said, looking up. "But it doesn't matter. Whoever's responsible, we have to do what we can for Arlo and his friends on our own, as Caledonia's always wanted to do."

Caledonia beamed. "Except for a few Master Milliners and tutors, adults are pretty useless, aren't they?" she said.

I'M GUESSING THIS WASN'T WHAT
THEY HAD IN MIND.

T he next day, a day of much weirdness, the four cadets waited until after evening exercises to make their way into the bowels of the academy for a secret strategy meeting.

"Did you notice how quiet the Banquet Plaza was?" Hatter asked.

"How could we *not* notice!" Caledonia said.

"It was creepy." Astra shivered. "The way so many of the Caps ate in perfect synch. Every bite, every chew. It was scary, actually."

Hatter had bumped into one of them in the South Needle: a possessed Cap whose expression was utterly blank, eyes glazed over, lifeless. After that, he'd noticed them everywhere.

"I heard some Master Milliners talking about how the new Caps are so much more disciplined than we were," Newton said.

Outside the detention room, Astra proved in part why she had been streamed correctly as a Spade: effortlessly, and with remarkable speed, she picked the lock. The cadets were no sooner in the room than Arlo materialized, as did four other souls none of them had ever met.

"These are my friends," Arlo explained. "Some of the others you are working to set free. They wanted to thank you."

"We haven't done anything yet. Thank us afterward," Hatter said.

"We might not be able to."

"Thank you for *trying*," one of the souls said—a small, round girl with fearful eyes. She appeared in a light-blue tunic, a blue cap over her pale-pink hair. The right side of her face was covered in a vine tattoo.

"This is Viola," Arlo said, introducing her. "She's from the orphanage, like me. Next we have Timber." A boy with a greenish hue to his scaly skin. "He's from a factory on the outskirts of the Boarderlands. No one knows exactly which tribe he's from, although we all think he's part Fel Creel."

"When the factory shut down," Timber said, "Shimmer offered employment to the workers."

"I'm guessing this wasn't what they had in mind," Hatter said.

"Here's Fallow, a Sirk through and through," Arlo said introducing an extremely tall, broad Boarderlander. Sirks were not known for wearing much clothing; they were almost beast-like men. But Fallow appeared in dark brown pants, no shirt, and a too-small jacket. He was the only one of the group who was an adult. "He was Timber's foreman at the factory."

Fallow grunted hello.

"And this is Poinsettia." Arlo gave the little girl a hug and picked her up in his arms. She was tiny, maybe around five years old, wearing a white nightgown. Her dark-blond hair was in braids. She shyly hid her face in Arlo's neck. It seemed, Hatter realized, that while humans and holograms couldn't interact physically outside the HATBOX, holograms could interact with one another outside the HATBOX.

"Hi, Poinsettia," Astra said, approaching cautiously. The little girl looked up for a moment and gave her a small smile. Then she hid her face once more.

"We're going to try and stay as you currently see us," Viola said. "The possessions are happening so quickly, and once we're in cadets . . ." She didn't finish her sentence, couldn't. "I haven't manifested like this for longer than an hour in a while."

"It'll be okay," Arlo said. "I've been doing it for a few weeks now. It's not easy, but you can do it."

Viola didn't seem so sure.

"So," Caledonia said, sitting down. Hatter, Astra, and Newton did as well. The holograms stayed floating in one spot. For the first time Hatter noticed that their feet didn't quite touch the ground.

"Sir Isaac Shimmer doesn't live at the academy," Newton said. "If the machine's running smoothly, what incentive does he have to visit? We can wait and hope that he just shows up, but then we'd better know exactly what we're going to

251

do and be ready to do it as soon as we know he's here. It'd be better if, when we're ready, we cause something to go wrong that requires Shimmer to come here and plug himself into the machine."

"We dispossess them," Hatter said. "If we dispossess even just a couple of cadets, that'll be a failure in the system. Shimmer will have to come back."

"What then?" Astra asked.

"He plugs himself in to find where the glitch is, and while he's hooked up, we somehow get him to initiate the shutdown program and I'll run the gauntlet. Not that I have a clear understanding of what the gauntlet is."

"It's an obstacle course of sorts," Arlo said, "a course that is specially created for whoever's running it. Part physical and part psychological. It uses the runner's memories, fears, insecurities to make itself exceedingly difficult, if not impossible, to suc-cessfully get through. As I said before, if the runner *does* make it through, he or she has access to the crystals that power the machine. Once the crystals are dislodged, the machine, the HATBOX, it all goes dark."

"Arlo, how do you know this stuff?"

"At first everything was confusing when they stole my soul, but I worked hard, thinking and learning inside the machine. And when Shimmer plugs himself into it, I have access to bits of his mind. We all do, really."

Hatter was impressed. Despite how mild-mannered he seemed, Arlo was a true fighter. It made Hatter want to help him all the more. Him and the others.

"Hey, here's a subject we seem to be avoiding," Caledonia said. "How do we dispossess cadets?"

"By letting Arlo possess one of us," Hatter said. "And the three who aren't possessed? We try to get Arlo out."

THEN WE TRIED VIOLENCE.

"I don't know if that's a good idea," Arlo said.

"But you can control it a little bit, right?" Hatter said. "You can possess us and stop possessing us. So if we can't do it, you can."

"I don't know," he said again, shaking his head.

"What if it does permanent damage?" Viola asked.

"It didn't seem to do any particular harm to Dogberry. I mean, it resulted in him getting beaten up, but that wasn't the hologram's fault," Hatter said.

"I'll do it," Timber said with that generally positive attitude of his. "I've never possessed someone, though, so I might do it wrong."

"Hey, it's all new to us too!" Astra said with a grin. "But with everyone working together, I'm sure we'll figure it out."

"You're definitely more optimistic than I am." Caledonia shook her head.

"I'm more optimistic than most people," Astra replied, and Caledonia couldn't help but laugh.

"So who wants to be the test subject?" Newton asked.

Hatter tried to sound casual and ignore the trembling in his hands. "It was my idea. I'll do it."

Timber stepped up to him. If it'd been possible, Hatter would have shaken his hand in a gesture of solidarity. Instead he just nodded at him, and Timber nodded back.

"And what exactly are we supposed to do?" Caledonia asked.

"Try to make me no longer possessed," Hatter said.

"I might have to hit you."

"I'd expect you to."

Caledonia shrugged and then cracked her knuckles. Suddenly Hatter felt a little more worried about Caledonia than he was about being possessed.

"Ready?" Timber asked.

Nope. Not a bit. "Yes." Hatter braced himself as if Timber were going to run into him. Which was exactly what Timber was going to do. Except it wasn't a metaphor; Timber was going to literally run *into* him.

Timber stared at him for a moment. He took a giant step toward him and then one more . . . Hatter closed his eyes.

And then he was opening them again. His face hurt, and he was lying on the floor. Caledonia had her hand extended for him to grab. Hatter blinked a few times and then took it.

She pulled him up to standing, and Hatter massaged his jaw. "What happened?" he asked.

"Exactly what we planned—Timber possessed you. We tried to unpossess you."

"You punched me, you mean."

"Well, first we tried to talk to you, tried to see if you were in there deep somewhere and could hear us," Astra said.

"Then we tried violence," Caledonia said.

"Did it work?"

"No," Newton said. "Timber had to step out."

Hatter glanced over at Timber, who gave him a small wave.

"Okay, well, I guess . . . " Hatter opened his mouth and moved his jaw around. "I guess, let's try it again."

"It's my turn," Caledonia said.

"No," Hatter said. "This was my idea, so . . ."

Caledonia placed a hand on his shoulder. "Maybe, but we're all in this together. Anyway, you need to rest. I've got a pretty solid right hook." She smiled.

Hatter smiled back.

"Okay, let's do this," she said.

They spent another half lunar hour, each taking turns, until they all were covered in bruises.

"I think that's enough. You all look terrible," Arlo said.

"Yeah, let's try again tomorrow," Newton said, rubbing his elbow. "It's getting late, anyway—we don't want to raise suspicions."

They all agreed and said their good-byes and snuck their way through one of the academy's seams until the girls turned north and the boys turned south. And they made their way back to the Needles. None the wiser, but worse for wear.

38

I'M SURE MANY OF YOU HAVE ALREADY PRACTICED WITH YOUR PARENTS' HATS, AND I HAVE NO DOUBT I WILL HAVE TO UNDO YEARS OF BAD HABITS.

The Brims had entered a general hat-focused portion of their studies. In History, Tutor Wren lectured on the evolution of hat-making. White Imagination class had become all about weaving orange hatbands with which they would imbue hats with strength, and Black Imagination class was nothing but warning tales about rogue hats. And in Hatter's dance class, several moves of the mock-turtle gavotte required the flourishing of a hat. He'd had to borrow one from MM Bliss's costumery—a strangely deflated-looking thing. It made Hatter angrier than ever at Rhodes for having sabotaged his work in the Textillery. He was the only Brim who had graduated from Caps without a hat.

"Why don't you use your father's?" Newton suggested one night.

"Because it's old, and it'll probably fall apart. Besides, I'll get in trouble because I didn't make it myself."

"I think you should try. It's better than nothing."

Hatter took his father's hat from under his bed, gave it a good dusting off, and set it on his head. He was surprised to find that while it was still too big for him, it no longer fell quite so far down as it had several lunar cycles ago.

In the morning, his father's hat in hand, he made his way to combat workshop and, trying not to feel self-conscious, waited in line with the rest of the Brim Hearts for MM Tornado. He caught Twist looking at his worn headgear.

"What?" he asked defensively.

"Oh, nothing!" Twist squeaked, whipping himself around to face the front of the room.

Hatter glanced at Twist's hat. It wasn't anything particularly fantastic, just a plain blue hat, but it was less worn than his was, that was for sure.

"Hey, you didn't get too badly injured the other day, did you?" he asked. "I mean, because of that whole providing-distraction-while-Newton-and-I-snuck-out thing you did? Which, thanks for that, by the way."

Twist beamed. "Any time. I wear my bruises as badges of honor."

"Hats!" said MM Tornado bursting in through the doors. "Every Milliner of every suit trains with a hat. In time you will be able to make your hat morph its physical form, track your foes, even warm you on cold nights."

The energy in the room was buzzing. Hatter too, despite his current hat concerns, was truly thrilled at the thought that someday his hat would be able to perform such incredible things.

"But. We're not there yet. Brim hat combat training focuses on the less glamorous but incredibly important hat basics. We will be testing to see not just how well you throw your hat, but also how well it's been constructed, how successful you are at weaving in the orange caterpillar thread that allows your hat to transform from soft silk to the sharpest steel. And each suit needs to learn them first. I'm sure many of you have already practiced with your parents' hats, and I have no doubt I will have to undo years of bad habits. So let us just begin with a basic toss."

A target shaped like a person appeared opposite each cadet.

"The key is all in the wrist." MM Tornado walked to the far end of the room. A target appeared opposite her, and she removed her hat. With a flick of her hand, the hat sped across the room and impaled the throat of her target. It happened so quickly it almost looked as if the hat had been stuck there the whole time.

"I shall walk down the row. When I say go, the first cadet will toss, and so on. I need to observe your individual techniques. Cadets, remove hats!" she ordered.

In one swift movement all the cadets removed their hats and held them before them in one hand, the other hand behind their backs. Even Hatter knew the move; he'd at least had the chance to practice on occasion, with Dalton's hat in the yard.

MM Tornado made her way down the line as they stood at the ready, correcting the form of this cadet and that. She pulled at Twist's hair to make him stand up taller but just glanced at Hatter before giving a satisfied nod. After thinking he'd pretty much ruined his reputation in her eyes by now, Hatter felt a real thrill at that small gesture.

"Go!"

Cadet Lin tossed her hat with a great deal of force. But it ended up grazing the top of the target's head and piercing the wall behind it.

"Go!"

Cadet Chullo seemed taken by surprise by the sudden order and threw wildly, sending his hat over the target to skid to a stop on the floor.

"Go!"

"Go!"

"Go!"

"Go!" Twist threw, and his aim was pretty good. He hit his target in the kneecaps. That could cause some serious damage.

"Go—wait!"

Hatter held his core in tightly to prevent himself from stumbling at her sudden change of mind. His body was tense all over, but he managed to stay entirely still as MM Tornado leaned over and examined his hat.

"Did you make this hat, cadet?" she asked, studying it closely.

Hatter could sense all his classmates listening intently. He assumed they all knew what had happened. He assumed it was well known throughout the academy. Rhodes would have seen to that.

"No, ma'am!" Hatter replied, his breathing growing shallow.

"Then where did it come from?"

"It was my father's, ma'am!"

MM Tornado looked at Hatter in the eye. "Stay after class, cadet," she said.

"Yes, ma'am."

"Go!" The order was so sudden that Hatter flicked his wrist before he could even aim the hat. It began to arch away from the target. *Please just hit it, anywhere, just hit it,* thought Hatter. To his great relief and mild surprise, the hat's arc straightened out and it landed low on the target's torso. Not an impressive hit, but at least a hit.

MM Tornado worked her way through the rest of the cadets and then marched back to the center of the room.

"Clearly something this basic requires extra attention. Target practice for the rest of the class!"

The cadets broke formation to retrieve their hats and returned to their starting positions. Everyone began tossing their hats and retrieving them and tossing them and retrieving them over and over. Hatter's aim improved immensely. He retrieved his hat from the base of the target after hitting it right in the throat and popped it on his head, feeling pretty much ready to work on the boomerang technique, which would send the hat to the target and bring it back in the same move.

We could try. The thought appeared in Hatter's mind almost as if someone else had said it.

No, don't be silly, no need to embarrass yourself further, he replied to himself.

Hatter removed his hat and aimed once again for the target. He could sense his fellow cadets getting as tired with the repetition as he was. Once more he aimed, this time right at the heart, and tossed his hat. It flew straight and true. It hit its target directly on the left side of the chest with such force that it flew through it and out the other side, curving suddenly as it did. Hatter suddenly realized the hat was flying back at him with great speed. In fear, Hatter jumped out of the way as it charged over his head and careened into the wall of the HATBOX behind him. It bounced off the tile hard and skidded to a stop on the floor, leaving behind a rather large dent.

The class stopped and stared at Hatter.

"Cadet Madigan, boomerang retrievals are not until next lunar cycle. You don't see anyone else showing off, now do you?"

"No, ma'am!"

"Get your hat and stand out for the rest of the class."

The humiliation stung. Hatter marched to the wall and picked up the hat.

But we showed her, he thought as he put it on, though he wasn't sure what he had shown and who he meant by "we." He moved to the far wall and stood at attention, watching the rest of class progress. He had no idea how it had happened in the first place; he hadn't even attempted to do such a toss. And he certainly had not attempted any White Imagination to make it happen.

Never hurts to try, he thought again. But that wasn't something he'd normally think. It can often hurt to try. And to disobey direct orders from Master Milliners. Hatter felt nervous.

There was something strange happening; he couldn't place it. Something familiar and also unfamiliar. It reminded him of when he'd spoken with the eeries. In fact, it felt remarkably similar.

Sorry.

Hatter suddenly had a very unusual thought. He dared not think it, and he pushed it out of his mind as quickly as he could.

Yes. The word came as an answer. Hatter tried to breathe slowly, tried to calm himself down. But the answer freaked him out even more than the question he had tried not to think. Especially as the question had been: *Am I having a conversation with my hat?*

THERE IS A DIFFERENCE BETWEEN WHITE IMAGINATION AND MAKE-BELIEVE.

lass was over, but Hatter was still standing at attention as the cadets peeled out of the HATBOX, leaving just him and MM Tornado.

Oh. And his father's hat.

MM Tornado motioned to Hatter and sat down cross-legged in the middle of the room. She gestured for him to join her here on the floor, and he did, feeling far too informal in front of a Master Milliner.

"Madigan, you can't use your father's hat—that's against academy rules," MM Tornado said.

"Yes, ma'am."

"I heard about your failure to make a hat in the Textillery class. I'm surprised you haven't sought to remedy that situation by working extra hours after class."

"I can't, ma'am. I have detention, ma'am."

"Well, maybe we can kill two jubjub birds with one stone then. Whom should I talk with?"

Hatter was surprised. He had assumed any efforts toward making a new hat would be his and his alone. "Tutor Wren, ma'am."

"He's a reasonable fellow. I'll speak with him. You need a hat, Madigan. And you shouldn't be using your father's."

"I know, it's—"

"Dangerous, yes," MM Tornado said, standing up and walking over to the door. She opened it. Hatter stared at her for a moment. He had been going to say *old*. *Dangerous* was quite something else.

Hatter didn't feel he was in any position to ask her meaning, though. He simply made for the door and gave her a respectful nod as he passed. As she began to close it behind him, Hatter suddenly wondered about MM Tornado. She seemed almost . . . nice. And very attentive to him in general. It went completely against her reputation. Maybe . . .

"MM Tornado?" he said.

"Yes?"

"Milliner hats. Everyone has one."

"Every Milliner. Yes." She eyed him with suspicion.

"And Milliners imbue White Imagination into hats."

"Yes." Her expression didn't waver.

"So, when there's all this imagination inside, it's like we can talk to our hats?"

MM Tornado's expression softened. "Ah. I see. No. It's not quite like that. Hats aren't alive. They don't have a mind of their own, obviously. The rare indigo caterpillar thread allows for a Milliner to make his or her hat do fantastic things, to

travel great distances, to do incredible tricks of combat. But it all comes from the Milliner's imagination. A hat cannot do something that a Milliner has not willed it to do."

"So you can't have a conversation with your hat?" he said.

"I'm not sure why you would want to. Cadet Madigan, why are you asking these questions?"

What could he say? He couldn't just tell the truth.

Make something up, replied a thought that wasn't his own.

"Some of the other cadets last night in the South Needle, they were talking about stories of hats being alive. I didn't believe them but—"

"Fanciful tales," MM Tornado said. "And unbecoming of Milliner cadets. There is a difference between White Imagination and make-believe. I'll let you know when I've rearranged your detention."

"Thank you, ma'am," he replied.

A short sharp nod. And Hatter took it as his sign to leave.

Hatter kept his hat off for the rest of the day, awkwardly carrying it from class to class as his fellow cadets looked at him in confusion. He set it on his desk while listening to Tutor Vim discuss the thirty-seven articles of being a royal bodyguard, which could essentially be boiled down to "Guard the royals." He took it with him to lunch, where he sat eating quietly as Astra went on and on about her camouflage exam. Hatter glanced up and looked over at the Caps. They all sat together in quiet clumps, not talking, not engaging, eating in a mechanical way, with the robotic demeanor of the possessed.

IS YOUR FATHER'S HAT USEFUL?

Did anyone notice that Hatter, Newton, Astra, and Caledonia never returned to the Needles until far into the evening, after their sessions with Arlo and his friends, during which they tried—so far, without any luck—to dispossess one another? The Master Milliners sure didn't care. Once the workday was done, they were done and gone. But the tutors—maybe they noticed? Then again, after having spent more than one detention in the tutor lounge refilling blueberrymint pipes and passing out carrot cake and lettuce tea, Hatter knew that the tutors were far more interested in reading and debating than in what the cadets were up to. Astra had even once accidentally spilled scalding tea on Tutor Libre's lap, but he hadn't noticed; he'd been too busy arguing about the technological revolution.

"No, no, no! Tutor Mars, you are completely old-fashioned. Why, look at the HATBOX and how it's helped improve combat training here at the academy. Technology can work completely in tandem with imagination, and—Cadet Vost, what on earth are you doing?"

"Just trying to mop up the spilled tea, sir," she had said, attempting to dab with her cloth the moisture on Tutor Libre's left leg.

"Oh, leave it! There are more important things in life than tea!"

"Like how technology is going to ruin everything that makes Wonderland great?" said Tutor Mars.

"Oh, please."

Tutor Mars stood up at that and pointed a long, white, bony finger at Tutor Libre. "Caterpillar thread and technology are not meant to be paired. They are essentially antithetical entities! The results of their combining could be explosive, literally!"

"Codswallop! When did you become such a fuddy-duddy, Mars?"

"Well, *I'd* like more tea," said Tutor Vim, turning to Astra with a small smile.

Hatter had watched the whole exchange in awe and found it strange that the tutors, who seemed so interested in the debate, were so oblivious to the real-life drama that the mix of technology and imagination was causing under their pointy noses. He wished he could just tell them what was going on, but he knew the tutors would be obligated to tell the Grand Milliner immediately. And that couldn't happen.

So it seemed that their little gang and the rebel holograms

could practice in relative safety from discovery, and it gave Hatter a sense of freedom he hadn't really ever felt before. It would even have been enjoyable if not for their continued lack of success in dispossessing one another. All that happened was they added to their individual collections of bruises and scrapes. Fortunately, at the academy, being all beaten and worn was a pretty typical look.

Finally, a week later, MM Tornado approached Hatter after class. "It's been arranged—your personal detention has been moved to the Textillery. Be there right after the end of classes today," she said.

It felt strange not to be spending detention with his friends for the first time in many weeks. Though none of them would tell Tutor Ampersand this, they all rather enjoyed the time they spent together in detention. It gave them a chance to figure out their plans. But Hatter knew the hat came first. He'd run back to his room during lunch so he'd have his father's hat with him while he made a new one. It had been Astra's suggestion, that having something to copy would make it a lot easier. After classes were finished, Hatter marched as quickly as he could to the Textillery.

He entered the empty hall. The suns were setting outside the windows, and the room was bathed in a warm glow. Hatter looked around and felt overwhelmed. He had assumed that someone would be there to help him, or at least welcome him. Maybe not Tailor Quince, but one of his undertailors. Someone.

Being alone in the Textillery was, he realized, an unusual circumstance, and Hatter wondered for the first time if there were something else going on. Why was MM Tornado helping him out like this? How had he managed to pass Cap level without completing a hat in the first place?

He placed his father's hat on the table and looked at it. It wasn't as if he hadn't actually made a hat in Caps—he had; but now that so much time had passed since then, he had forgotten some of the basic technique.

Hatter glanced around the still, empty room and placed his father's hat on his head.

"Tell me, hat," he said quietly, "where should I start?"

Hatter felt a little ridiculous, but he thought, *Maybe? It's a hat, after all. It should know how it was made.*

A design is a good place. The better the design, the better the hat.

Hatter felt a little scared and a little relieved. The weirdness of the situation did not escape him.

It's odd for me too.

"Is it? Didn't you and my father have conversations?"

No. He made me very powerful, though. He was a good person.

There was so much in that response. Too much. Hatter whipped off the hat and pushed it a little farther away.

A design, yeah, like with everything. Like with the C-blades he was working on. And he set to it, on his own, without any help, not even from his hat.

By the end of the hour he had created what he thought was a pattern that would wind up making a more-than-serviceable hat. He nodded and put his design away, hiding it in his trunk beneath the metal pieces he had only just managed to attach together. Now they looked a right mess, not C-shaped at all, and he was still attempting to file them into shape. He took a moment and stared at them, disappointed in his job. Why was he so terrible at making things?

"Missed you in detention today," Caledonia said when Hatter joined his friends at dinner.

"Yeah, well, it was pretty lonely in the Textillery all by myself," Hatter replied.

"Is your father's hat useful?" Astra asked.

More than you'll ever know, Hatter thought. "Yeah. It is. Good idea." He took a big bite of food so he wouldn't feel the urge to tell her what exactly he meant by that.

"Can I see it?" Astra reached out, and Hatter looked at her carefully. He wasn't sure what he thought would happen exactly. But it made him nervous to pass his father's hat over to her. Still, it was Astra. And the hat had said it didn't normally talk with anyone else. Hatter picked it up off the seat beside him and held it out over the table for Astra to take.

"I remember this!" said a familiar voice, and the hat was whisked up into the air by a third hand.

"Rhodes, just stop it," said Hatter. He was trying very hard to stay calm, but the fury was building already within him.

Rhodes stood above him holding his father's hat. Next to him were Nigel, Benedict, and Drummer. West lingered behind them, watching the scene with a furrowed brow.

"Yup, just as old and worn as I remember. What a piece of garbage," Rhodes said, turning the hat over in his hands. "Why do you even have this thing out with you, Madigan? I'd be embarrassed to be seen with it!"

"Give that back to him!" Astra said.

"Little Miss Perfect, star pupil. How are your C-blades coming along?" Rhodes asked with a grin.

"Just fine. Had to start all over today; they'd gone missing. It was weird. But I handed them in by the end of class," Astra replied, folding her arms across her chest. A strange expression flickered across Rhodes's face, but it quickly returned to that smug smile.

"Don't you have anything better to do?" Newton asked.

"Look who it is. The charity case. Haven't missed you one bit, Newton." Rhodes took off his hat, and put Hatter's father's hat on his head. "How do I look, boys? Pathetic and orphan-y?"

"Pretty much," said Nigel, laughing loudly, which was most unbecoming of a Milliner. Other cadets looked over at their table. All except the Caps, who maintained their rhythmic eating pattern. Hatter thought a bit about the Millinery code, remembering Astra's questions, and for the first time he wondered whether "To contain and control all emotion" was actually that great an idea. Because of course the Caps this term were praised far and wide for their emotional discipline. But no one was asking exactly why they were so stoic.

Hatter rose. "Rhodes, give me my father's hat. This is really immature. We're Brims now."

Rhodes stepped away. "There's only one way you get to take it back. And this time, Madigan, I won't be taken by surprise." Rhodes raised his fists and stood in ready position.

Hatter swallowed hard. He had to keep his feelings in check. Why did Rhodes get to him like this? Rhodes was an idiot. And Rhodes's father was an idiot too—a bloody traitor was what he was.

Hatter rushed forward, but Rhodes ducked out of the way, punching Hatter in his ribs. It hurt, but not more than in a regular combat workshop. Hatter ducked down, swept his right leg along the floor, and tripped Rhodes, who landed hard on his back, the hat remaining firmly on his head. Hatter was ready to jump on him when Nigel and Benedict grabbed his arms.

Caledonia was up on her feet at once, and without Hatter exactly knowing how she did it, she freed Hatter from their grip, and he rushed toward Rhodes once more. Another arm appeared and grabbed him, and Hatter batted it away easily.

"No, Hatter," Astra said, raising her arm again and holding tight to his shoulder. "He's not worth it. You're doing what he wants."

Hatter stared at Rhodes, who was laughing so hard he was bent over. Then he looked at Astra, who appeared very calm and serious. It was unusual to see her look like that. It made him pause.

"Oh come on; you're pathetic!" said Rhodes. "You're going to let a Vost stop you?"

"Why is it," Hatter asked, "that I'm always called out for showing my feelings, but you get to be as angry and laugh as much as you want?"

Rhodes stopped laughing instantly. "Because I can control it," he replied. "You can't. You're an embarrassment to your family and to all Milliners. It's just too pathetically easy with you, Madigan."

Hatter wanted to run at him again, but Astra's comforting hand on his shoulder helped keep him calm.

"Give me back my father's hat," he said slowly.

"No."

Rhodes stared at him defiantly. Squinted. Flinched. Shook his head a little. He stumbled backward and reached up as if he wanted to pull the hat off his head. But he didn't. He pulled at it, but it didn't come off.

"Ow!" he said. "Ow, ow!" And then he swore so loudly that a few Caps actually turned their heads and blinked in his general direction. Rhodes staggered around the plaza, now screaming in pain. "Help!" he called out, falling to the floor. "Help! Get it off me!" Drummer rushed over to him and tried to pull the hat off his head. Nigel and Benedict joined the efforts. West stayed where he was and continued to watch the action. "Get it off get it off get it off!" Tears were streaming down Rhodes's contorted face.

"Do something!" Astra said. Hatter looked at her. What was he supposed to do, exactly?

He rushed over to Rhodes and pushed the others to the side. Then he placed his hands on either side of the hat, expecting quite a struggle. But the hat slipped off Rhodes's head so effort-lessly it sent Hatter flying backward into a table of Bonds.

"What kind of Black Imagination was that?" Rhodes yelled, pointing at Hatter.

"I didn't do anything!" Hatter yelled. "And the hat doesn't have any Black Imagination in it, so shut up!"

"You'll pay for this, Madigan. You'll pay!" Rhodes scrambled to his feet and flew out of the plaza, followed by Drummer, Nigel, and Benedict. West watched them run and then turned and headed over to the dessert stall.

"He always threatens me like that," Hatter said, dusting off his father's hat and rejoining his friends at their table.

"Why couldn't he get the hat off?" Caledonia asked.

"No idea." Hatter placed the hat on the chair next to him again.

"No?" Newton sounded very casual, but Hatter knew it was a pointed question.

"No," Hatter replied with an edge to his voice.

The rest of their meal was uneventful, and Hatter was happy that nothing had happened to his father's hat. But he couldn't help wondering if what Rhodes had said was true. All this time he'd assumed the hat was on his side, was good because it was his father's hat. But how could he know that for sure? What if—what if the reason the hat could speak to him, could attack Rhodes without Hatter willing it to, what if that *was* because of Black Imagination after all? And what would that say about his father?

I HAVE A DARKNESS!

O ver the next several days, Hatter made good on a new-found resolve to focus his attention where it was due. He set his father's hat aside. Not only for the pragmatic reason that if the hat did possess Black Imagination, it was very dangerous for him to wear it, but also because if there was anything worse than being taken over by Black Imagination, it was being taken over by emotions. So instead, Hatter put all his extra energy and thoughts toward finding the key to dispossessing someone and stopping Shimmer's evil work, and also toward making himself a new hat.

Making a hat might have seemed like a secondary task to be concerned with, but his education was now reaching a crisis point; he wouldn't be able to progress much further without his own headpiece.

In White Imagination class they were deep into imbuing hats with the ability to fly longer distances than a Milliner could throw, and Hatter had to put all his efforts into a practice hat that didn't belong to him and that had clearly had so many different colored hatbands over the course of its existence that it had been imbued, unimbued, imbued, and so on so many times that the thing just got plain confused. Not that hats could actually *be* confused (aside from maybe his father's hat); it just seemed as if they could. It would fly backward instead of forward or fall like a stone to the ground when even without any imagination it should have flown several feet at least. He had to resort to hand-to-hand combat and that meant he wasn't learning how to effectively fight with a hat.

And so, every day, by himself in detention, he worked on his hat. And worked. It was such slow going because he really didn't know what he was doing. He'd try to remember the next step, then he'd do that, but then it wasn't quite right, so he'd have to undo it. Why was this so hard? He'd made a hat once before! Well, half-made one. Rhodes had pretty much made that hat.

Which just made him hate Rhodes even more.

Then came the day when he pushed open the Textillery's large, heavy doors and found Astra waiting at the table for him.

"What are you doing here?"

"I'm here to help," she said, smiling.

"How did you get out of detention?"

"I have my ways."

Hatter shook his head. Astra really did make a good Spade.

"Okay, let's get to work," she said, clapping her hands.

For the first time—ever—working in the Textillery was

282

actually kind of fun. Astra was so effortless with the materials and so patient with him as she showed him step by step how to complete his hat.

"Ooh! Let's add a little decorative heart at the seam of the hatband!" she said, and without waiting for Hatter's approval (although he did like the idea), she did exactly that. It was subtle, hardly noticeable, but it made the hat uniquely his.

The hat done, Astra helped him finish his C-blades. Watching the sparks fly as she filed her own blade as a demonstration was a truly odd experience. She was so sweet, so bubbly—and yet in her goggles, playing with fire, she looked pretty intimidating.

"Your turn!" she said, pushing her mask up onto her forehead. And Hatter took the torch from her.

They worked through dinner, and by the time they left the Textillery, Hatter had completed his first pair of C-blades. Astra had made three. They were on their way to the detention room for their nightly dispossession practice session when Hatter stopped her with a touch on the arm.

"Hey, Astra, I'm really sorry."

"For what?"

"For thinking—for acting—just . . . for thinking that whole no-Vost-has-ever-made-it-past-Cap-level thing." He felt his face get warm.

Astra shook her head and laughed. "Thanks, I guess! But it's okay; everyone was thinking it. And why would they think any different? It's true! I'm . . ." She took a step toward him and lowered her voice: "I'm kind of the weirdo in my family. They aren't that happy that I want to be a Spade and am continuing at the academy."

"Really?" asked Hatter. What Milliner parents wouldn't want that?

"Yeah. I haven't heard from them since I made it to Brims." She pressed her lips together so hard they nearly turned white. Then she took a step back and smiled brightly again. "But once I'm home over hiatus and we can have a talk, everything will be okay."

Hatter didn't doubt it.

ϒ

"Okay, now that everybody's here," Caledonia said as Hatter and Astra entered the detention room, the last to arrive, "who's first?"

"Before we start . . . I've been thinking," said Newton. "We haven't been successful just trying to force the holograms out. We need a new strategy."

"What do you want us to do? Say please?" Caledonia asked.

"I'm just saying maybe violence isn't the answer," Newton replied.

"Violence is always the answer."

Astra sighed. "Oh, Caledonia."

"Wait," Hatter said. Everyone turned to look at him, even the holograms. "What if there was a way to get at the brain?" he said. "Get at thoughts. Make the person who's been possessed reclaim his or her own mind."

"What do you mean?" Caledonia asked.

"I don't know. Maybe something deep down, like our deepest fears or the things that make us sad. They keep saying feelings are dangerous at the academy because they distract you. But maybe that's what we should use to dispossess someone—a little distraction."

Astra looked at Caledonia, who shrugged. "I guess . . . why not? What do we have to lose?"

"So who goes first?" Caledonia asked.

"Me," Astra said with such certainty that it surprised Hatter. As if sensing his surprise, she added, "Come on; who else is so free with their feelings? I'm the easy target!"

"I don't think you are," Newton said.

"Of course I am!"

"You're a happy person, and sure, you show it all the time, and that's not usual here at the academy. But your darker feelings, if you even have them, they aren't on the surface. They aren't raw."

"I have a darkness!" Astra insisted while bouncing up and down on her heels.

"But mine is on the surface." Hatter knew he was the one Newton was talking about. Newton nodded, and Hatter stood up. "I'll go first."

"And I'll try to dispossess him," Newton said. His volunteering made Hatter surprisingly nervous. He realized then that he'd always thought Newton understood him better than anyone. His little comments, his pointed observations. It was possible Newton could really go for the gut with this one, and who knew what the others might learn.

"I think Caledonia and I will step out into the hallway," Astra said.

"Why?" Caledonia made a face.

"Just . . . let's give them some privacy." Astra gave her a stern look.

"Oh. Yeah. Okay."

The girls left the room, and Hatter stood up. "So who's going to possess me this time?"

"It's my turn," Arlo said, stepping forward.

Hatter nodded and walked over to where Newton was sitting. "You ready?

"Are you?"

"I am." And before Hatter could even give him a sign, Arlo made his move.

Darkness. So much darkness. But an awareness of darkness. Oh no, it's not darkness. Grief, anger, pain. Needing to scream. Needing to cry. He didn't understand. What was happening? Where was he? A fog before his eyes, a white whirling fog like that night out on the cliff with the Wellingtons. More anger. Then a boy. Dalton when he was ten. Was he dreaming? It didn't feel like a dream. It felt like pushing against a door that was blocked on the other side. Yes, that's exactly what it was. A door. Plain. A light wood color. His door. From home. Was it his door? How did he know it was his door? It was so long ago. It was opening a crack. If he just pushed it harder.

He was possessed! Arlo! Yes, he was in detention. He was

possessed and had to fight it. Of course! *Just keep pushing the door. Push harder and harder. The door is almost open.*

"Hatter! Are you okay?"

Hatter opened his eyes and saw Newton standing before him. Hatter stared for a moment, completely disoriented. He reached up and touched his own face. It was wet. He looked around and saw Arlo standing to the side, smiling broadly.

"You did it!" he said.

"I did?" asked Hatter.

"I couldn't stay inside. I don't know what you did, but you did it."

"I don't think it was me—I think it was Newton." Hatter turned back to look at his friend.

"Let's call it a team effort," Newton said. He looked shaken, not his usual confident self.

"What's wrong?" asked Hatter.

"That wasn't fun, and I'm so sorry, Hatter," Newton said, sitting down.

"Hey, don't apologize. I don't know what you said; I just felt things. You did a good job."

Newton nodded but didn't seem convinced.

"Let's call Astra and Caledonia back in," Hatter said, changing the subject. He was glad he had no idea what had caused the dispossession. He could still feel an ache in his heart from something profoundly sad.

The girls rejoined them and were quickly let in on the success. After a small moment to rejoice, everyone began taking turns. They partnered off: Newton and Hatter, Caledonia and Astra. They gave each other privacy each round. It was hard at first. And Hatter found it tricky to know what to say to Newton, realizing he didn't know Newton nearly as well as his friend seemed to know him. But there was one thing he knew he could attack—his lack of sight. Though it hurt him so much to do it. As he mocked Newton, he felt so many horrible feelings well up, but worst of all was the familiarity. It felt like back at the beginning of the year when he'd been friends with Rhodes. A hot, nasty feeling, but at the time it had also been a feeling of pride. And remembering feeling good about being mean to Newton just made Hatter all the more miserable.

They then switched partners, and that was harder still because Hatter didn't know Astra or Caledonia nearly as well. But by the end of the session they had started to really get the hang of it. There were certain common fears everyone seemed to share: failing at being a Milliner, not living up to expectations. There was also the fear of losing a family member or a pet. They were all such horrible things to make someone else feel, but by the end, Hatter felt oddly closer to them all. And even more than that, he recognized that he wasn't alone in his fears.

"Well, that was intense," Viola said, and the other souls nodded quietly.

"It was." Caledonia turned her head to wipe her face dry.

"Do you think you're ready?" Timber asked.

Hatter looked at the others. They were each sitting at a desk at a different spot in the room. No one wanted to be too close to the others. Everyone looked worn out, emotionally drained.

"We're ready," Hatter said.

42

I'M CALM. I MEAN, NO I'M NOT, BUT IT DOESN'T MATTER.

This was the day Shimmer would return. The day of dispossessions.

Breakfast. Hatter and his friends stood on the periphery of the Banquet Plaza, scanning the crowd.

"Did you ever think bullying would have any possible use?" Newton asked.

"No. Can't say I ever thought the Rhodeses of the world would be an inspiration," Hatter replied.

"You guys ready to be terrible?" Caledonia wanted to know.

"Oh, don't put it like that," Astra said, distressed.

"Don't feel too badly about it." Caledonia put a reassuring hand on Astra's shoulder. "One each ought to be enough to get Shimmer back to the academy."

"Let's do it," Hatter said.

They fanned out into the welter of cadets. Hatter made for the egg station, looking for a possessed Cap who, for no reason he could articulate, he thought might make an easy target. As he stood in line for food, he heard a kind of wail, and he, along with the other cadets, turned. Caledonia had her arm around a tiny Cap boy who was positively weeping. Wow, she worked fast. What was even more impressive was that two other Caps were standing beside the boy, trying to comfort him. Clearly, seeing their friend upset was enough to make them upset as well. If she'd done three, did that mean the rest of them didn't have to do any?

Hatter took his tray and crossed to their table, sitting next to Newton. "Caledonia just got three!"

"So I heard," Newton replied.

"We have to catch up."

"Well, I did one. I don't feel a need to do any more just to compete," Newton replied, taking a sip of juice.

"What? Already? Who? How? Tell me what to say."

"All you have to do is share your story about being blind and all the difficulties you've had growing up, and how people bullied you, and how no one thinks you should be a Milliner, and you're golden," Newton said.

"Thanks," Hatter replied, not meaning it at all.

Caledonia sat down just then, a rare smile playing on her face.

"Good work," Hatter said.

"Newton did one too."

"I know."

"Anyone seen Astra?" Caledonia asked.

Hatter looked around, saw her talking very sternly to a Cap girl.

"Yeah, she's over by the fountain," he said. "She's being pretty aggressive. I'm not sure it's going to work." But just as the word *work* came out of his mouth, the tall girl slumped and looked around the room in complete confusion; Hatter noticed tears in her eyes. Then the tall girl looked at Astra and gave her a big hug. Astra spoke with her a moment, and then the tall girl walked over to a table where the trio Caledonia had been with and another boy were sitting. Meanwhile Astra wandered over and smiled sadly at Hatter.

"It's done," she said.

"Who was that?" Hatter asked.

"A friend of the family. I don't know her that well, but I thought if I told her she wasn't living up to her potential and was really harsh with her, the difference in me compared to my usual personality would be so shocking and upsetting that it would break her."

"Clever," Hatter said.

"Yeah." Astra didn't seem happy about it. "How did yours go?"

"I haven't tried yet."

Hatter surveyed the plaza and made his way over to a table full of Caps eating in that creepy, ultra-efficient way of theirs. He approached them hesitantly. He so didn't want to do this. All he could remember was what he'd said to Astra so many lunar cycles ago, and how horrible it had felt to see her tear up. He wasn't sure he could do that again, even for the greater good. But suddenly, in one swift movement, the table of Caps rose and turned to leave the plaza. Hatter heard the *screech* of

291

metal chairs against the marble floor behind him, and another table rose, and then another. The Caps all marched with speed toward the exit and were gone. The only table that stayed behind were the five dispossessed Caps.

Hatter stood where he was, stunned and also a little relieved.

"How much you want to bet the machine recognized that something was wrong?" Caledonia said. Hatter turned and saw that she, Astra, and Newton had joined him.

"That means it won't be too long before Shimmer returns," Hatter said.

"Like no time at all. He's already here." Astra exulted. "And troubleshooting the machine at the end of the day!"

"How did you find out already?"

"I kind of forgot to go to class. I've been sneaking around the seams you showed us, keeping watch."

"It's not like you to skip classes," Hatter said.

Astra shrugged. "Sometimes people don't even notice me when I'm around, so sometimes they don't notice when I'm gone. I don't know why. But it was always a useful tool when I was little. Anyway, I've been staking out the main doors and I saw him come in, so I followed him to the office, and I convinced Bill I needed to speak with the Grand Milliner, so he let me in through the doorway way, not the trapdoor way, although he tried, and then I listened. I just listened. And here's the weird thing—I don't think the Grand Milliner is involved in any way. Shimmer just talked about how the machine wasn't working right and he needed to fix it, and the Grand Milliner was annoyed and said fine, but he'd have to wait until after classes were over for the day. No mention of possessing Caps or a plan to take over the queendom and you'd think they would mention that stuff in private. You know?"

"Okay, okay," Caledonia said. "Calm down a bit."

"I'm calm. I mean, no I'm not, but it doesn't matter." Astra sat. "So he's here. What do we do now?"

"We confront him in the machine room," Hatter said.

43

YOU HAVE TO BELIEVE.

Hatter led his friends down the administrative hallway, through the foyer to the Diamonds exit. He stopped and looked at it for a moment. Then he turned around and made for the well-trod red diamond mat on the floor. He pulled it up, revealing a trapdoor beneath. One by one, they slipped into the darkness.

He led them down into the seams and they began to race through them, not exactly sure how long Shimmer would be down there and fearing they might miss him.

"Are you sure we're heading the right way?" Caledonia asked.

"Not really." It was the truth, but Hatter knew he had to continue heading down, that if he focused hard enough . . .

The ground leveled out. He skidded to a stop at a fork. Which way should they go? He couldn't even remember there having been a fork in the seams last time.

"What's happened?" Newton asked. He had been holding on to Astra's arm and let go to approach Hatter.

"Nothing. I just . . . " Hatter thought for a moment. Then he snapped his fingers. "Yes! This is where I heard the voices. The vent to the machine room is down there"—he pointed to the left—"so a door to the room should be . . . come on." He started down the right-side tunnel.

"That's a good sign," Astra said. "It means your intuition is working together with your imagination. Trust it."

Hatter tried to follow her instructions, focused and closed his eyes and felt that feeling of calm. He opened his eyes again. This was all new. He didn't know how to get out of the tunnels now that they were beneath the HATBOX. They continued to walk slowly and carefully. Hatter reached out and placed his hand on the wall. Pushed. A small door creaked open.

"That's impressive," Caledonia said.

Hatter had to agree.

They slipped out the door into a wide, dark hallway. It looked very similar to the tenders' hall—plain, purpose-built. There was no sign of a room anywhere. "Keep your eyes peeled," he said quietly.

They walked along, carefully scanning each brick in the walls as they passed. Hatter even took to examining the ceiling.

"He's in there," Newton said suddenly.

Everyone stopped.

"Where?" Hatter asked, turning.

"There." Newton pointed to his right and walked toward the wall. He pressed his ear against it. "Or at least someone is. There is definitely the sound of someone moving around in there."

The other three joined him and listened. Hatter could hear the faintest of scufflings from the other side.

"So, the question is," Caledonia said with her ear pressed against the wall, "how did he get in there?"

That most definitely was the question.

There had to be a secret door. Hatter touched the wall, closed his eyes, and felt . . . not brick and mortar, but thread and embroidery, thread that he'd known his whole life. He walked along, feeling the weave and texture of the fabrics, until—

His index finger sussed out a seam in the cloth.

He opened his eyes. The seam was small, possibly just a minor imperfection in the fabric. He pushed down on the spot. Nothing happened.

"Maybe pull?"

Hatter jumped. He hadn't realized Astra was at his shoulder. He pulled the thick fabric. The seam began to grow, and slowly the frame of a door materialized. Hatter put both hands into the seam and pulled harder. And harder. And suddenly it was open.

Sitting on the floor attached to the cables, just as he'd been that time when Hatter had stumbled upon him secretly, was Sir Isaac Shimmer: motionless, eyes closed, rivers of light running from one cable, through his body, and then up through the other cable.

"How do we get him to initiate the machine's shutdown without disturbing him?" Caledonia asked.

"Newton," a voice said. It was Arlo. "Newton, you must talk

to Dr. Shimmer. You must talk *at* him, in much the same way that you talked at Hatter when you successfully dispossessed him. If you can make Dr. Shimmer doubt himself, his intelligence, his invention . . . his mind hears even if his body appears not to. You are uncommonly smart. You can do this, can cause him to feel insecurity about the cleverness of his plan to take over Wonderland. His own insecurity will beget insecurity for his invention, for the machine, and when it does, the gauntlet will manifest in the HATBOX arena."

"I don't know if I deserve your compliment, Arlo," Newton said, "but I'm flattered. While I'm getting the bad doctor here to question his self-worth, the rest of you should be up at the HATBOX, ready for the gauntlet."

"The gauntlet is for one individual at a time," Arlo said. "One only."

"And I'm that individual," Hatter said. Caledonia started to protest, but he cut her off. "You both have families, you and Astra. I have my brother, sure, but he's busy with his new life. My parents are gone. I'm alone. Let me do it."

"You are *not* alone," Astra said.

"No," Caledonia and Newton echoed.

"You are not," Arlo said, and his friends materialized at his side: Viola, Poinsettia, Fallow, Timber. "There is a specialness about you, Hatter. At first I thought I was drawn to you because of your emptiness, but the longer I am around you I feel a some-thingness deep inside the nothingness. A thread of something that connects you to Wonderland in a unique way."

Hatter wasn't sure he understood what Arlo meant by this,

298

but he thought of his non-story, the empty book. He thought of what the eeries had said to him.

"You have to *believe* you can turn off the machine or you won't be able to do it," Viola told him.

Remembering what Arlo had said about the gauntlet, Hatter was less concerned with its physical trials than its psychological ones. So many fears. Of not being good enough. Of not living up to his family name. Of not doing Dalton proud.

"I can do it," he said, his voice firm and steady. "I *will* do it."

Caledonia didn't protest.

"If you don't succeed," Arlo warned, "you will become like us—no longer counted among the living. I should probably tell you that nobody has ever successfully run the gauntlet, but then, nobody has ever tried."

"The machine's always been on?"

"Yes. Some version of it has been in operation ever since Dr. Shimmer created it."

"So the power crystals in the lid of the HATBOX, that I need to remove to turn the thing off—"

"You'll know them when you see them."

"Now that everything's settled," Newton said, "I'd like to remind everybody that there's a group of possessed Caps on the premises. Not to mention Benjamin and any other souls who might still be inside the machine and want bodies again. Once the shutdown program is initiated—if not before—they'll all realize something's going on. They won't like it. You guys should gear up, arm yourselves with as many weapons as you can."

ARE WE READY?

Hatter, Caledonia, and Astra briefly went their separate ways, to gather what weapons they could. Alone in his room in the South Needle, Hatter started to feel anxious. It didn't seem quite real, what he was about to do. Sure, if he succeeded, it'd be for the good of the academy and all of Wonderland, but did he really think he had the skill and strength and maturity to run the gauntlet and shut down the machine? He'd only made it to Brims, after all; there were still so many things to learn before he could even hope to be a fully commissioned Milliner. And if he failed to run the gauntlet, what would Wonderlanders say about him? Probably that he'd been young and arrogant, that he'd had an inflated sense of himself and should have stayed in the kitchen with Cook, where he belonged. The worst, though, was thinking about how disappointed Dalton would be—embarrassed by a little brother who'd gotten himself killed because he mistakenly believed he could save the queendom.

Hatter outfitted himself with his newly made hat and the C-blades he'd fashioned in the Textillery.

"It must be a relief to have finished it," Newton had said the first time he saw Hatter wearing the headgear that'd been so long in coming. "I know how much you don't like your father's hat."

"No, I like it," Hatter had said. "You were right, it's . . . better than I thought."

"That's good. Nice to be proud of something your father owned, isn't it?"

Without pondering for too long, without considering the pros and cons, without even asking himself *why*, Hatter now retrieved his father's hat from under his bed. He placed it on his head and tossed the new one on his desk.

"Don't say a word," he ordered his hat. And the hat didn't say anything. Which would be normal for any other hat, but which Hatter nonetheless took as a positive sign from his.

Astra and Caledonia were waiting for him in the academy foyer with C- and J-blades hanging at their hips.

"Where'd you get those?" Hatter asked, meaning the J-blades.

"I made mine," Astra said. "Kind of a secret side project. So was this." Her hand went to a long, braided loop of multicolored material clipped to her belt: what might have been a lasso. "Knitted it from scraps of caterpillar thread the Peaks left in the Textillery. All five caterpillar colors."

"Borrowed mine from a Cobbler," Caledonia said.

"And when you say borrowed . . . ?"

"She won't even know it was missing," Caledonia said. "Are we ready?"

Hatter saw Astra's eyes flick up toward his hat. She smiled at him and gave Caledonia the thumbs-up. He nodded.

It was time to get to the HATBOX. Past time. They approached a tapestry depicting a collection of teapots, but before they entered the academy's seams, the spout of one of the pots expanded to the size of a Wonderlander, and out stepped West.

"I've been following you," West said, seeing their surprise. "Twist told me you'd been sneaking out every night."

"And I thought he wanted to be friends," Hatter rued.

"He does. He believed he was helping you guys by telling me. He's worried about you."

Caledonia's voice was as sharp-edged as the J-blade she gripped in her hand. "What do you want?"

"To know what your immediate plan is."

Silence.

West turned to Astra. "Cadet Vost, as your Top Hat, I order you to tell me what you're about to do."

Astra's eyes opened wider than Hatter had ever seen, and that was saying something. She turned and looked frantically at the rest of the group.

"You don't have to tell him anything," Caledonia said, placing a hand on her shoulder.

"But . . . but . . . I do, don't I?" she said, her whole body quivering.

"Aren't you the one who questions everything?" Hatter asked. "Aren't you the one who doesn't believe in all the absolutes a cadet lives by?"

Astra sighed hard and chewed at the inside of her cheek.

"Oh, come on!" West said. "I'm not a bad guy! I want to help!"

"Yeah, right," Hatter said bitterly. "You're a Wellington. You're good friends with Rhodes. We can't trust you."

"Listen," West said. "For weeks now, I've noticed strange behavior in a lot of the Caps. And then there's what Dogberry did to me. Something's obviously going on. And then I saw all of you trying to be secretive at your table, and I thought maybe you were up to something. So even before I talked to Twist, I'd heard more than a few of your conversations, and honestly, as a Taper let me tell you, it would be wise to stop making top-secret plans in public."

Hatter and his friends stared at him in shock.

"You're lucky I'm the only one, it seems, who thinks Brims aren't young and foolish, because quite frankly, anyone else could have easily spied on you. Even other suits; not just Spades. I know about the possessions. I know about Shimmer and the machine, but I don't know what your plan is and I really do want to help. Madigan, have I ever given you reason to think I was like Rhodes, or even like Nigel and Benedict?"

"It doesn't matter—you still keep their company."

"It's so easy for you, isn't it, Madigan, to be all self-righteous. Some of us have been Wellingtons since our very first day at the academy. Some of us have parents who were

Wellingtons too. Grandparents. Some of us had an okay time of it until Rhodes showed up; we were able to tolerate Nigel and Benedict because they had a friend in your brother. I can't leave them now, not when I'm to graduate so soon. Excuses maybe, but . . . well, there it is."

West stopped talking.

"I think I trust him," Astra said. "Don't you guys? Besides, he's got a backpack and wrist-blades and the whole official set of Millinery weapons. That's pretty useful, isn't it?"

No one said anything, though Hatter grudgingly admitted to himself that yes, it might be pretty helpful to include Cadet Trilby.

"I'm making an executive decision." Astra turned to her Top Hat. "We're going to turn off the machine. Hatter is, I mean. Caledonia and I plan to keep guard while he's in the HATBOX, because once the gauntlet starts, he can't be interrupted if he's going to make it through, and we think it's pretty much guaranteed that the possessed Caps will try to stop him."

"Right. Let's do it." West turned to the tapestry from which he'd just emerged. Paused. Stepped aside. "After you, Madigan," he said.

Hatter took a long deep breath, walked past West, and ducked into the seams.

45

WE WON'T LET YOU DO IT.

Now that Hatter knew the way, it took him little time to lead his friends and Cadet Trilby through the seams that coursed down and around and down again to the HATBOX's antechamber. Not wanting to stop and give himself more time to think, to doubt himself, he pushed open the door to the arena. Inside, all was vast and blank. The souls of Arlo, Viola, Timber, Fallow, and Poinsettia were waiting for them. Astra introduced Spade Top Hat West Trilby, and—

"How will we know if Newton's getting anywhere with Shimmer?" Hatter asked.

But Arlo had no chance to answer, because a gang of HATBOX sparring partners, boys and girls, materialized. Benjamin stood at their head, as intimidating as ever with his scarred face. The others in his gang were pretty menacing in their own right: their clothes rugged, coarse; their calloused feet either poorly shod or not at all; hard luck in their faces;

and in their dirty fists weapons ranging from lead pipes to double-edged J-blades.

"We know what you're planning," Benjamin said. "We won't let you do it."

"But you'll be free," Astra said.

"Free to be what?" Benjamin scoffed. "Nothing? Nah, we barely had a life before the doctor came along. Now we've got a chance to live again, as one of *you*. No one's going to take that from us."

"Did Shimmer send you to stop us?" Hatter asked. Then, turning to Arlo: "Does that mean Newton wasn't able to—"

"We're part of the machine and we're ourselves," Benjamin said, echoing words Arlo had once said to Hatter. "We're also part of one another."

"They *did* have help," Timber said, leaving Arlo's side to join the ranks of Benjamin's gang.

"A spy!" Viola cried.

Fowler growled.

"Arlo, you've always been a soft touch," Timber said. "Don't know why Shimmer thought your soul would be useful. Or any of yours, for that matter."

"But why would you—?" Arlo started.

"I spent my life in Boarderland, working a miserable job, living a miserable life, and then getting my soul taken. Not fun. But getting to be a Wonderlander? A warrior? That'll be fun."

"It isn't about fun!" Hatter fumed. "Being a Milliner's about standing up for what's right, for those who can't stand up for themselves. Possessed Caps have it as bad as you did back in

Boarderland. Maybe worse, because they don't even know they're slaves. It isn't right."

"Not everything happens because it's right," Timber said, an ax materializing in his hands.

"I'm tired of all this talking," Benjamin said.

He snapped his fingers and a wild-eyed girl beside him charged Caledonia, and before Caledonia knocked her to the floor in an unconscious heap, the rest of Benjamin's gang attacked, manically swinging pipes and J-blades.

IT'S COMING!

The HATBOX sparring partners had a couple of advantages over Wonderlanders: Although they apparently felt pain and could be wounded, even knocked unconscious, they quickly recovered to full health. And they could appear and disappear at will. Hatter threw a punch at Benjamin, who was directly in front of him. His fist passed through air, and Benjamin was at his back, clocking him in the head. Frustrated, struggling to land a single blow, Hatter dropped low, swept his leg out behind him, and spun, knocking Benjamin onto his back. He grabbed two C-blades and stabbed the shoulders of Benjamin's coat, pinning the kid to the floor. Benjamin grinned, vanished.

Caledonia and West—each were taking on a couple of Benjamin's Boarderlanders simultaneously. Arlo battled with Timber, Viola with the wild-eyed girl, and Fallow swung out at anyone who tried to get at Poinsettia, crouched in fear as she was between him and a wall. Astra, meanwhile, was holding

311

her own against a pipe-wielding Boarderlander—a kid who, no matter how he swung and lunged, couldn't quite hit her, so acrobatic were her defensive moves.

"Arlo, is *this* the gauntlet?" Hatter called as one of Benjamin's gang, sword in hand, rushed him.

"No, I told you," Arlo said. "It's only for a single runner. Just keep fighting."

Hatter, holding his father's hat tight to his head with one hand, somersaulted clear of the incoming sword; it lodged into one of Benjamin's own. Blades were slicing the air all around him. He rolled up on one knee and stabbed a hologram in the gut with a C-blade. It vanished. Hatter got to his feet. He was surrounded by half a dozen of Benjamin's Boarderlanders.

Let me help.

No.

Let me help.

Well, desperate times . . .

Fine.

Hatter took off his hat, flicked it into a disc of rotating blades, and sent it flying. With a precision that he knew had nothing to do with his skills, the hat flew in a perfect circle, taking out all six of his adversaries—who dissolved to nothing as soon as they were hit—and returning to his hand.

Clangkrssssh!

Hatter turned to see Astra locking J-blades with one of Benjamin's Boarderlanders. Two more were moving toward her. He threw his hat; the J-blade enemy fell first. The hat boomeranged back to him and he immediately sent it toward

Caledonia, to dispatch the scruffy tomboy who seemed very much her equal in hand-to-hand combat.

"Madigan! Some help here!" In all of the fighting, West had never taken on fewer than two combatants at a time, but there was only so much he could do against four. So it was fortunate that Hatter's disc of coptering blades scared West's attackers so much, they disappeared before they could feel the cold cut of its Wonderland steel.

Hatter caught his weapon as it circled back to him, with a flick of the wrist returned it to what looked an ordinary piece of haberdashery, and doffed it at the Spade Top Hat.

"Effective piece you've got there," West said in appreciation.

"They're gone," Astra breathed. "Why are they all gone?"

But the HATBOX was empty of Benjamin and his gang for no more than the blink of a spirit-dane's eye. They rematerialized, armed with spears and double-weighted tripchains.

Arlo, Viola, and Fallow didn't wait—and ran at them with a ferocity they'd never shown during combat workshops: Arlo, normally so mild-mannered in his misfortune, let out a yell that might've been a tribal war cry as he closed with Benjamin. And just as Fallow was showing what his large fists could really do—

The door to the HATBOX flung open; possessed Caps rushed in, wielding knives. With his own hat flattened into a shield and with help from Caledonia, West butted them back out to the antechamber. And while Arlo, Viola, and Fallow battled against Benjamin and his gang, West and Caledonia defended the HATBOX door, which remained open. It was impossible to see how many Caps there were. A lot. No way was it a fair fight.

"Go," Hatter said to Astra. "Help them."

She went. But fighting a bunch of Wonderlanders without getting or causing serious injury wasn't so easy. The Caps didn't know what they were doing; they were innocent; they just needed to be held at bay long enough for Hatter to run the gauntlet and turn off the machine.

Amid the skirmishing, Hatter heard Poinsettia's small voice. She was standing next to him.

"It's coming," she said.

"What?"

Then he felt it: the entire HATBOX shook as if from an impossibly heavy footstep.

"It's coming," Poinsettia repeated, closing her eyes tight.

Again came the footstep. Closer this time. Heavier. Then again. Closer and heavier still. All the fighting stopped—arms and blades raised, clubs held in crosswise defensive postures—as if the action in and around the HATBOX had been put on Pause.

"What's *that?*" Caledonia asked.

It seemed to be originating from behind a giant tile in the arena's north wall—a steady, determined pounding.

Thump. THUMP. THUMP!

The HATBOX shook as if from an earthquake. The wall tile swiveled 180 degrees and there it was, in front of them: a giant beast with iridescent wings, clawed feet, a tail powerful enough to demolish houses, and a massive head on a long, thick neck, its eyes as red as fire and its mouth full of flesh-gnashing teeth.

YOU ARE READY FOR THIS, HATTER MADIGAN.

"Jabberwock!" Hatter said as the beast roared, scorching the air with its hot breath. He'd only ever seen jabberwocky in books. "What about this? Is *this* the gauntlet?" he called to Arlo.

"Not sure!"

"Aaah!" Benjamin cried, and the fighting resumed, Arlo, Viola, and Fallow vying against Boarderlander souls eager for bodies, Caledonia and Astra busy with the possessed Caps.

"West, no!" Hatter yelled, because the Spade Top Hat ran past him, straight for the jabberwock.

West knew that because of the jabberwock's size, the closer he was to it, the harder it'd be for the creature to maneuver against him. He ducked under a jet of its torch-like breath, reached its underbelly, and shrugged open his Millinery backpack: swords and daggers, J-blades and corkscrews sprouted to the ready. He took hold of a pair of swords and thrust them up through the jabberwock's crusty outer skin. The beast jerked in pain, bellowed, and clacked its slobbery teeth. Its tail whipped against the walls.

He's going to be trampled, Hatter thought.

West reached into his backpack for more blades. The jabberwock reared up and, with one of its hind feet, its claws unsheathed, kicked the cadet out from under him. As if shot from a catapult, West's body skidded to a stop clear across the arena.

"West!" Hatter ran to the Spade Top Hat and crouched over him. He saw a big gash in his left side. "West, can you hear me?"

"I hear you," West said weakly. "I think . . . I made a mistake. Don't try to fight it. If you use violence, it wins. There has to be another way." West wasn't a Spade Top Hat for nothing. "Go on, Hatter. I'll be okay."

Hatter stood and faced the jabberwock. He couldn't manage the thing alone. He shouted for Astra and Caledonia, and as they ran toward him, Fallow took up the defense of the arena door.

"That rope you made with caterpillar threads," Hatter said to Astra. "I need it."

She handed it over without asking why, noticed Fallow having a hard time fending off the Caps by himself, and hurried back to support him, slashing her J-blade at any of Benjamin's gang who tried to stop her.

Hatter handed one end of the rope to Caledonia. "I hope it's long enough," he said.

"For what?"

"Run at least twice around the jabberwock, clockwise. I'll run counterclockwise. Meet me near the tail."

The jabberwock swiped at them with its front feet, wrenched its neck this way and that to bite at them. As Caledonia rounded the beast the first time, one of its teeth snagged her, catching between her body and the belt that held her J-blades, and suddenly she was in the air, being shaken back and forth like a chewtoy but somehow holding on to her end of Astra's rope.

Hatter ducked under the jabberwock's flailing front legs and reached for his hat, but Astra spun away from a Cap she were fighting at the arena door and winged a C-blade that lodged in the jabberwock's nose. The beast reared, dropping Caledonia, who regained her feet before Hatter could even ask if she were okay.

"One more time around, right?" she said.

Again they ran, circling the enraged jabberwock— Caledonia in the clockwise direction, Hatter counter-clockwise. They dodged its swiping claws, jumped clear of its fiery breath. Caledonia reached the tail first, and Hatter was still a few strides away, about to yell "Pull!" because the rope needed to be as tight around the jabberwock's legs as they could get it, when—

The end of the beast's tail whipped around and knocked the wind out of him. He lay on his back, gasping for air. The jabberwock lifted its right rear foot to stomp on him. The cracks and crevices of its hardened sole were the last things Hatter would ever see.

Sorry, Arlo. I tried. I—

Caledonia yanked him to safety as the foot thunderously hit the arena floor.

"Thanks," Hatter said, coughing, standing.

"If this is where I'm supposed to say something witty," Caledonia said, "forget it."

Within moments, the rope was as taut as they could pull it around the jabberwock's legs, limiting its mobility. Caledonia swatted at the creature's side to hold its attention. Hatter took both ends of the rope in hand and, with a running leap, launched himself up its hindquarters and onto its back. With the rope as his reins, he rode the jabberwock as it bucked and twisted and exhaled fire, trying to throw him off.

Hoping, praying that his thoughts and imaginings were infused with the powers of the braided blue, orange, yellow, red, and green caterpillar threads he held so tightly, he spoke soothingly to the jabberwock. Unsure if the beast could hear him, he imagined that he was actually speaking jabberwock as he called it friend and promised that there was nothing to be afraid of, absolutely nothing. "There now," he said. "It's okay. Shhh. Calm down. That's right. That's it." And eventually, the beast settled down on its haunches, its wings gently pulsing. It remained that way even after Hatter jumped from its back.

The possessed Caps had fallen still, but not Benjamin and his gang. They fought with increased aggression against Astra and Caledonia, Viola and Fallow.

"Look." Arlo had materialized at Hatter's side.

In the northwest quadrant of the arena, a woodsy path

snaked out of sight into the distance. WITHIN THE BEGINNING: THE END read a banner above the path's entrance.

This was definitely it. The gauntlet.

"Whatever Newton's saying to Shimmer, I guess it's working," Hatter said.

"You *are* ready for this, Hatter Madigan." It wasn't a question but a statement. Arlo reached out and placed his hand on Hatter's chest—his palm flat and his fingers spread, feeling the pump of Hatter's heart beneath skin and bone. It was the sole time the two had touched in friendship. Together in the HATBOX, they'd only ever sparred. "What you're about to do . . . it's the most generous thing anyone has ever done for me," Arlo said, his voice quivering. "For Viola or any of us."

"Yeah, well . . . your choosing me?" Hatter said. "It means everything. Assuming this works, you'll be gone before I get back?"

"I hope so. No offense."

"None taken."

The two embraced.

"You *will* be free," Hatter said. "You will be surrounded by love."

"Good-bye, my friend."

Hatter took a last look at Viola and Fallow, who were too busy fighting Benjamin's gang to notice him. But Poinsettia—standing so tiny and fragile-seeming amid the violence: she waved to him.

He stepped onto the path and it began to move under

his feet, quickly, like a treadmill. He had to run to keep from being thrown backward. The landscape on either side of him morphed from woods to desert to jungle to moonscape. Figures blurred past him—some in Millinery overcoats, others having the shape and build of card soldiers. He kept his father's hat in hand, ready for anything. But none of the blurred figures made a move at him. He ran and ran, beginning to think that the gauntlet's purpose—this part of it anyway—was to physically exhaust him, because overexertion might cause him to lower his emotional guard. How far had he gone? How long had his arms and legs been pumping him along? He felt as if he'd run the equivalent of four times around the academy. At least. But just when he was sure he couldn't run any farther, the path ended. Hatter fell to the same woodsy ground that had flanked its entrance, coughed, struggling to catch his breath until—

Everything went black.

48

WHY DO YOU HATE US?

Hatter opened his eyes, found himself standing alone in a square red room. The floor, the ceiling, the walls— everything was red. He didn't see a door or a window, and nothing that suggested where he might locate the crystal that powered the machine. Was this the HATBOX or his own mind? He wasn't sure.

"You're wasting time," a voice said.

He spun around: nobody. *Okay. A voice in my head then.*

He walked up to a wall and touched it. It felt very wall-like. He turned back to the center of the room. A desk was there, with Bill the lizard, the Grand Milliner's secretary, standing on top of it.

"Can I help you?" Bill asked, looking up at him from behind those large round glasses.

"I need to turn off the machine. Do you know where the power crystal is?"

"Is this it?" Bill pointed at a button on his desk.

"I don't think so. I think that's the button for the trapdoor."

Bill pushed the button. The room began to spin slowly, and Hatter realized, as it slowed to a stop, that he wasn't in a square room at all, but a diamond-shaped one. Just as he was about to articulate this observation, the floor began to tilt upward, creating a steep decline behind him. He grabbed the desk just in time as papers and pencils began to slip off it toward him. Bill took a few steps back so that he was now standing upright on the legs of the desk. He looked down at Hatter, who was hanging off the desk, gripping it tightly.

"That was unexpected," Bill said.

"Help me!" Hatter said. The small lizard looked at Hatter and raised his nonexistent eyebrows.

"No, that would be silly." Bill looked over the edge of the desk. "Oh, look! There's the trapdoor!" Hatter glanced down and saw a black hole at the point of the diamond far below him. "You need to let go now!"

Hatter tried to pull himself up higher onto the desk.

"No, that's not letting go," Bill said. He wandered over to Hatter's left hand and looked at it for a second. Then he leaned over and bit it hard.

Hatter yelled in pain and lost his grip. Dangling now by just his right hand he watched as Bill casually wandered over and stared at it.

"Don't!"

"You need to let go now." Bill opened his mouth wide and clamped down hard on Hatter's right hand.

Hatter let go of the desk. As he fell, he stared up at the little lizard, who nodded approvingly.

Red whooshed past him, and then he was surrounded by blackness. He fell and fell, and as he did, he heard a faint sound below him, a distant roar building and building. He wasn't sure what it was, but his muscles tensed and the roar got louder. It started to sound like clanging metal, like explosions, like yelling, all mixed up together, yet each sound distinct.

Hatter landed on something hard. He looked beneath him—damp matted grass. He looked up. A brown sky and fallen soldiers on the horizon. Chaos as bodies ran this way and that.

"On your feet, soldier!" said a loud voice.

Hatter turned and saw a card soldier, a Three of Clubs, staring down at him, holding a J-blade out for him to take. Hatter pushed himself up to standing and reached out slowly.

"Hurry, they're attacking from the west!" The soldier pushed him, and Hatter turned and saw a line of card soldiers bracing themselves against the distant shadow of an enemy marching down a green hill.

He began to run while the soldier kept pace with him.

"Excuse me, sir," Hatter said.

"Not now, soldier," replied the playing card.

"I need to turn off the machine!" Hatter said, his voice full of exasperation. Why wouldn't anyone help him?

"You can't do that here," replied the playing card.

"Then where?!" Hatter said just as they broke through the

line of card soldiers and were standing in the front, weapons at the ready.

The enemy army came into view, a host of boys and girls dressed similarly to Benjamin and his gang. All in torn trousers and suspenders and caps, their shoddy weapons obviously made from whatever they could find. A cudgel with nails sticking out of it, a broken bottle at the end of a rope, knives and shields made of scrap metal.

"This isn't a fair fight," Hatter said, looking down the rows of card soldiers in their armor, holding their gleaming blades.

"Fight them!" the soldier said as the kids started to attack.

"I can't just—" A boy who looked exactly like Timber rushed at him.

Hatter was now fairly certain that this was all in his head, that his body lay in the HATBOX, collapsed at the end of a woodsy path. So he imagined himself as the greatest warrior who had ever defended Wonderland. He leaped into the air, sailing over the line of kids and landing on the other side. He charged them from behind and tripped up an entire row so that they were down for the count. He spun just in time to meet the blade of a girl with a fierce scowl on her face. He disarmed her easily and pushed her so that she went flying backward until she was out of sight.

He spun and parried and sliced and diced until suddenly there was no one left standing. He panted for a moment and looked around. The card soldier nodded his approval. "You are definitely one of us," he said.

For some reason Hatter looked down at himself then and noticed he was wearing a dirty shirt and torn trousers held up by suspenders. Instinctively he reached up and touched the top of his head and felt a cap.

"I'm not one of you," he said quietly. What had he done? Why had he done it? He had been fighting for the enemy! What did that mean? He rushed over to the kids and saw Timber sprawled on the grass, breathing hard. He knelt down beside him. "I'm so sorry."

"Why do you hate us?" Timber sucked in a deep tortured breath. "You hate us all."

"I just want to turn off the machine."

"Why? You're one of us now," Timber said. Then his head dropped to the side and he stopped breathing.

"Hatter, we need to go," the playing card said, but his voice was softer than before.

"I can't just leave him," he replied.

"The battle still rages—you need to leave this instant!" The voice had changed. It belonged to a woman, and Hatter, in surprise, turned to look up at her.

Staring down at him, her soft brown curls blowing across her face, was the familiar and yet unfamiliar face of his mother.

WE ARE SO DISAPPOINTED IN YOU, HATTER.

Hatter stared at his mother in stunned silence. He couldn't move. He couldn't think. His heart felt as if it might explode out of his chest.

"Hatter, now!" she ordered, holding out her hand for him.

Dazed, he grabbed her hand, and she pulled him to standing. "Follow me," she said. "Fast!"

Hatter reminded himself that this was all the creation of his own mind. But the feel of his mother's skin . . . it was so real. Maybe he was wrong. Couldn't it be at least a little bit real?

A whipsnake grenade exploded next to him, and Hatter was running after his mother. They dodged fighting playing cards and knights on large white horses and more hologram kids giving as good as they got. A row of Milliners riding tiger-size beetles with shiny blue-and-green armor was marching in lockstep toward a new group of kids coming over the horizon. Complete and utter chaos reigned. Finally, Hatter and his mother reached a copse of trees and tore into the shady quiet. Instantly, the sounds of battle were silenced, and all that could be heard was someone rhythmically tapping on a drum.

"What is that?"

"Hurry!" replied his mother, taking his hand once more and pulling him quickly through the trees. They seemed to be in a thick, gloomy forest, but then the trees gave way to a small clearing in which a tent was standing. A flag flew at its topmost point. It bore the Heart family crest. And the entrance to the tent was shaped like a heart.

They ran up to the entrance and burst into what was a large high-ceilinged room covered in gold leaf. A grand ballroom. The floor, a gleaming white marble, reflected the golden light back upward. Mirrors ran the length of the walls, but as Hatter walked by them, he noticed he had no reflection. His mother did, though.

Running down the center of the room from one end to the other was a long table, set as if for a banquet of two hundred guests. All the seats were empty except for two at the very far end.

"Sit here," his mother said, indicating a chair at the opposite end from the other two people. Hatter sat. From his vantage point the two people at the other end of the table were little more than dark spots. His mother left him and made her way to join the figures, growing smaller and smaller until he would not have recognized her except for the fact that he knew it was her.

Hatter glanced to his left to stare at his non-reflection. He quickly returned to looking down the long table at his mother.

"What do you think you're doing?" a familiar voice asked. Though the person was far off, the voice was crystal clear, as if he were sitting right next to Hatter.

"Dalton?" Hatter asked in shock.

"Answer the question, Hatter," said his mother, her voice so far away now.

"I'm trying to turn off the machine."

"Why are you trying to do that?" a different voice said.

"I—I—" Hatter stammered, and then fell silent.

"Answer your father, young man," his mother said.

His father. His father was sitting there. Just down the table from him. Hatter was on his feet in an instant and making his way down the length of the table.

"Sit down!" his father ordered.

Hatter stopped walking and turned to head back toward his seat when he saw he was suddenly standing right next to it. He sat down.

"Answer your father, young man," his mother said again.

"I—"

"You already said that, Hatter." Dalton's voice was strained and full of exasperation.

"I'm trying to turn off the machine," he said again. He was starting to sound almost like a machine himself, the way he just repeated the same sentence in a sort of monotone.

"But why you?" his mother asked.

"Because . . . because I have to. For my friends. For myself."

"What arrogance," Dalton said. And even from such a dis-tance Hatter could see him shaking his head.

"You should've let the grown-ups handle it," his father said. "We are so disappointed in you, Hatter."

"You are ruining the Madigan name," Dalton added.

Hatter felt his heart drop. In fact, it felt as if it slipped right out of his body. He looked down toward the ground and saw a heart, bloody and still beating, squeezing blood with every heartbeat out of its arteries and shooting it out in squirts onto the gleaming marble floor.

He looked down at his chest. There was a gaping hole in his left side. Black and empty.

"Now look what you've done!" Dalton said. "It's making a mess everywhere!"

Hatter stared down at the heart.

"Pick it up, Hatter," his mother said coldly.

"But," he replied, looking up, "where do I put it?"

"Where it belongs—on your sleeve," his father replied even more coldly.

Hatter leaned down and picked up the heart. It felt warm and slippery in his hands. He looked at his sleeve and, sure enough, there was a little pouch sewn into it, the perfect size for his heart. He slipped it into the pouch.

"Now it's time to go back to the academy," Dalton said.

"And stop trying to be a hero," his father said.

Hatter could feel tears welling up in his eyes. Were they

right? Was this all to prove a point? That he belonged at the academy? That he was meant to be a Milliner? That as a Heart, he could be just as good as a Spade?

There was a *crash* as part of the roof suddenly broke off and fell onto the table in a cloud of dust and debris. Hatter coughed and waved away the white and saw that a piece of ceiling in the shape of a spade had landed at the far end of the table, obscuring his parents and brother.

"Mother, Father!" he cried out in fear. "Dalton!"

Hatter was up on his feet, but this time he climbed onto the table. No more tricks: he was going to run across and see his family. But as he ran on the crisp white linen toward the spade, he could sense he wasn't getting anywhere. No matter how fast he went, he just couldn't get any closer to his family. It didn't matter. He wasn't going to give up. He had to get to them. If he got to them, he knew, he just knew that they would help him. Even if it weren't to turn off the machine. Even if it were just to get out of there and return to the South Needle, to being a cadet and dealing with the simple things in life.

Hatter tripped and went flying toward the fallen part of the roof and his family. He flew right off the other end of the table and landed in a heap on the floor, painfully and hard. He looked up. He had passed the chairs, and he saw his parents sitting with their backs to him. Hatter scrambled up and rushed to the center chair where his father sat.

Sitting in the chair was Grand Milliner Victus.

Hatter stumbled backward and fell into his brother's lap.

He looked up at him, but saw instead Rhodes staring down at him. He pushed himself away, and with terror and panic he ran to his mother. In her place was Shimmer.

Slowly Hatter backed away from all three toward what ought to have been the far wall, but at that moment he noticed he was no longer in the grand ballroom. He stood in a large space of black nothingness. There was no table. There were no mirrors. There was nothing in the room except for the three chairs on which the Grand Milliner, Rhodes, and Shimmer sat.

"Where are my parents?" Hatter asked.

They said nothing.

"Where is my brother?"

They said nothing.

Rhodes started laughing hysterically. His face turned red—he was gasping for air. Tears ran down his cheeks. The Grand Milliner just stared at Hatter, his eyes narrowing.

"You're ours now," Victus said.

"That's not true!"

Hatter felt suddenly as if he were being pulled backward. He fought the sensation, flailing his arms out before him, but it was too strong. His feet slid across the blackness beneath them; he flew backward away from Victus, Shimmer, and Rhodes, away from the small spotlight of white in which they sat, farther and farther and farther away until they disappeared.

Hatter forced himself to turn in the direction he was flying. And he saw he was falling once again, but falling into the real world. Below him he saw Caledonia fighting off half a dozen

Caps and Astra taking on the holograms. He felt a sudden urge to attack not the holograms nor the Caps they were fighting, but his friends. He sensed it was wrong, but it also felt incredibly right.

He was going to fight them. And he would win. He knew their weaknesses; he knew their strengths. And when he won, he and the others would take over the academy. No! This wasn't happening—he wasn't going to let it happen. It wasn't real. It still wasn't real. None of this was real. Hatter forced himself to stop falling; he stopped in midair, still far enough above the fray that no one noticed him. But he felt a strange pull then, somewhere deep down inside, as if something had grabbed hard onto his guts. No, not his guts . . . his soul.

It's mine, not yours! He was not going to become like Rhodes or Benjamin. He looked at the heart on his sleeve as it lay resting there, limp and brown, producing an effortful, squishy single *thump*.

It was imperative that he feel something.

Hatter closed his eyes and tried to dredge up some dark emotions. He thought about never being as good as Dalton. He thought about his fear of not living up to the family name. He thought about Rhodes and the Wellingtons, of fitting in for once, of finally being someone, and then suddenly not fitting in. He thought of his parents. How everyone else seemed to know them but he'd never had that chance. He thought of his story. That he didn't have one. That his book was blank. That he was a freak. That he was scared. That he didn't want to be a Heart. That everything was wrong. He opened his eyes and stared at his heart. It still lay there, barely registering a single emotion.

Oh, come on. Now when he needed to feel something, now when he needed it most of all . . .

Something small registered in the back of his mind. A small thought.

Hatter closed his eyes and changed his tactic. He thought of Newton and his wry sense of humor. He thought of Caledonia and how she stood up for those who couldn't stand up for themselves. He thought of Astra and how she saw the best in everyone. He remembered them taking him in, being his friend even though he'd been so mean to all of them. He remembered Cook and the free snacks. He remembered Tutor Wren teaching him and Dalton, even though he didn't have to. He remembered Dalton's protectiveness. He remembered Weaver.

His eyes filled with tears, but not from sadness. It was a kind of joy, a kind of gratitude. A kind of love.

Hatter didn't need to look at the heart this time. He felt it beating hard against his arm.

50

I CAN HELP.

Everything vanished around him and he felt as if he were floating in space. The strange pulling sensation had ceased. Looking down, he thought he saw Arlo and the others fighting against Benjamin's gang. Then he realized: he wasn't in space; he was in the HATBOX. The surrounding blackness lightened to reveal that he lay on the leafy ground at the end of the woodsy path, high on a hill in the northwest quadrant of the arena.

Arlo had said that the power crystal was in the HATBOX lid, but that to dislodge it, he had to be *outside* the facility. Hatter wasn't yet sure what this meant, but he at least knew that he had to go *up*, to get above the ceiling which he'd never been this close to before; now he could see that what looked like an evening sky full of twinkling stars was a mosaic of crumbled crystal.

The grass under Hatter's feet, the shelter of trees: it was all the same as at the beginning of the path, only now the arena

335

walls weren't hidden by foliage. He walked over to one of the wall tiles. The jabberwock had emerged from behind a tile exactly like it. And back when Dalton had demonstrated for the entire student body what the HATBOX could do, Hatter had seen floor tiles flip over and produce chessmen. Didn't it mean . . . yes, it had to. There was another layer. The arena that he knew, that he was standing in: it was a box within a box.

He put his shoulder to the left edge of the wall tile and pushed with all his weight and strength. The tile swiveled, and he slipped through the opening into . . . the industrial armature of the combat facility. Girders, supports, mechanical workings everywhere.

Hatter climbed, working his way up a crisscrossing array of struts and supports until he was above the arena's ceiling but not yet outside the entire HATBOX. Silken threads, thousands of them, draped down from a skylight to the crumbled crystal ceiling of the arena.

Not a skylight. The power crystal.

Hatter flung his father's hat. Its spinning blades severed every thread that connected the crystal to the arena ceiling, the hat repeatedly coursing up and back as if with a mind of its own until finally returning to Hatter's waiting hand. He wasn't sure if the power crystal were still providing energy to the machine and HATBOX, but he wanted to be thorough.

Only how did he get to the roof? A crawl space on his left led into blackness. He approached, heard a mishmash of angry, whispering voices. He noticed an air duct across the room, large enough for him to stand in, and he started toward it. The power crystal rained sparks on him in intermittent bursts. The severed ends of the dangling caterpillar threads popped and sizzled. Carefully, Hatter picked his way to the air duct. Angrier than ever, the whispering voices swirled around his head. A flash of light from the malfunctioning power crystal illuminated a ladder at the far end of the duct—a ladder leading *up*. Within a blink, he was on it, three-quarters of the way to the hatch that he figured must provide access to the roof, but—

Something moved above him: Benjamin, on the ladder's top rungs, blocking his way.

"You've done more than enough damage," the Boarderlander hissed. "Now it's my turn."

Benjamin dropped onto his back. Hatter gripped the ladder as best he could, but with the added weight, and Benjamin pulling at him, his fingers kept slipping.

I can help.

Hatter still found it unsettling that his father's hat talked to him, but hey, if it could help . . .

He jerked his head so that the headpiece could get a flying start. It retained its hat shape, looped around and tumbled into Benjamin's gut. The Boarderlander cried out and let go of Hatter, but it was too late. They were both in the air. They landed in a clump, and then Benjamin was on top of Cadet Madigan, punching him again and again. But the Boarderlander's fists didn't always make contact.

The ever more ghostly representation of a faulty connection, of power on the fritz, Benjamin was coming in and out of focus, dimming and brightening. And then—

Hatter stopped getting punched altogether. Benjamin still sat on him, still swung his fists, but he was completely without substance.

"No!" the Boarderlander yelled. "Noooo!"

Hatter stood and picked up his father's hat, went to the ladder and climbed.

"Noooooooooo!" Benjamin wailed.

Hatter pushed open the hatch at the top of the ladder, stepped outside.

The power crystal was a flat dial, five average-size Wonderlanders in diameter, embedded in the roof. Cloudy specks and lightning flashes played under its surface.

How was he supposed to dislodge *that*? He tried to grip it anywhere along its edge, in case by some feat of imagination he could actually lift it. Nothing doing. He jumped up and down on it. It was too large, too secure.

Again, I can help.

His hat flattened into rotating blades, Hatter sidearmed it out over the power crystal. It swooped down and rolled on its sawlike edge, rolled along the perimeter of the crystal at great speed, round and round it went, cutting a deeper and deeper groove . . . creaking, the sound of straining Wonderland steel . . . until, with a series of small explosions that signaled the crystal's ultimate disconnection from the HATBOX, the power source fell, crashed down to the floor below, and broke into several large pieces.

They're free.

Hatter thought he saw them, thought he saw Arlo, Viola,

Fallow, and Poinsettia flicker ever so briefly before him, but he couldn't be sure. He stood there, alone on the rooftop, nothing but a cold wind blowing for fanfare.

♣

♥

♠

♦

ϒ

"You did it!" Astra gushed.

It'd taken him a quarter lunar hour to climb down from the HATBOX roof, to push open a wall tile at ground level and enter the arena, where Astra and Caledonia were being questioned by Grand Milliner Victus and Tutor Wren, and healers were tending to West, whose torso was wrapped in Astra's handmade rope. In the antechamber, dazed Caps were being examined by healers.

"One second they were here," Caledonia said, "and the next they weren't. Your jabberwock friend too. And the Caps"—she gestured toward the antechamber—"all of them fainted. We knew you'd done it." She couldn't have been happier if she'd managed the feat herself.

West excused himself from the healers and limped his way to Hatter, held out his hand. "Excellent job, Madigan."

"Thanks. Where's Newton? And what about Shimmer?"

"I'm here," Newton said, entering the arena with the help of his cane. "Shimmer's in the chessmen's custody. No need to worry about him anymore."

"But what'd you say to him to get him to initiate the shutdown program?"

"I don't know what specifically did it," Newton said. "I just asked over and over again, in a hundred different ways, if he really thought he was fit to rule Wonderland when he couldn't even dress himself properly. I mean, what kind of ruler only wears dirty pajamas and gross slippers? It must have cracked his confidence enough to boot up the program. Viola briefly appeared in the machine room to say that the program was running and so I just kept at it, questioning Shimmer. And then, when you did whatever you did to the power crystal, the machine started to whirr down and Shimmer let go of the cables, looking quite defeated. I think by that point he *wanted* to be taken into custody."

"Now that everyone is caught up on the latest," the Grand Milliner said, approaching the cadets with Tutor Wren, "I will tell you that your behavior tonight was exceedingly dangerous and antithetical to the Milliner ethic, which calls for strict adherence to command hierarchies and discipline. As talented a cadet as West Trilby is, you and your friends, Hatter, should have informed your more qualified adult superiors about all of this, instead of leaving the entire academy at risk."

"But we tried—" Astra started.

"I don't need to hear the ill-informed, twisted, and completely pathetic excuses of a Vost," snapped the Grand Milliner.

Astra fell silent.

"And while I'm thankful that, in this instance, tragedy has been avoided, I must inform four out of five of you that you are now expelled from the academy. Cadet Trilby, as a Top Hat of rare reputation, I am granting you a reprieve from this punishment, though you should have known better. The rest of you will immediately pack up your things and leave. Oh, except for you, Hatter Madigan." Victus turned to look at him. Though his face was stone, there was something gleeful behind his eyes. "You will have the honor of returning to your room in the tenders' quarters. You will be trained as a tender, and I believe you'll find the company far more to your liking."

Hatter felt tears well up in his eyes. He also felt a surge of rage. *No, don't feel. Don't feel.* But why not? Feeling was *good*. Without giving himself the leeway to feel, he wouldn't have made it through the gauntlet.

Suddenly, his hat flew off his head and into the Grand Milliner's face, knocking the man off his feet and onto his backside.

"Madigan!" Victus yelled, turning a bright shade of red.

Hatter wanted to apologize. But not really.

"Enough!" boomed the usually calm and soft voice of Tutor Wren. "Hatter, you never, ever attack unless your life or the life of the royal family is in danger. If you thought you might get out of detention for this final week of classes, you certainly won't now. Grand Milliner, that's a very fancy speech, but yet again you seem to have forgotten the ways of the academy. No one can expel a cadet except the eeries. It is up to them whether this foursome should stay or go. And now it is time for the cadets to return to their quarters. For all of us to return to our quarters. There has been enough excitement for today."

While West was escorted to the Healing Room, Hatter and his friends made their way out of the HATBOX, up the mountain, and back to the Needles. Hatter glanced at Astra; there

341

was a little something around her eyes that suggested she was worried.

"It'll be okay," he whispered to her, not entirely believing it himself.

Astra nodded and tried to smile. "That's usually my line."

I GUESS . . . GOOD-BYE.

The following days were odd ones at the academy. The Caps were back to being themselves, but after having been possessed for so long, they were so far behind in their studies that Hatter wasn't sure what would happen come the next level. The rest of the cadets could speak of nothing other than their fantastic fighting skills when they had fended off their possessed fellow cadets. Rhodes in particular had created several fanciful tales that actually included his killing one of them. Of course, when Twist produced the Cap in question, all the boys in the South Needle had a good laugh at Rhodes's expense. It was the beginning of the end of his reign of terror, it seemed, because a bully is only as powerful as others allow him to be. No one felt like letting him get away with it now. But odder than all of that was the return to normal life for Hatter and his friends. Classes. Training. Even detention. There was a marked lack of grand plans and hanging out with holograms. It was a little silly to think this way, now that safety and order were restored, but Hatter kind of missed the excitement, and that worried him. A Milliner was meant to keep the status quo, and if he got a thrill from the status quo being disturbed, what did that say about him?

But there were larger issues to worry about. His status as a cadet was on shaky ground and it was all in the hands of the eeries. He hoped that when he next saw them, he would be able to convince them he should stay. In every private moment over the next week he practiced the speech he would make to them, preparing himself for the final day of classes.

Which arrived all of a sudden and far too soon.

The booming, disembodied voice made the announcement just as he was adjusting his new hat in the dorm room mirror. "All current cadets—Brims through Tapers—will have a morning meeting in the following locations. Tapers, the Grand Foyer. Crowns, the Banquet Plaza. Bonds, the Yard. Cobblers, the Textillery. And Brims, the HATBOX. You have five minutes."

Hatter glanced at Newton and said, "The HATBOX?"

"Let's go."

Hatter grabbed his story from under the bed and shoved it inside his vest, ready for his meeting with the eeries. He glanced briefly at his father's hat sitting on the foot of his bed but then shook his head. He followed Newton out of their room.

They joined the general rush of cadets spilling out of their dorm rooms and onto swifties and marched with them in as efficient a manner as they could, with so little time to prepare, into the academy. They then peeled off toward their respective destinations.

Hatter and Newton made their way into the HATBOX and went to stand with their suits. The HATBOX no longer had that warm glow but was instead lit more harshly by a single floating orb at the center of the room. It made the room feel lifeless. Maybe it wasn't the lighting creating the sensation. Hatter felt a lack of energy; no pulse was coming from the ceiling and walls.

MM Tornado entered the room and stood before them. The cadets all rose to attention in one sharp movement.

"If I call your name, be it known you have not made it to Cobblers and will be asked to leave directly after the conclusion of this meeting." MM Tornado pulled a list from inside her jacket and began to read.

What? No. Weren't they supposed to speak with the eeries again? Hatter needed to talk to them. Needed to explain everything that had happened, and why. And he thought maybe he could ask them about his father's hat this time—whether it meant something. Like his story. It was impossible to think that MM Tornado was just going to read some list written down on paper.

"Cadet Boshi, Cadet Gat . . . "

Hatter felt his heart start to pump faster as she worked her way through the list of cadets who had been cut from the academy. He took it as a good sign that Caledonia's names had been skipped though. She was past the *Hs* now and had just announced, "Cadet Hennin." This was it. The moment he would find out the truth. Hatter could sense Rhodes looking at him, but of course he wasn't really. That would be breaking form. No, he could sense Rhodes hoping his name would be called. He wondered if Rhodes could sense that Hatter was hoping *Rhodes's* name would be called. As she approached the Vs, Hatter suddenly hoped more than anything that Astra's name would not.

"To the rest of you, congratulations! You've all made it to Cobblers." MM Tornado turned and walked out of the room.

Wait, what? What just happened?

The cadets broke rank, and Hatter looked around, kind of stunned. He saw half a dozen cadets in tears and knew they had not made it to the next level. But he hadn't heard his name. That meant . . . that meant . . .

"Empty threat. Tutor Wren was right," Caledonia said, approaching him.

"Wow," Hatter said.

Newton joined them. "I think the Grand Milliner will not be happy to learn the eeries have superseded his powers."

"I bet Rhodes ran off to tell him right away," Caledonia said, shaking her head.

"Hatter, aren't you happy?" asked Astra, who had been standing quietly beside him.

"Yes, I am. I just thought . . . I just thought we'd get to talk with the eeries in person, is all."

"I guess not," Caledonia said.

They stood quietly together for a moment.

"So . . . " Astra said. "What happens now?"

"All cadets," the disembodied voice announced, suddenly booming once again through the academy, "please go for breakfast and resume your regularly scheduled day until you are summoned for the Peaks' graduation ceremony."

"That answers that," Astra said with a smile. "And a good thing too. I'm starving."

Their last day of classes was relatively uneventful, though considering everything they had just been through, it would be hard to consider classes as being all that eventful ever again.

And then classes were done. And all levels were seated in the Wonderground, ready to watch the graduating Peaks walk across the stage, their Millinery placements read loudly for all of the cadets (and their parents) to hear. Hatter sat next to Newton.

The alphabet being used at the ceremony was the one that began with A and went by first name. As such they had to wait a long time before they finally got to West. He crossed the stage on crutches, and Hatter wanted to cheer or do something to honor him. West had been through so much this year. He saw Caledonia stand up a few rows down, and Astra did almost immediately after.

"Stand," Hatter whispered to Newton, who nodded, and they did. Slowly other cadets rose too, more and more, until everyone was standing as West crossed the stage. He stared out at them all, as stoic as ever, and nodded slowly. Then he sat with his fellow graduates, and the rest of the cadets sat too.

Then it was over and time for everyone to return to their dorm rooms, pack up, and make their way to the foyer, where they'd be picked up by their parents. Ready for the solemn march down the winding gray hill.

Everyone, that is, except for Hatter.

"So," Caledonia said, shouldering her large duffel bag and glancing over at a tall blond couple standing by the massive academy entrance doors. "I guess this is good-bye for now." She shook everyone's hands efficiently, though Astra insisted on hugging her. "See you in Cobblers!" she said, as she peeled off her friend. She turned and marched over to her parents, and they gave each other a brief, formal nod.

"You know, I think I'll go back to my room," Hatter said, starting to feel really uncomfortable. "It's kind of dumb for me to be standing here, in everyone's way."

"Whatever you'd like to do," Astra said, glancing nervously toward the doors. Hatter put a hand on her shoulder.

"Your parents are going to be so proud of you, especially after everything that happened," he said. Astra didn't look back at him, just kept staring at the doors. And Hatter sensed that for the first time since he'd known her, she was attempting to be stoic. "Can I get a hug good-bye?"

Astra turned and looked at him, tears shining in her eyes. And then she smiled hugely, overjoyed that Hatter wanted a hug from her. She grabbed him tightly and then did the same to Newton. Then, with a determined huff, she took her flowery suitcase and walked off into the crowd.

"I guess . . . good-bye," said Hatter to Newton.

"It's only two weeks. I think we'll survive. I know I will," Newton said. He stuck out his hand, and Hatter grabbed it. They shook. Then they stood there for a moment in silence. "Man, I'm usually okay with the not-seeing thing, but sometimes I wish I could read your expressions. I bet some crazy stuff happens there." He gestured toward Hatter's face.

"Oh, just go already," Hatter said with a laugh.

Newton laughed too and turned toward the front doors, where Hatter noticed an older, gray-haired couple had just arrived. As Newton approached them, Hatter determined it was just too much. He turned away and made his way back toward the hallway and away from all the reunions.

He walked against the stream of cadets flowing into the foyer. He passed the Grand Milliner standing outside his office and saw the man actively avoid making eye contact with him; Hatter felt a little smug.

He walked out the heart-shaped doorway, through the yard, and into the now-empty common area of the South Needle. It was so quiet. So still. The last time he'd seen it like that, he'd been a little kid sneaking in during hiatus.

He went to his room and wandered to his window. Though it didn't face in quite the right direction, if he twisted his neck enough, he could see the line of cadets and their families winding their way down the Gray Cliffs and out of sight.

And he was left behind.

What was it like having parents to pick you up? To ask you about your experiences? To be proud?

"Hi, Hatter."

Hatter turned and was completely floored to see Dalton standing in the doorway. It was something he hadn't even thought was a possibility, what with his new job and everything.

"Why are you here?" he asked in shock.

"Good to see you too," Dalton said, shaking his head and stepping into the room.

"I just don't understand why you're here. That's all."

"It's hiatus. I thought it might be nice to see you."

"And?" He knew his brother too well, and his brother was not that sentimental.

Dalton sighed. "I heard about what you did. All of Wonderland is buzzing about Shimmer's upcoming trial. You'll probably be asked to come in as a witness."

Hatter nodded. He had indeed considered that possibility, and it both thrilled and terrified him.

"I thought we should maybe talk about it."

Of course Dalton had an opinion about it all. And it likely was not going to be one Hatter would like.

"Sure." Hatter turned back and continued staring out the window as the tail end of black vanished behind a bend. He sighed to himself.

"You know, of course, that I think you should have been punished."

"I heard."

"Disobeying the direct orders of the Grand Milliner is a huge violation of cadet conduct."

"I know."

"And I must say, I was deeply disappointed that you—"

"Stop it!" Hatter turned around and stared hard at his brother. Dalton for his part looked sincerely shocked, which was sincerely shocking for Hatter to see.

"Don't speak to me that way," Dalton said. His voice was quiet, but there was a tinge of emotion to the voice. It made Hatter feel kind of good.

Hatter took a deep breath and spoke in a calm even tone. "No. You need to stop telling me all your opinions all the time. I know. I've never been good enough. But you know what? Because of that I spent too much time trying to prove myself this year and not enough time just being myself. All thanks to you." Immediately after he'd said it, he realized how much, exactly, he meant it. He'd never really thought of it that way, but there it was. He felt a wave of exhaustion pass over him and turned and sat on his bed.

"Now see here—"

"I'm sorry, Dalton—it's not all your fault. But I'm proud of what my friends and I did. Given the chance, I'd do the same thing over again. And sometimes I wonder if all of the rules we are told to follow were created for the right reasons." There was Astra in his brain again; he could almost see her approving grin.

Dalton stood, towering over Hatter for a moment. Hatter didn't look up, just felt the shadow looming. Then Dalton sat

351

next to him and put an arm around Hatter's shoulders. That made Hatter finally look at his brother. He couldn't remember the last time his brother had touched him with more than a handshake.

"Our father always pushed us—do you remember?"

Hatter nodded ever so slightly. "When we asked for help, he always made us find a way to do it ourselves."

"Yes," Dalton said. "But you were so little, you don't know. The pressure he and Mother put on me to be the best—"

"Me too!" Hatter interrupted. "I might have only been little, but me too."

"As I was saying," Dalton said, "to be the best older brother. The perfect older brother. 'Hatter looks up to you. Whatever you do, he'll do too. Lead by example.' That kind of thing."

"Oh. I didn't know."

"Why would you? I had to be perfect. I had to follow all the rules. And when they . . . went missing . . . I knew I had to be even better. I'm sorry that I've made you think you weren't good enough. You've always been good enough. Better than good enough."

Hatter nodded. He was worried that if he tried to talk, he would just start crying instead.

"My point, I'm beginning to realize, is that even if I lead by example, you're not me. And you know things I don't. It concerns me, and I don't know how I feel about it, but you are being hailed as quite the hero out there. So . . . " Dalton struggled for a moment with the thought. "Maybe we do need a rule breaker in the family."

352

Hatter swallowed hard. He didn't want to hear that—that's not what he'd meant at all. "I like rules too. I want to be a soldier of Wonderland. I believe in obeying orders and being good. I can be good."

"Of course! But you wouldn't be the hero of the day if all you did was what others told you to do."

His brother squeezed him gently, and Hatter nodded again. He didn't really know what to say and wasn't sure he wanted to say anything anyway.

"Okay!" said Dalton, standing up. "Let's go to the kitchens and have some lunch. Cook's already insisted I stay for a proper meal, as if the chefs at the royal palace are incompetent or something. Besides, I want you to tell me everything about your adventure."

Hatter rose and smiled. "What about being the queen's bodyguard? What's it like? Is it dangerous? And what's it like living in the palace?"

Dalton smiled his small reserved smile, a smile just big enough that Hatter could tell he was in a good mood, though others might not have been able to see it.

"Slow down, slow down. I'll tell you all. Though I will say, all those dance classes? They actually do come in very handy."

"Oh no."

Dalton's smile grew a quarter of an inch. He glanced down at the foot of Hatter's bed. "Father's hat," he said, picking it up. "You've been taking care of it. Good."

"Of course." Hatter wondered if he should ask. If there were a way to ask. "Dalton, did you ever wear it?"

"Not to class, but I did on my own. Maybe as a way of connecting with Father."

"And what was that like?"

"Wearing his hat? It was like wearing a hat. Except not like Milliner hats. More like the hats a typical Wonderlander might wear. Just another piece of clothing. I think once upon a time it was considered a fashionable style."

"Okay, because I wasn't sure if I should wear it. In case," lied Hatter.

"In case?"

"I dunno, if Father had left some kind of imagination properties in it or something that would be dangerous or . . ."

"No, it's safe, little brother. It's just a hat." Dalton placed the hat back down on the bedspread and looked at it for a moment. Then he turned to Hatter and said, "Shall we?"

"I'll be there in a second. I just need to . . . I'll meet you there."

Dalton looked at him for a moment, and Hatter looked back. Then Dalton gave a sharp nod and left the room.

Hatter walked to the edge of the bed and picked up his father's hat. He stared at it, turned it around in his hands. *It's just a hat. That's all. Just a hat.*

That talks to him and has a mind of its own.

That's all.

Hatter sighed deeply, and then bent over to hide the hat once more under the bed. Only it didn't really feel as if he were hiding it. More as if he were keeping it safe and ready—in case.

In case of what? He had no idea. He pulled out his story from his inner pocket and placed it next to the hat. He leaned over the edge of the bed and stared at the two objects side by side, feeling a confused wave of emotions flow over him, a combination of fear and something else, something kind of thrilling. Something . . . special.

He really hoped that, as a Cobbler, he'd finally be able to control his feelings better. To channel them into his work.

Hatter stood up and straightened his uniform. Then he took the hat he and Astra had made together and placed it on his head. Well, there was no time like the present. Hatter closed his eyes and visualized putting his confused feelings away under the bed. Hiding them away. Not disposing of them, just keeping them for when he'd need them next. Just not dealing with them right now. He opened his eyes and nodded and left the room. Secure in the knowledge that his feelings were tucked away nicely.

Safe in the dark.

Next to an unwritten story.

And a most remarkable hat.

TWITTER @FrankBeddor

INSTAGRAM FrankBeddor

FACEBOOK TheLookingGlassWars

Visit Frank on the web: FrankBeddor.com